The Trouble with Tomboys

by

Linda Kage

The Trouble with Tomboys

COPYRIGHT © 2010 by Linda Grotheer

Cover Art by *Angela Anderson*

The Wild Rose Press
PO Box 708
Adams Basin, NY 14410-0706
Visit us at www.thewildrosepress.com

Publishing History
First Champagne Rose Edition, 2010
Print ISBN 1-60154-790-0

Published in the United States of America

"I heard about five minutes ago that someone had knocked up B.J. Gilmore."

That finally evoked the response he'd expected. Her face drained of color and she dropped her bag of popcorn, spilling kernels around her bare feet.

"Who told you that?"

Grady folded his arms and stared hard. "I overheard Gabe Watson telling Ulrick Pullson about it at Herb's Quick Stop. Both of *them* already knew."

"*Who?*" she demanded, and then she shook her head furiously. "I...I just wasn't sure *how* to say it," she answered quietly. "I mean, was there any way to break it to you easily?"

Grady opened his mouth, but B.J. hurried to add, "One thing was sure, I definitely wasn't going to tell anyone *else* until you knew."

She stopped suddenly as if just realizing something. Then she scowled and pressed her hands to her hips, snapping, "Wait a second. What even makes you think this is *your* kid?"

She'd already given it away, but his answer was a quiet, heartfelt, "Because I'm not that lucky."

B.J. looked like she was going to cry, and he felt like a heel for saying such a thing. He wasn't typically a rude man. But B.J. wasn't the type to break down and bawl when her feelings were hurt either. So why did the two of them together seem to bring out the worst in each other?

God, he wanted to scrub his face with his hands and mutter, "What a disaster," but he didn't want to hurt her any further. She already looked like she was on the edge and might crumble any second. He sighed then and really did scrub his face with his hands.

"I guess we'll need to get married," he announced, sounding none too pleased.

Dedication

For Kurt Karl

Chapter One

B.J. Gilmore clamped a fat cigar between her teeth and studied the hand of cards in front of her as she sat backward on a rusty kitchen chair.

God, she loved playing poker. Didn't matter if she wagered with cash or matchsticks, five-card draw was one game where you could always count her in.

To her left, a slimy drool of sweat dripped off Ralphie Smardo's face while he eyed his own cards, then glanced at the pile of cash in the center of the table. B.J. had to admit, she felt a little moist around the edges herself. Not a lot of air circulated to the back corner of her family's airplane hangar, and a stale July heat hovered over the group, making the grease-scented air stick to every seam and collar.

However, the droplets gushing from Ralphie's pores led her to believe he wasn't just hot. He was damn nervous.

Across from her, Buck grumbled as he lifted his hip and pulled a billfold from his back pocket. B.J. glanced at her oldest brother for any telltale signs, but Buck merely looked annoyed about having to dig up more cash for his bid.

"Hell, I'm out," Leroy muttered next to him, tossing down his cards and sending a scowl to the other members of the game.

Well, praise the Almighty. B.J. didn't much care to play against her second brother. Leroy had a penchant for cheating, and as stubborn as she was, she usually called him on it, which led to a lengthy yelling match and meant her beloved poker game would come to an end.

Leroy was as mean as a rattlesnake and, out of her three brothers, B.J. liked him the least...mostly because of the time he'd taunted her with an actual rattler when she was ten and she'd spent the night in the hospital. Damn snakebite had left a scar just under her armpit.

Buck used to be as cruel as Leroy, chasing her around their homestead with all sorts of creepy crawlers, but he'd softened a lot in the last four years since he'd gotten hitched. He'd turned into even more of a pansy when his wife had their first baby two years later.

Out of her three brothers, Rudy—who was probably still passed out from the night before or nursing a hangover at three in the afternoon—was her favorite. Maybe that was because the Buck-Leroy combo had picked on him as much as they had her. But she'd always been protective of him because, truth be told, the boy was more effeminate than B.J.

Not that she had a feminine bone in her body.

"I'm done in too," Pete Smardo announced with a tired sigh.

The sigh matched his weathered features. Pete probably wasn't a day over sixty, but he looked more like he was approaching eighty. His sun-ripened face was full of wrinkles and age spots from sitting outside in front of his junkyard on a rocking chair three hundred and sixty-five days a year.

His son, Ralphie, ran the yard with Pete, and Ralphie's pale skin revealed how little he sat with his old man. His colorless cheeks also indicated how antsy he was when he glanced over to watch her meet the bid and raise it.

The four men surrounding her sat up in interest as the bill she flung out settled onto the rest of the pocket change. Pausing at the sudden silence, B.J. frowned and looked as well. She almost pissed her pants when she saw Alexander Hamilton grinning back. But damn, she'd only meant to throw out a single dollar, not ten.

"She's bluffing," Leroy said, eyeing her intently.

She lifted her gaze and shot him a challenging look. "That why *you* cut out so early?"

He glowered, and she dismissed him with a snort, turning toward Ralphie to catch his next move.

Ralphie was two years her senior and, to her eternal shame, the last man she'd slept with. A few years earlier, they'd gotten tanked one night, snuck into a nearby watering hole and gone skinny-dipping. After the swim, he'd been frisky. B.J. hadn't been with a guy in almost three years, so she'd given in to his pathetic seduction—and she was only calling it a seduction for lack of a better word.

It ended up being one of the most God-awful experiences of her life.

Luckily, Ralphie hadn't been that impressed either, and they'd somehow remained friends. In fact, she'd pretty much roped in his current girlfriend for him. He and Nan Lundy were probably going to tie the knot one of these days, if the idiot ever got around to proposing. Ralphie continually told her how grateful he was for her matchmaking, and they remained tight.

B.J. took a swig from a Styrofoam cup of cooled coffee and thoughtfully eyed him as he threw down the cash to meet her bid.

Her attention swiveled to Buck. He growled, "Fold," and B.J. silently sighed in relief. That left only Ralphie to defeat.

"Okay," she said, ready to wheel and deal as she turned fully toward the pale, sweaty man. "If I win, I get that set of ten-ply tires you snatched from Rick

Hopper's wrecked truck."

B.J. adored her souped-up four by four, three-quarter ton Dodge diesel, and the tires from Hopper's old truck would look sweet on it. They were exactly what she wanted, but she couldn't cough up the cash when her current set worked perfectly fine. She was a real miser that way.

Ralphie glanced at his old man and winced as Pete scratched his gray-black beard stubble with a frown. Then Pete shrugged. "If you lose us those tires, boy, it's coming out of your wallet."

Ralphie didn't look too reassured. He glanced at B.J. "And if I win?"

She lifted a brow. "Name your price." When Ralphie fell into intense contemplation, she sighed and rolled her eyes. "Sometime today, please. I got a job to do here pretty soon."

"Speaking of which..." Buck motioned toward the opened doors of the hangar.

B.J. turned and froze.

At first, all she saw was a silhouette. The lean, slim-hipped form entering carried an overnight bag slung over his shoulder. Tall and surprisingly graceful, he wore a cowboy hat, Wranglers, and some kind of tucked-in, long-sleeved shirt.

She could hear the echoing click of his boots against the concrete floor as he walked with a slightly bow-legged stride. The whole scene screamed George Strait in that movie *Pure Country*...only ten times sexier, because this was real.

The man made a mouthwatering picture, that was for sure, and she could only gape as he strolled into the place with the confidence of an alpha used to being in charge. The female inside her took immediate notice. Good God, he was gorgeous.

Grady Rawlings had always been great-looking, though. There had to be zero percent of body fat covering him from head to toe. But while he had a lean build, he still appeared fully ripped. He was pure muscle, bone, and steel, and it looked damn fine on him. In high school, football and baseball kept him in shape. These days, he lifted heavy machinery daily, what with working in his oilfield.

When he stopped just inside the doors and turned to the side as if seeking assistance, B.J. hollered from her chair. "We're back here."

He turned at her call, and her girly organs leapt to attention, startling her with their enthusiasm.

Good Lord, she must need to get laid. Seeing a guy look her way should *not* have that kind of effect. But as he started toward her voice with his sexy male stride, she felt the impact all the way to the tips of her steel-toed boots.

Forcing her attention back to the game, she cleared her throat and told Ralphie, "Well, hurry up already. I gotta go."

Grady approached, and she couldn't help but glance toward him one more time. When he was close enough for her to make out the features in his face, she drew in a quiet breath. Since his wife and unborn child had died two and a half years earlier, he'd become hardened and withdrawn.

He'd always been fairly serious, yet these days, nothing made him smile. He was a lot tanner and his clothes fit a little loose, yet he was still as hot as hell. That look in his eyes, though, like he didn't have a friend left on earth, that was what hooked her the most.

B.J. hated to see people in pain, and Grady Rawlings was in a great deal of agony. Posttraumatic stress had leashed a collar around his neck, refusing to let go. He'd become so aloof, other people grew uncomfortable around him. They didn't know what to say or do. B.J. had heard if someone tried to talk about his wife with him, he'd get nearly violent with his irritation before storming off. With every step he drew closer, B.J. could actually feel the guys around her tense into awkward idiots.

Grady stopped ten feet from the table and planted himself.

No one gave him any kind of greeting, so B.J. cleared a couple more cobwebs from her throat. "I'll be right with you. Just as soon as tortoise here makes his bid—and I wipe the floor with his face—we can be on our way."

He jerked his attention toward her like he was surprised by her declaration. "You're flying today?"

Though his low voice shot an overdose of pure lust into her bloodstream, she frowned. "You got a problem with that?"

There'd been occasions when customers had refused to ride with her because, well, she figured it was because she was a woman. It could be because she wasn't very polite and had somewhat of a sour disposition, but she reasoned it probably had more to do with her lady plumbing. Some people just couldn't trust such a little woman—though B.J. was five ten—to fly such a big, masculine plane.

Grady sent her a level look, and his blue eyes penetrated another feminine part she hadn't even known existed, making her hormones shudder.

"No problem," he said quietly. "I just wasn't aware of who the pilot was going to be this trip."

The last time he'd hired their family's service, he'd had the misfortune of getting Leroy as his pilot. She guessed he was merely relieved he didn't have to ride with that maniac again.

B.J. nodded, hoping she understood the situation, and said, "Why don't you take a seat. I'm almost ready, but...who knows when Junkyard here's going to make his damn bid."

"I'm thinking," Ralphie snapped.

Grady remained standing apart from the group.

B.J. took another drag from her cigar and eyed Ralphie until he squirmed.

Buck finally found the courage to say, "H-hey, Grady," which sounded totally lame, coming this late.

The others, all except B.J., chipped in next, mumbling stuttered, uncomfortable greetings.

Grady gave a brief nod. "Fellas."

No one asked how he was or how his oil business was doing, and he certainly didn't start any small talk with them. B.J. was about to say something just to fill the silence when Ralphie finally spit on the floor, sent a skittish look Grady's way, and muttered, "Okay."

She rolled her eyes. "Good Lord in heaven, he's going to make his move."

A couple of the guys chuckled.

Ralphie said, "I want five hundred," and the laughter at the table intensified.

B.J. sniffed. "Damn, Ralphie, I could buy a brand new set of tires for that."

"Well, then, why don't you?" he retorted.

Still frowning, she relented. "All right, fine. But I want you to put 'em on my truck for free if I win."

"And I want you to take one of them aerial pictures of my mama's place so's I can give it to her for Christmas if *I* win."

"Deal," B.J. said, studying her cards. "Add another hundred to my bid."

At her immediate compliance and raised wager, Ralphie shifted and cringed down at his hand. He scratched his ear and glanced with one eye squinted at his father.

"Damn," Pete said, puffing on his cigar. "If she's offering free service, she must have a good hand."

B.J. chewed on her own cigar and grinned at the old man, sending him a conspiring wink.

"Well, hell," Ralphie muttered. With another

curse, he threw down his cards and forfeited his hand.

Letting out a deep whoop, B.J. triumphantly tossed her fist in the air. "Yes!" she hollered, then stood and stubbed out her cigar. "Boys," she told the table of men as she leaned over to rake in her booty. "It's been a pleasure."

"Well, what'd you have?" Ralphie demanded.

When she ignored him, he surged to his feet and reached across the table to snag her cards. B.J. let him have at them.

He stared at them with a saggy jaw a good five seconds before he yelped, "A pair of twos? A pair of *twos*!"

B.J. beamed and sent him a two-fingered salute. "What can I say? My lucky number's two. And when I get two twos, I figure, hell... Might as well bluff, huh?"

Ralphie's face turned flamingo bright. He threw his hat off, exposing a head three-quarters gone bald. "I had three jacks!"

B.J. whistled, impressed. "Gee, then maybe you shouldn't have forfeited," she told him. "Oh, and by the way, I'm free tomorrow afternoon. Will that be a good time for me to swing my truck by for the new tires?"

Ralphie was so flustered he couldn't even talk. Finally, he turned to his father. "What the hell's the matter with you? 'B.J.'s betting free service. She must have a good hand,'" he mimicked. "Good hand my ass."

"Oh, cry me a river, Ralphie," B.J. butted in, stuffing her new wad of money into her back pocket. "You threw in your hand."

"I'm never playing poker with you again." He sounded like a scorned child who'd just had his ice cream cone taken away.

"I won fair and square." She glanced toward his

dad. "You see me cheat?"

Pete shook his head. "No, ma'am."

B.J. snorted. "Ma'am? Who the hell are you calling ma'am? Your old lady just walk in?"

While Pete chuckled, B.J. finally returned her attention to Grady. He'd been passively watching the scene. She had no idea what was going on behind those cool blue eyes of his.

Ignoring the insistent tug in her loins, she arched him a look. "Let me grab my gear, Slim, and I'll be ready to go. 'Kay?"

He nodded, and she left Ralphie to complain to the others. She wouldn't be surprised if he reneged on the tires. But if he managed to cough them up, then hey, that'd be okay too. She wasn't too concerned about it. She'd won fair and square, that was all that mattered to her.

She was still glowing over her victory when she came strolling out of the back room with her cap on forward and her dark hair pulled through the hole in the back. Wearing reflecting aviator glasses and chewing on sour apple bubble gum, she slung a beat-up green duffle over her shoulder and led Grady toward her plane.

Since his meeting was supposed to last late into the evening, this was going to be an overnight run. Ready for a long, boring stay in her hotel room, she climbed into the opened back doorway of her plane. After tossing her gear inside toward a corner, she looked over her shoulder at Grady, still standing on the tarmac behind her.

"Ready?" she asked, giving him one last chance to make a pit stop before they went wheels up.

Again, he merely nodded. B.J. held a hand down to him. He frowned at her palm, looking confused.

"Your bag?" she prompted.

He lifted his clear blue gaze and quietly said, "I got it."

She barely restrained herself from rolling her eyes. Now there was an honest to God gentleman for you. He'd probably cut off his arm before letting some woman lift his load.

Shrugging, she muttered, "Suit yourself," and slithered inside the belly of the plane, leaving Mr. Gentleman to follow. She settled into the cockpit, tugged on her headset, and checked the panel controls. Just as she started the engine, Grady slid into the seat beside her, grabbing his own headset.

She glanced over and thought, *Holy Hell*. How was she supposed to make it through an hour-long ride with him alone in such a tiny space and be expected to keep her hands to herself?

Chapter Two

Having already walked through her pre-flight inspection before the poker game, B J. was ready for takeoff. Daring a second glance Grady's way as he pulled on his safety harness, she told herself to focus her attention on her job. But she'd never felt someone's presence so much in her life; it made her want to crawl out of her skin.

Assuming a joke would help her little funk, she watched him situate his seatbelt into place and said, "That's not going to do you much good if we crash."

At his short frown, she cleared her throat and quickly turned away. Loudly popping her gum, she released the brakes, and they slowly rolled forward.

She was successfully able to ignore him as she contacted the tower and started toward the runway. But when the plane first lifted into the air, she noticed Grady's hand clamp around his knee, his short nails digging into dark denim.

She made a point to look at his white-knuckled grip. "Not too keen on flying, huh?"

He glanced over, and she wondered how anyone could look so miserable. "Not really," he answered, which made her feel bad about the crashing joke.

"So, why didn't you just drive to Houston?" she wondered. "It's only a five, six hour run."

Grady gave a slight shake of the head. "I had a meeting here this morning. There wasn't enough time. Besides, I hate driving in Houston more than I hate flying."

B.J. was a little shocked he'd actually spoken three sentences to her...in a row. She'd never heard him talk this much. Not in the past couple of years, anyway.

She nodded. "Yeah, big city driving ticks me off too. There's just too many people who get in my way. Too bad they arrest you for running over dumbasses. You know?" She hitched an ornery grin his way, but Grady didn't respond. Not even an amused smile. B.J. sighed to herself. Tough crowd.

She waited for him to say something else. When he remained silent, she returned her attention to the air. She was used to all different types of riders. Usually, customers sat in the back unless they were the chatty or curious type; then they rode in the co-pilot seat and gabbed away as she flew them to their destination.

But Grady was neither. She figured it was a control issue with him. He needed to be up front where everything transpired, to see what happened. That way, he could get a handle on the situation. She couldn't blame him there. She hated being a passenger, would rather be the one driving—or flying, as in this case. And man, she loved to fly.

There was a small load of cargo in the back, so she would've been making this flight even if Grady hadn't needed a lift. But it was nice to have another presence beside her, even if he didn't talk. What wasn't so nice was the way her hormones honed in on the poor, depressed widower—a widower whose dead wife used to be her babysitter back in the day.

Striving to keep her dirty thoughts at bay, she attempted to start a conversation.

"How's the twins?" she asked of his two younger sisters. Jo Ellen and Emma Leigh had been a couple of years older than her in school. She hadn't been close to them, but, hey, what else was there to talk about...beside the fact she wanted to put the plane on auto pilot and jump his bones at thirty thousand feet?

"They're fine," Grady answered.

B.J. nodded. "I haven't gotten around to seeing Jo Ellen's kid yet. It was a boy, wasn't it?"

Grady nodded. "Tanner," he said.

B.J. glanced at him. "Beg pardon?"

"His name's Tanner," he explained. "Jo Ellen's son."

"Oh..." B.J. nodded. Then, "Right. Yeah, I think I knew that. Probably a good-looking tike." Both his parents certainly were.

"He has a lot of hair."

"Well, huh," B.J. said, wondering what the hell else there was to say about a kid. She knew squat about ankle-biters. The only child she'd ever really been around was her niece. And Buck's daughter was an honest-to-God brat. "That's...that's good. I guess."

Grady didn't bother to elaborate; she wondered if he was thinking about his own baby, the one who'd been born dead, the one who'd taken Amy's life when it'd tried to make its entrance into the world.

Starting to feel ill at ease, she squirmed in her chair to get more comfortable. Grady kept his face turned away from her as he stared out his side window at the scenery below.

"Can you see your house from here?" she asked.

When he glanced at her, she winked. But he merely turned away again and continued window gazing.

B.J. took a moment to study him, wondering if it was possible to describe someone as skinny and muscled at the same time. He looked like an Ethiopian on steroids, minus the potbelly. Okay, it wasn't quite to that extreme, but he was pretty thin. He'd always been a slim man. Now he looked...hollow. He was definitely leaner than when she'd last seen him, which had probably been about six months ago.

Before she realized what she was going to blurt out, she commented to herself, "Amy must've been a good cook."

But no sooner did the words leave her tongue than she snapped her mouth shut, wishing them away.

Grady's head whipped around so quickly B.J. swallowed her gum.

"What?" he said in a strangled voice.

She froze for a good three seconds. Oh, damn, oh, damn. She'd forgotten Amy was a taboo topic.

Feeling like she should apologize or something, B.J. stalled a moment by checking all her gauges and making sure everything was still running smoothly. But just as suddenly, she felt like a big weenie. What the hell did she want to apologize for? This was her plane, and B.J. never watched her words. She had a right to talk about her old babysitter if she wanted to.

Lifting her chin in stubborn rebellion, she nodded her head in his direction and found a fresh piece of gum in her front shirt pocket to stuff inside her cheek. "You ain't so meaty around the ribs anymore. I just figured you might be missing out on your three square meals."

There. She'd shown him. She hadn't backed down from the formidable Grady Rawlings. *And* she'd dared to mention his wife.

He was quiet a moment before he answered with a quiet, "I get by."

Thinking back on Amy, B.J. let out a quick laugh. "I remember when she used to babysit Rudy and me. She never did cook much, but this one time it was Pop's birthday. She wanted to bake him a cake and, man..."

She paused to shake her head at the fond memory. "She didn't check the oven before she turned it on. Preheated it to three hundred fifty degrees. But not two minutes into whipping the batter, she stopped and sniffed the air. 'You smell something burning, B.J.?' she asked me. So, we ran to the oven and pulled it open, only to find a stack of magazines catching fire.

"I guess since no one ever used our oven, Leroy had been hiding his porn in there. I couldn't tell who was more upset over the whole ordeal. Leroy because all his good smut was charred black, or Amy because she was afraid she'd ruined our stove."

Grady looked a little shell-shocked, like he couldn't believe someone other than he had a memory of Amy tucked away inside them. He frowned thoughtfully. "I remember her telling me about that."

"That's right," B.J. said, her shoulders slumping because her story wasn't as original as it could've been. "I forgot. You were seeing her back then too, weren't you?"

"Yeah," he returned. "I was."

The way he said "was" about broke her heart. She wasn't typically such a softy, but she didn't understand why people had to suffer. If an animal was in pain, you put it out of its misery.

Once she'd gone with Pop to the vet when they'd had their old, cancer-ridden dog, Charlie Horse, put to sleep. She remembered feeling relieved Charlie wasn't going to hurt anymore. But B.J. didn't know how to deal with humans in pain. Couldn't exactly put them to sleep when they hurt too much.

It bothered her more than she could describe to watch someone's feelings bleed out. Since Grady Rawlings' wound was over two years old, it was even more disheartening.

B.J. didn't do sympathy well, so she shut her trap for the rest of the ride.

****

If a pair of white-hot needles had been jammed

into each of his temples, Grady didn't think his skull could ache any more than it throbbed now. But flying always did that to him, messing with his equilibrium until his head felt like it was going to internally combust.

By the time his meeting let out, all he wanted to do was crawl back to his hotel, find a bed, and overdose on some Tylenol so he could fall into a coma-like state for a week or so.

As his buyer pushed to his feet, he did the same, ignoring the persistent pulse behind his eyes. They both moved out of the way of the table and toward the exit.

"Always good doing business with you, Grady," Hammond Weatherly said as he thrust out his hand for a hearty shake.

"You as well," he murmured, accepting the Texas-sized grip Weatherly strapped onto his palm.

"Been a while since you came around here, though. I'd been dealing with your dad so much lately, I kinda figured you'd stepped out of the family business."

"No," Grady said. He probably would've tacked on a few more comments if his head weren't so sore. Then again, he really didn't want to get into any of the reasons *why* he'd been off the grid in the past few years. "I've been around," he finally supplied with a lame attempt not to sound rude.

"Well, I don't know how long it's been since I last saw you," Weatherly mused more to himself, scratching his chin and frowning a second before his face cleared. Then he snapped his fingers and pointed at Grady. "Now I remember. Your wife was expecting her first last time we met up." He grinned. "Was it a boy or girl?"

For a second, Grady couldn't talk... couldn't breathe. Agony clogged his chest, and he forgot about the hammering in his temples. His vision blurred, going foggy and slanted. He concentrated on sucking oxygen back into his lungs and blinking until the world veered back into focus.

Weatherly didn't know. About Amy, or the baby, or any of it.

Grady cleared his throat, lowered his eyes to the floor and mumbled, "It was a boy." Which wasn't a lie. It *had* been a boy. A dead boy, but Grady didn't particularly want to divulge that detail and make the both of them uncomfortable.

Weatherly chuckled and slugged Grady companionably on the shoulder. "Guess I owe you a belated congratulations, old son. Had any more since the first?"

Unable to speak, Grady shook his head. He lifted his face and managed a tight smile. "I need to go." His voice sounded like shredded gravel, but at least he'd managed to utter understandable words.

"Oh, sure, sure," Weatherly said, taking a step back to let Grady pass. "You got a long drive ahead of you."

Grady didn't mention he'd chartered a plane for the trip. Instead he nodded and said over his shoulder as he moved toward the exit, "I'll make sure our secretary gets back to you on that tax issue."

"Thanks, Grady. See you around."

In the outer office, Grady nodded toward the receptionist and strode straight for the exit, looking neither left nor right. He held his briefcase stiffly down at his side as he pushed his way out the door. The transportation service he'd made arrangements with before coming to Houston already had a car waiting at the curb. The driver held the back door open for him, and without a word, he slid into his seat.

The ride back to his hotel was a silent misery. He stared out the side window, waiting until he could close himself alone in his suite. If he could keep it together until he got to his room, he knew he'd be okay. But traffic was a bitch. They had to take two detours before reaching their destination. Nearly an hour passed before his chauffer pulled to a stop.

Grady managed a brief thank you and exited before the man could come around and open his door. He walked through the overly long lobby, feeling as if everyone was staring at him, thinking he must look miserable, like some kind of defeated widower. An urge rose inside him to stop under the jeweled chandelier in the center of the vestibule and shout at the top of his lungs for everyone to look somewhere else. He was fine. But he knew he was merely being paranoid. No one stared. No one here pitied him. And no one paid him any attention as he pressed the elevator button to wait for the doors to open.

Thankfully, no one entered with him, and the mirrored cubicle remained empty as he stepped inside. The doors slid shut, and finally he was alone. Grady's shoulders sagged a fraction of an inch, letting out some of their starch. He closed his eyes and leaned to the side to rest his cheek against the cool surface of the elevator walls.

Peace.

Well, mostly peace. After Weatherly's mention of Amy and the baby, the visions swimming around his brain were filled with blood and death, tears and heartbreak. But at least no one else was around to aggravate the agony any further. By himself, he could deal with the memories. Around others, he always had to be so damn strong and unaffected. He much preferred the private pain.

Images swirled through him until suddenly he could see Amy as a teenager, standing in the Gilmore family kitchen where he often visited when she was babysitting. Her light blonde hair was pulled up into one of her impossibly neat ponytails. She looked so young, it made his chest hurt. When she grinned, a dimple dipped the right side of her cheek.

"I tried to bake Jeb a cake yesterday," she told him before throwing back her head and laughing.

Grady sucked in a breath; his eyes snapped open only to find himself alone in the elevator. He could remember her telling him about burning Leroy Gilmore's porn as if it'd only happened yesterday. She'd laughed so hard as she recounted the story, he'd barely understood a word she said.

She'd been young and happy then.

Grady closed his eyes again and tried to recapture the image. It'd been over two years since he'd envisioned her smile. But in his desperate attempt to grasp a happy memory, the only scene imprinting itself on the inside of his eyelids was of her panting and crying as yet another deadly labor pain struck.

Sweat trickled down the side of his face. He opened his eyes and wiped the perspiration away with the back of his hand as the elevator doors opened. Grady took a step forward but jerked to a stop when he spotted the woman standing in front of his room door.

He didn't recognize her at first with her back to him. In cowboy boots, lean form-fitting jeans, and a pale yellow short-sleeved blouse, she could've been anyone. A dark mass of brown hair hung most of the way down her back, held together in a high, sloppy ponytail. She had a nice, feminine figure full of healthy curves in all the right places. Grady narrowed his eyes, wondering who the hell she was and why the hell she was standing in front of *his* door, staring at it as if she'd just knocked and was waiting for an answer.

Obviously growing impatient with her wait, she cocked her hip to the side and rested her hand on the generous curve, letting out a loud sigh. Finally, recognition set in. Putting that attitude in her stance, she told him exactly who she was.

The Gilmore woman. B.J.

Grady winced and glanced around, hoping he could spot some kind of deliverance to save him from having to gag through another encounter with her today. They weren't scheduled to see each other again until eight the next morning when they were to meet at the airplane to return home, and he wanted it to stay that way.

Not that he minded B.J. Gilmore. He'd never much cared for her family as a whole, but he'd never had any problem with her alone. Maybe that was because Amy used to babysit her, and he couldn't despise anyone who'd been partially raised by the love of his life. Though, admittedly, her younger brother, Rudy, had been one of Amy's wards too, and Grady didn't have much use for that lazy drunk. The two elder Gilmore boys were equally worthless, one a total dumbass and the other so mean and wild he was scarily unstable.

The one thing Grady remembered about the only female sister was her mouth and how much she liked to use it. She could talk a person into the ground. Since talking was the last thing he cared to do, avoiding her seemed like the best plan. But slipping past her without being spotted and escaping into the blessed silence of his room would to be the real trick.

Suddenly wishing he hadn't booked their two rooms adjacent to each other, he decided to stay put and pray she wasn't hanging around his next pass. But the stupid elevator let out a blaring ding before the doors began to close. B.J. lifted her head and turned his way. Caught, Grady gritted his teeth and stepped between the closing doors and into the hall. He lowered his face, thinking she might not recognize him if he kept walking by.

"There you are," she called.

Damn.

He glanced up and fell to a pause. She'd moved closer to him, was only about five feet away. A pair of big brown eyes hit him full in the chest. She blinked as if startled to see him dressed in his business gear. Her gaze ran down his suit, missing nothing as it slid over his jacket and slacks. The blatant female appreciation in her stare made his throat constrict. He itched to tug at his tie and breathe again, but refused to show her any sign of weakness.

She licked her lips before meeting his eyes. A strange sensation rushed up the back of his spine and neck as he watched the dart of her tongue. The feeling tickled the base of his skull, but he wasn't sure what it was. Could've been his own awareness of her, he guessed, but it'd been so long since he'd felt anything—toward anyone—he dismissed the idea as soon as it came.

Grateful she'd moved away from his door, he nodded his hello and pulled a key card from his pocket as he stepped around her and approached his room. Hopefully, she'd realize he wanted to be left alone.

No such luck.

She turned as he passed her, falling into step with him. "I was fixing to head downstairs and find myself some vittles. You hungry?"

"I've already eaten." He unlocked his room to emphasize how much he wanted to be alone.

She set her hands on her hips. "Well, you look like you could do with an extra meal here and there. Why don't you come along? Keep me company."

He shook his head. "I'm not hungry."

Sighing, B.J. tugged his briefcase out of his hand and tossed it into the opened door of his room. He frowned but didn't react. If his head didn't hurt so bad, if he hadn't been thrown off track by the incident at the end of the meeting with Weatherly, if he could only see Amy smile again when he closed his eyes, he probably could've come up with a suitable comment to scare her off. Something scathing and dry. But his head went blank, so all he could do was gape at her for her daring.

To further confound him, she hooked her arm through his and started walking them toward the elevators. He could've been rude and pulled away. But for some reason, he followed.

"Don't matter none if you're not hungry," she said. "You just sit there. I'll eat enough for the both of us. I hate going to those fancy, shmancy hotel restaurants by myself." She grinned at him. "I won't even make you talk if you don't want. Hell, I've been known to carry on a whole conversation by myself. So you don't have to worry about a thing. Just having a presence like you around will do me well enough."

"It's been a long day," he said as she stopped to press the elevator button. A last attempt for escape. "I'd like some rest." He unhooked her arm from his.

She grinned up at him, her brown eyes hopeful and encouraging. "You can sleep the whole way home tomorrow if you like," she told him. Then her grin faltered, and the gleam in her eyes died. She gave him a serious, probing look. "Just don't make me eat alone tonight, Rawlings."

Grady froze as a sensation similar to pity slammed through his windpipe. He knew exactly what it was like to eat alone every night. He preferred it that way, sure, but it didn't stop the wistful hope to sit across from Amy again, sharing just one more meal with her.

22

Realizing B.J. could probably see the empathy in his gaze, he glanced away. "Why don't you just order room service?"

"Thought of it," she said before shrugging. "But I had to get out of there for a while." Pausing, she patted his arm. "Don't take that to mean I don't appreciate such sweet lodging, Slim. I already snarfed down the chocolates on my pillow and dumped the free goodies from the bathroom into my duffle bag. But I can only take so much of being penned in one place before I start going stir crazy. Know what I mean?"

He knew he was beginning to go a little stir crazy himself, wanting the privacy of his room for some tranquil silence.

But B.J. stared at him with that probing look again; he couldn't tell her no. He figured he owed her. She'd been the one to remind him of Amy burning her brother's magazines. She'd been the one to help him drag up the vision of his wife smiling after missing it for so long.

With a sigh, he tugged at his tie. "Okay," he relented. "But I want to change out of this suit first."

Chapter Three

Supper proved a lot more difficult to come by than B.J. had originally thought. The hotel restaurant was one of those classy digs that required a certain dress code. As she and Grady approached, the hostess looked at B.J.'s shirt and jeans and black cowboy boots in disgust, but refrained from remarking.

Instead, she turned to Grady and promptly said, "I'm sorry, sir, but you need to wear a suit and tie to eat here."

Truth be told, Grady looked a lot more spiffed up than B.J. in his Wranglers, boots, and a neatly pressed plaid top, so the whole suit-and-tie rule sent her a little over the edge.

"Look, we only came here to eat, lady. Our money'd be just as green if we were naked, so why don't you just shove it up your lily white—"

"It's fine," Grady said quietly to the hostess, reaching for B.J.'s arm to draw her away.

She jerked her elbow out of his reach. "No, it's *not* fine," she growled, glaring at the hostess. "If you want to pick on somebody's clothes, why don't you go after me, sister? I'm not—"

"B.J.," Grady said sharply.

His tone surprised her. She lifted her face to catch his hard expression.

"We're leaving."

"But I'm freaking starving."

"This isn't the only restaurant in the city," he grit out, taking her arm before she could evade him again.

Keeping close to her as if he didn't trust her to obey, he ushered her toward the exit, not once letting go of her until they were outside.

A wave of memories assailed her as her nostrils filled with his scent. He smelled exactly as she remembered. It was so startling, she didn't even think to resist as he pulled her along. She'd forgotten she'd ever been close enough to him to smell his scent before, but as she breathed in the fragrance, she suddenly recalled the days when Amy used to babysit her and Rudy, and a teenage Grady would unexpectedly show up at their door.

As the nostalgia hit, she remembered distinctly what it'd been like to form her first crush on the seventeen-year-old football captain. She recalled the sharp feeling of excitement she'd experienced, spying on Grady when he didn't know she was watching, and how she'd lie awake at nights, hugging her pillow, imagining it was him.

The adult version of him didn't hit upon those little girl fantasies of wanting to hold his hand or primly lay her head on his shoulder. No, now she wanted more...she wanted a long, hot, hard roll in the sack, and she wanted it bad.

Hoping to escape his enticing presence, B.J. took a step away as soon as they were outside. But even from five feet, she still felt the pull. Sucking in a deep breath, she looked up into the sky. Though it was night, the city was full of light.

Momentarily forgetting her agenda, B.J. paused to take in all the action around her.

"God, I wish I was home," she murmured, thinking she should've just let him hide in his room. Or better yet, she should've stayed in her own and ordered room service. "At least it's actually dark at night there, and you can see the stars."

Grady paid her no attention. "There's a restaurant," he said, pointing across the street.

"Oh, good," B.J. said, following him as he made his way toward a crosswalk. "I hope they have a dress code too. Maybe I can break a Guinness record and get us thrown out of the most eateries in one night."

He arched her a warning look that ordered her not to cause trouble.

Yeah, she remembered that about him too. He was a rule follower. He didn't break protocol, and he didn't engage in scandalous, spur-of-the moment actions.

Prepared to insult his moral sensibilities, B.J. was a little surprised when the next hostess merely smiled at their approach. Damn, there went her opportunity to cause another ruckus.

"Is it just the two of you tonight?" the perky woman asked, already grabbing a pair of menus.

Grady nodded and moved aside to let B.J. precede him. It felt funny, being the recipient of his chivalry. He'd opened two doors for her already, and now he was letting the lady go first. It was disconcerting and boldly reminded her how male he was.

When they were seated near a dance floor, B.J. rolled her eyes and plopped down in her seat before he could do something really crazy, like hold out her chair for her.

"Jesus, I hate dancing," she muttered and watched the couples on the floor swinging and swaying about, though she had to admit, dancing with Grady Rawlings would be an experience. She could already imagine herself in his arms, pressed against him, showing him just how much of a woman she was under all that tomboy.

She caught him looking at her oddly and frowned. "What?"

"Is there anything you *do* like?" he said.

"Yeah," she grumbled. "I like medium rare

steak, ice cold beer straight from the bottle, and a heaping pile of onion rings."

That was exactly what she requested too when a waitress approached seconds later. After putting in her order, she glanced toward Grady. "You want something to drink, Slim? I'll pay since I dragged you out here."

He shook his head and glanced at the waitress. "I'll take a glass of water."

B.J. rolled her eyes. "Get him a Bud...Light."

Grady didn't say anything to contradict her, so the waitress moved away with a nod.

Finally, he asked, "Should you be drinking while you fly?"

B.J. wrinkled her nose. "You see me flying?"

When he merely gave her a don't-be-a-smart-mouth-with-me frown, she sighed. "We're not leaving till eight in the morning. As long as I quit by midnight, you'll be okay. I won't stumble onto the plane tomorrow, slurring and slobbering, so just relax, Slim."

Grady glanced away. As he watched a pair of dancers, she couldn't help but wonder if his thoughts veered toward Amy. She remembered seeing the two of them dance together. Amy had loved to dance, and he'd loved to make her happy.

Half tempted to stand, shouting for the music to stop so he wouldn't be assaulted with any bittersweet memories, B.J. latched onto her beer as soon as it arrived and proceeded to guzzle.

He turned from the dancers and surprised her when he said, "Why did you order me a light and not an ultra?"

B.J. took a long draw before setting her bottle down and letting out a refreshed sigh. "I don't know," she said. "You look like a light kind of guy." He held himself back, as if not wanting to enjoy life to the fullest. "Why? Was I wrong?"

"No," he murmured and studied his own drink thoughtfully.

"Then what's the big deal?"

A half shrug later, he answered, "Just curious."

But she could already guess the reason. He didn't like a woman knowing too much about his tastes and preferences. It was an only-my-wife-should-know-how-I-take-my-coffee kind of thing. Such intimacy with another female didn't sit well.

B.J. swallowed when he silently reached out to catch a trail of condensation dripping off the side of his bottle. How he could make the move look as sensuous as it did, she'd never know. But, Lordy, she wanted to experience the feel of those long fingers trailing down her skin that way.

Finally, he lifted the draft for a long drink. She sensed he was ending a drought as he swallowed the first gulp. She wondered why he'd been without for so long. Was it because of Amy? Had he hit the cups too hard after her death? B.J. didn't think so. For one thing, she hadn't heard any rumors about him becoming an alcoholic, and more important, he didn't look guilty about drinking. So she had to figure he was clear to proceed.

She found herself watching his gaze move around the room, studying the different tables and different people. He had such a detached expression, he'd be awesome at poker. She could see his mind work but couldn't even guess what thoughts emerged from his detailed inspection. She found herself resting her chin on her hand and her elbow on the table to watch him scrutinize his surroundings.

The boy was in dire need of a haircut, but she liked the shaggy look he had going. He was incredibly gorgeous...in a sad, depressed sort of way. She just wanted to give him a hug and wipe the hair out of his face. While she was touching him, she wouldn't mind undoing the top button on his collar to give him some air.

Hell, while she was at it, she might as well shed him of his whole shirt. This was her daydream, wasn't it? She could think about stripping him naked if she wanted. And, well, yeah, she really did want to.

She shook her head. God, what was wrong with her? This poor man had lost his wife and child, and she could only wonder what he looked like naked? How sick was that?

And what *did* he look like naked?

She continued to study him, awed by his composure. Sure, he'd had two and a half years to get over the loss of Amy and the baby. He'd had time to deal, but still...there had to be a gaping hole right smack through the middle of him.

He must feel so lost. She couldn't remember a time when Grady and Amy hadn't been together. They'd been two halves of one whole. It was a wonder he made it through each day without her.

B.J.'s food came before she could gawk too much longer and make a total fool of herself. Grateful for the distraction, she tucked into her meal, cutting the beef into bite-sized pieces and drinking deeply from her beer to wash it down. She told herself to leave him alone. He looked like he wanted solitude. She was already torturing him enough by hauling him out on the town with her.

But she couldn't keep her eyes off him. He'd started on his drink again and sat quietly across from her, looking content in doing just that, though he did rub at his forehead like he had a killer headache.

She pointed her steak knife at him and, with her cheek full of meat, said, "You sure you're not hungry?"

He shook his head.

"Need an aspirin?"

That earned her a sharp glance, his eyes a little shocked, probably because she'd noticed his pain. But he answered, "I'm fine."

"Great," she said sarcastically. "Well, then, if everything's just hunky-dory, order yourself another beer." She nudged his empty container with the fork in her other hand. "Your bottle's empty."

Grady looked equally surprised he'd finished his entire drink.

As the waitress approached, B.J. pointed at both their empties. "We need refills please, ma'am."

She'd downed two more by the time she swallowed her last bite. Feeling relaxed and loose around the tongue, she grinned at Grady and sat back in her seat, patting her flat belly. "Let me ask you something, Slim. If it's too personal, just tell me to shove off. 'Kay?"

He looked at her warily. "It's too personal."

She laughed and leaned forward, her voice low and confidential. "But I haven't even asked yet."

He edged a centimeter back. "If *you* think it might be too personal, then it is."

"Yeah," she agreed morosely. "You are a sight more modest than I am." Then she ordered them both another round as the waitress came to clear her last plate.

"I don't want any more," Grady informed the woman.

"I'll drink his for him," B.J. spoke up.

He pinned her with a disapproving wince like he wanted to warn her to slow down. But he kept his thoughts to himself, which made B.J. want to blurt out all of hers.

"You see, the thing is," she said. "I'm curious, is all. I want to know if the first time you were with another woman after...you know, after Amy died, did you feel guilty like...like you were cheating on her or anything? Did you have to close your eyes and imagine her face?"

Grady just stared at her; B.J. lifted a hand in apology.

"Okay, I know," she slurred. "'Shut the hell up, B.J.'"

She made a zipping motion across her closed mouth but then kept talking. "I just thought that would have to be the hardest thing to deal with after your spouse passed on. Admitting you're still alive even though they're not and having to move on without 'em...*God*." She shivered. "That must've sucked. How long did you wait before you slept with someone else?"

Grady's mouth fell open. "Excuse me?"

"How long—"

"I heard you the first time," he growled, his lips barely moving.

"Then why aren't you..."

Her question died at the vulnerable flicker in his blue eyes. But then his jaw hardened and his nostrils flared. He jerked his gaze away, and she watched his throat work while he swallowed.

Suddenly, it became clear.

"Oh...my...God," she whispered, stunned mute for a moment before she was able to yelp, "Holy shit, Slim. You mean, you haven't had sex since—"

She realized she was talking too loud when a couple at the next table over stopped eating to send her a scandalized scowl. Grady glared at her like he might reach across the table and strangle her.

She lowered her voice to a hiss and leaned across the table. "Good God. Amy's been dead for over two years."

"I know exactly how long it's been," he snapped, his eyes flashing hot.

B.J. pulled away immediately, realizing how rude and obnoxious she sounded. "Okay, okay," she said. "I'm backing off. I've definitely overstepped my bounds."

She closed her mouth, shutting up for about two seconds before she said, "It's just...*damn*. What're you trying to do to yourself? Win the monk of the year award?"

Through gritted teeth, the words "I thought you said you were backing off," rumbled from deep within his chest.

But B.J. had drunk one beer too many. "Well, I can't, okay. Frankly, I'm worried about you. I mean, Jesus, Slim. This is *not* healthy. Men have to have sex. I grew up with four guys. I know. They can't function without it. You just need to find some anonymous woman and get yourself laid, man."

Grady made a sound that wasn't quite an incredulous laugh and not quite a sob. "I can't believe I'm hearing this." He lifted his eyes and defensively retorted, "Guys go without sex all the time."

"Yeah," B.J. snorted. "They're called priests. And priests aren't the normal, average guy. They got some extra spiritual thing going on that makes them high on God and not women. Now, you may be a good Christian boy and all, but you ain't *that* holy. You're a normal, red-blooded man, and I'm telling you, you need sex or you'll turn into a...a serial killer or something."

Grady shook, looking feral, like she might be his first victim.

"Damn it," she continued. "Don't you think Amy would want you to move on and someday marry again? Or do you think she'd want you to dig a hole next to her and bury yourself in it for the rest of your life? Because, personally, I think she'd want you to go on and live a full, happy life."

Starting to breathe hard, he sent her a pointed glare. "Why don't you mind your own goddamn business and stay out of mine?"

He pushed his chair back and jerked to his feet. B.J. swallowed as he glared down at her. She wanted to apologize, but apologies had never come easily from her. Frankly, she was too ashamed to even speak. Lowering her face, she listened to him snort out a scathing mutter before he strode off.

"Everything okay?" the waitress asked, appearing at B.J.'s side.

"Yeah," B.J. mumbled. "Just dandy."

She rose to her feet and pulled enough money from her wallet to more than cover the bill. Glancing over, she watched Grady stride from the restaurant and gritted her teeth. Damn it. Everyone had been pussyfooting around him for two and a half years. It was time he woke up and faced reality. Amy was never coming back. He *had* to move on.

Suddenly angry with him for making her feel so shitty, B.J. tossed her wad of cash at the surprised waitress and hurried for the exit.

Chapter Four

Grady had already made it to the hotel by the time B.J. exited the restaurant.

It had started to rain, and a light drizzle coated her face. Pushing her drooping bangs out of her eyes, she dashed after him, streaking across the street and jaywalking to catch him before he made it to his room. She was soaked by the time she hit the entrance's overhang and caught sight of him through the window. The miserable shower had drenched him too, but a heedless Grady marched determinedly toward the bank of elevators. She entered the fancy foyer and took off in pursuit.

Never one to bother with propriety, she cupped her hands around her mouth and yelled, "Hey, Rawlings."

He didn't break stride, pause, or give any indication he'd heard her. But she knew he had, mainly because everyone else in the lobby stopped to glance curiously her way.

B.J. ignored the others and raced after Grady. As he stepped into the elevator, she hollered, "Hold that door!"

Another man entering glanced back. When their gazes met, he spiked out a hand, accommodating her request.

"Thank ya, sir," she said breathlessly, slipping inside and settling herself next to Grady.

He must've known it would look childish to hop off, so he merely stood stiff as a board, hands fisted at his side, and studied the numbers above the door as they lit one after the other.

B.J. exploded. "What the hell is wrong with you?"

The other passenger lifted his face, his eyes wide and startled, before he no doubt realized she was ripping on Grady and not him.

"I was actually racing after you to apologize. But you know what? Screw that. I'm not sorry about what I said, because it's about time someone threw an ice cold glass of reality right in your face."

When he refused to meet her glower, she set her hands on her hips. "You make everyone in Tommy Creek uncomfortable whenever you're around because you freeze folks out like they should all feel ashamed they're alive and your wife isn't. Well, you know what? That's just the way it happened. Time to move on."

He continued to stare at the numbers, but his jaw worked furiously, tightening and loosening, tightening back into a knot and then loosening again. "Go to hell," he said in a low, warning baritone.

The third occupant of the elevator backed against the wall and darted skittish glances from Grady to B.J.

"No. *You* go to hell," she countered, jabbing her finger his way. "I'm trying to give you helpful advice on—"

"I don't need your *advice*," he snarled. "I just want to be left alone."

B.J. snorted. "Well, I can't. Amy was important to me too, you know. She'd be devastated if she knew I was letting you pretend you're not alive. You need to join the real world again, Slim. Quit wallowing—"

He whirled toward her so quickly she jerked an intimidated step back. From between clenched teeth, he hissed, "I'll live my life however I damn well please."

When she sucked in a breath, he blinked like

he'd just realized she was cowering. Letting out a low growl, he reeled away and raked a shaky hand through his hair. "Jesus," he whispered. "Why can't everyone just leave me alone?"

B.J. could tell his control was splintering. But she fully believed it'd be healthy for him to lose it. For once in his life, he needed to let out some of the pressure. He needed to alleviate the pain that had been brewing inside him since the moment his wife died.

He needed to go a little crazy.

"It's probably because you bring it on yourself," she said.

He glanced menacingly at her. "Excuse me?"

She rolled her eyes. "Oh, come off it, Slim. If you really wanted everyone to stop feeling so sorry for you and treating you like some kind of wounded animal, you'd stop *acting* like one."

Shock filtered across his cheekbones with a red tinge. His mouth fell open. "What? I do not—"

But his gaze landed on the wet shirt clinging to her breasts, and the words died in his throat. Looking taken aback by the fact she was nipping, he gaped at her with slack-jawed shock. On pure impulse, she pulled her shoulders back a fraction, pushing her chest forward to goad him. For the briefest of moments, his lashes lowered, and he sucked in a quiet breath through his teeth. Then he tore his eyes away, muttering a curse.

B.J. blinked, taken aback. She'd just gotten a response from the ice man. Grady Rawlings had looked at her with sexual awareness. Thinking this might be good for him, she licked her lips and quickly planned her next move.

The elevator stopped on their floor; he shot through the doors as soon as they began to open.

B.J. stuck to his heels, grabbing his arm.

"Don't," he said and shrugged her away, not

36

once stopping his long-legged stride.

She clutched his wet, slippery sleeve again, ignoring the warning.

With a snarl, he swung around, grabbing her wrist in a bruising grip and ripping her hand off him. The scorching heat in his eyes was deadly. "I do *not* ask for anyone's sympathy. The last thing in the world I want is for everyone to treat me like some kind of—"

Ignoring his tirade, B.J. rose onto her toes and stamped her mouth against his, moving so fast, she gave him no time to back off or evade her before their lips were firmly sealed together.

He froze on contact, making a muffled sound of irritation. B.J. tasted his surprise, but she only pressed closer until the front of her soaked shirt clung to his. Then, lifting her hand, she touched the side of his neck. He jerked his face to the side, dodging her.

Not wanting him to break their connection, she bit down on his bottom lip.

In response, he growled and gripped her face in his hands, trying to pry her away, but not succeeding because she dug her teeth in and refused to let him go.

He buried his fingers under her ponytail and balled his hands, capturing two fistfuls of hair and grasping them tight like he was wrapping horse reins around his knuckles. Knowing he intended to yank her off him by the roots of her hair, she retreated instantly, letting go of his lip with a sob of surrender.

They both froze, gaping at each other, chests heaving. His hands remained buried deep in her hair, ruining her ponytail all to hell. Her mouth trembled, moist and swollen. She tasted blood. His blood. Needing some semblance of order in her scattered brain, she licked the salty flavor off her bottom lip.

For some reason, that was his undoing.

With a moan that wasn't quite human, he tightened his fingers in her hair until she gasped. Then he attacked, dragging her back to him and kissing her senseless. He took control, becoming the aggressor. His mouth punished as it moved against hers, bruising and savage. When she opened for him, he plunged his tongue deep, letting out an agonized, hungry sound and ravaging the moist, hot cavity within.

He grew hard against her stomach. She whimpered, envisioning the heated length of him buried deep inside her.

"Grady," she moaned. But his breathless name on her lips must've alerted him to reality because he yanked away, wheezing furiously, and spun blindly toward the wall to brace himself with one arm.

She panted too, gaping at him through her wet lashes. Oxygen chugged into her lungs so fast it burned her chest. His shoulders lifted and fell with their own erratic, unsteady rhythm.

He wouldn't meet her gaze as he held up the wall. But when he blew out a shuddered breath and turned, she saw his side profile and caught sight of a flushed expression with glazed eyes. Pulling himself together, he cleared his throat, stepped past her, and once again started for his room, staggering unsteadily.

B.J. wasn't about to let him go. "You responded to me," she said, hurrying after him. "Are you just going to ignore that?"

He didn't answer.

"Well, I'm not going to let you. I'm not going to let you just walk away from this." She tugged him around. "You're still alive, Grady. You have to accept that."

"Don't," he whispered raggedly, gritting his

teeth like he was in pain. His command was part plea, part order.

Taking her wrist, he weakly pulled her hand off his arm. But he didn't let go of her. Instead, he tightened his grip and looked down at her body. His ragged breathing intensified, and his eyes dilated as they focused on her pouting nipples pushing against wet cloth.

B.J. swallowed. She wanted his mouth on those hard, throbbing peaks. She wanted his tongue stroking her. An electric current spiraled up the insides of her thighs, growing damp and heavy between her legs.

Stepping toward him, she gently pulled her wrist from his captivity and slid her hand around the back of his neck. He was taller than her and certainly stronger. If he wanted to escape, he could. But he merely watched her warily as she drew his head down.

He closed his eyes and lowered his face to receive her. She eased her lips back to his.

This kiss was soft. So soft, she couldn't take it. Thinking her point proven, she moved back, giving him mercy, or maybe giving herself mercy. But his lips followed hers. Her skin buzzed with awareness, and an almost painful tightening began in the bottom of her stomach. He cupped her face and drew her back, opening his mouth and demanding more.

Their tastes melded; she groaned and sank against him, deepening the contact. Feeling primal as she pushed her tongue into his mouth, B.J. wrapped her arms around his neck and arched against him. Grady pulled her closer and devoured her, leaving her no air to breathe, only hormones jazzed and ready for action.

He stroked his hands down to her waist, then grasped the hem of her shirt and jerked it up, cupping her breasts through her bra and finding the pouting tips that had first taunted him. She groaned and shivered.

"God damn you," he managed to hiss against her mouth only to use his tongue to invade and his hips to grind hard against hers. "Damn you to hell for this."

He freed one nipple and rolled it between his thumb and index finger, making her cry out.

She swallowed and choked on the sound, suddenly realizing what was happening.

Whoa. Wait. Public hotel hallway.

"My room," she wheezed before he sealed his mouth back to hers and continued to torment her.

She backed toward her door, which was only a few steps behind her. He followed, crowding her space and stroking her nonstop. Though she had no idea how she managed to unlock her room without coming up for air, the door slipped open, and she and Grady tumbled inside, not once breaking what was fast becoming the greatest kiss of all time.

A slight glow emanated from the bathroom where she'd forgotten to turn off the light before leaving to go down to supper. But otherwise, they kissed in the dark. She barely had the door shut before he pushed her against it and worked open the top button of her damp jeans. He only broke the kiss to nip at her jaw with his teeth. Not bothering to flip on a light, B.J. kicked off her boots and reached for his belt buckle.

She barely unzipped his trousers in the time it took him to shed her jeans and underwear in one mighty tug. He didn't say anything, but he did let out a groan when he covered her mound with a hot palm and kneaded her once before pushing a finger inside to find her soaked and dripping.

B.J. gasped, clutching his shoulder for support. Her body quivered with every bone-shivering caress he gave. He barely nudged another finger in, brushing the inside of her thigh with the back of his rough knuckles, and she almost came.

She dove her hands into the waistband of his underwear and cupped his ass before slipping them and his jeans down. As soon as they dropped to free his penis, he lifted her, spreading her knees to either side of his ribs, and buried himself deep, plunging all the way to her core.

Her head fell back, and she hit her skull against the hard door.

"Mother of God," she cried, unable to decipher if she was cursing the pleasure of him stretching her sensitive passage, the pain in her head, or both.

They were doing this. They were really doing this. Of all the times she'd dreamed of being with Grady, she'd never imagined this...this all-consuming sensation: the dampness of his skin clinging to hers, the fall of his breath on her neck, the thickness of his hair in her hands. It was more than she could process.

He didn't slow his pace—not that she wanted him to. He surged back, harder and faster, pushing them both to the brink.

Her body went taut and hot while he rode her with deep, confident thrusts, only to pull nearly all the way out before surging back in. She clung to him, clawing his back, and fought to keep from coming too soon. It felt like she was being pulled apart by a string. When the wire snapped, the explosion inside her was like lightning, zapping through all four limbs and coming out the ends of her fingers and toes.

"God," Grady growled and bucked one last time, grabbing her hard as he joined the fireworks. "God."

Afterward, he stayed motionless for a couple of seconds before easing out and sliding limply to the floor. Still in shock from experiencing such an earth-shattering climax, B.J. collapsed next to him, too limp to move.

As her breathing slowly settled, she stared wide-eyed into the dark room and listened to Grady suck in air beside her.

Well. She'd done it now.

Wondering what was going to result from her wild, unplanned seduction, she closed her eyes and set a hand over her heart. If he hated her, she wouldn't blame him. She'd forced him, pushed him beyond his control. Grady Rawlings was one controlled individual. He wouldn't take her manipulation lightly. Intentional or not.

In memory of his dead wife, he'd kept his body as pure and chaste as a church for the past two and a half years. But it'd only taken a matter of minutes for destructive B.J. to come along and desecrate his saintly temple. Satan was no doubt grinning up at her, giving her a conspiring wink and the thumbs-up as she lay next to Grady.

This was too unreal.

Abruptly realizing her breathing had returned to normal while he still gasped for air, her heart plummeted.

Oh, God. What had she done to him?

"Grady?" she whispered, reaching out. He jumped when her hand found his arm. Body shaking, he was cold and clammy to the touch.

"No," she uttered and crawled closer, "Sweetie, don't. Please, don't." She put her hands on either side of his face, moving her thumbs to the corners of his eyes to make sure he wasn't crying. When she found the skin dry, she felt like bawling herself because he wouldn't. "I'm sorry," she whispered.

Instinctively, she put her arms around him and laid her cheek against his chest.

Her voice broke. "I'm so sorry."

She felt terrible. He was probably reeling in guilt because he'd just cheated on his dead wife, and it was all her fault.

She sniffed like she was going to howl any second. Then she awkwardly patted his hair and rubbed his back, having no idea how to help him, or comfort him, or stop this pain she'd caused.

"I'm sorry," she said again, feeling pathetic and useless. For someone who usually choked on apologies, this one gushed off her tongue like water from Niagara Falls. "Please. I'm so sorry."

Lifting her face, she leaned in to kiss his cheek but missed and caught the corner his mouth instead.

In response, he turned...and not away from her. Seeking her, his warm breath fell on her lips a split second before he kissed her hungrily, sucking from her nectar.

Unprepared for the hot torrent of his mouth, B.J. gasped; her body responded immediately. She forgot her worry and regret, and gurgled out an unexpected cry when his hands came up to feast on her breasts. Obviously irritated with her damp, tangled shirt in his way, he stripped it off and went about shedding her bra. All the while, he continued to kiss her, the contact morphing from greedy to curious and then to explorative.

Once she was entirely naked, he cupped her bare breasts she'd unknowingly been pressing against him. A sob rose in his throat. He nudged her down onto to the floor right there by the door, kicking his pants and underwear off his ankles and keeping his mouth against hers the entire time. Their lips became permanently fused as he finished unbuttoning his own shirt and shrugged it off.

He broke from her mouth to dip his face and kiss his way down the center of her body, starting in the hollow at the base of her throat and working his way south, not even pausing between her breasts or navel. But he did falter when his lips lowered to about four inches below her belly button. She tensed in expectation, waiting for him to move lower. But that was as far as he went, making her body burn for more.

Oh, God. Who would've known Grady Rawlings would be such a tease?

His fingers followed the torture next, as he skimmed them over her clavicle and around her breasts, caressing close to her most sensitive points, but never providing direct contact. It had to be the most sensual moment of her life, and yet he seemed perfectly content to turn a little PG, driving her insane by exploring safe zones.

Pausing at her old snakebite a few inches under her arm, he bent and kissed the healed wound. It felt very intimate to reveal such a scar to Grady. He didn't ask about it, only lavished it with loving attention and then moved to the next scar he found on her knee.

Then, damn it, the man turned cuddly. He shuddered out a breath and lay on top of her, making sure every inch of his skin pressed against hers from their ankles to their necks. Sighing, he relaxed against her. His arms came around her as he rested his face by her shoulder, lying there quietly like he was soaking in the sensation.

He was...he was hugging her, she realized, and burying his face in her hair like he was hiding from the fact he needed such contact...such comfort. But this was definitely an embrace. She swallowed; tears pricked her eyes at the sweetness of the moment.

"Touch me back," he whispered. Manually taking her hand, he pressed her palm against the side of his ribcage. "Please."

She did, uncertain at first while she ran her fingers up the back of his shoulders. Shuddering out his pleasure, he closed his eyes and let his head roll back, allowing her to explore him as he had her. She traced the sculpted plane of his stomach and abs, and he investigated the curve of her hip before trailing his short nails up her spine.

The pace slowed to a drowsy tempo, neither rushing as they learned the contours and curves of their partner. When Grady finally abandoned her mouth, he only moved his lips to other body parts. His tongue and teeth lavished her. She sighed and threaded her fingers through his damp hair.

He kissed and touched like he was making love. There was no humping or screwing or any kind of degrading term like that with this man. Once he was in control of himself, he was all about gentle and soft. It was so damn precious she mimicked his kindness, touching him tenderly, rubbing her fingers up his arms and over his elbows, investigating places she'd never gone on a man, simple places like his wrists and earlobes, but places that suddenly seemed incredibly sensual.

This was how a married couple made love, she thought. But then, he *was* a married man, wasn't he? He wouldn't know any other way. Jesus, he was probably thinking of his wife as he nuzzled her neck with his nose, trying to forget he was with—

"B.J.," he groaned, barely lifting his voice, a low rumble that vibrated through her and made her shiver.

So, okay, maybe he wasn't thinking about Amy, which only made this better...and so much worse.

"Can I..." he started to ask and then hesitated.

"Yes," she answered with no pause whatsoever.

Yes, he could do anything he wanted.

He lifted her leg, wrapping her thigh around his hip, and sunk himself inside her with an achingly slow plunge that had her gasping and bowing against him.

Slipping her hands ever so softly over his back and gracefully lifting her hips to meet this thrust, B.J. closed her eyes and pretended this was exactly what it felt like: making love.

His pace filled her with agonizing frustration. It didn't take long for her to crave the speed again. She yearned to drown in the sensations, dive into the storm. But he took his ever-loving time like he relished discovering each inch of her with his mouth and hands, like each instance he moved within her, he needed to savor the feeling with concentrated deliberation.

B.J. squeezed him tight with her thighs, digging her heels into his ass and holding him deeper, urging him on and trying to coax him into cooperating and going faster.

"Hurry," she rasped.

He looked down at her with sweat beading his brow and his lips tight with focus. "I want slow," was his steady command.

She shook her head...or more like thrashed it from side to side. "I can't—" Oh, God, she was going to die—or go insane—if he didn't hurry. "Grady, I can't."

"You will," he said, and, damn it, she did.

She came slowly, feeling it methodically work its way up her toes and the insides of her thighs, until it hit her g-spot. Then she came and came and came...and came. Above her, Grady gasped and tensed. Picking up his pace and pounding into her, he released himself, joining her orgasm. He gritted his teeth, telling her just how hard he strained as he gave that last plunge. Then he groaned deep and long, holding his large, quivering body taut as he closed his eyes.

The silence that followed was deafening.

B.J. didn't think she was ever going to stop shuddering from the aftershocks, not even when he collapsed heavily on top of her, his limp deadweight making her wonder if he'd physically passed out.

Just when she decided she liked the warm,

blanketing load, he picked himself up and rolled off her. She instantly chilled, missing his heat. Closing her eyes, she wished him back, and then jumped when he actually curled his arm around her waist and tugged her against him.

They held each other close, like a pair a frightened children huddling in the dark and worrying about the scary monster coming for them. And, damn, she did feel terrified out of her mind. Reality could be one mean bogeyman.

Not sure what had just happened between the lines of all that moaning and orgasming, she clutched him for dear life, thinking he was the only thing solid and real in this crazy, mixed-up situation.

He kissed her hair and stroked her arm, settling her nerves. She wasn't sure if he knew she needed his tender touch after that explosion of raw feelings and need, but he provided exactly the kind of tranquil comfort that eased her. Relaxing and closing her eyes, she inhaled the smell of his sweat that oozed what could only be called a Grady pheromone.

Lounging against him so peacefully, she imagined a husband and wife this way, all happy and satisfied after making a baby together.

She paused.

Baby?

Her eyes jerked open; she stared up at the ceiling, feeling frozen.

"Did you wear a condom?"

What kind of stupid question was that? Of course he hadn't...in either round. She'd been there the entire time. She knew perfectly well there'd been no pausing for prophylactic safely.

Grady went tense. He sat up and looked down at her with wide eyes.

"Shit," she said and sat up as well. "I...I should

clean this off...or something."

She couldn't see him clearly in the dim light, but she could tell he wasn't moving.

"Not that it would make much difference," she added as she pushed to her feet. "But washing's better than nothing...don't you think?"

He didn't respond.

She felt stupid, explaining herself and asking his advice. But what the hell was she supposed to say? She'd never had unprotected sex before. She'd never completely forgotten about safety. She'd never coerced a man into deserting his vow of chastity and, damn it, she'd certainly never experienced two orgasms right in a row like that.

She was completely at loose ends over how to handle any of this.

Feeling stiff and suddenly sore, she moved toward the bathroom and hobbled inside, quietly shutting the door behind her. Once alone in the brightly lit chamber, she let out a breath and pressed a hand to her quaking stomach. She met her own gaze in the mirror. Large, dazed brown doe eyes stared back. She looked like a woman who'd just taken a long, hard tumble with a very potent lover. Her naked skin was red and chafed from his five-o'clock shadow while her hair, which had come free from its ponytail holder, was mussed in a ratted, mangled mess. Her lips were swollen and bright rose in color.

B.J. blinked and lifted a hand to touch her mouth. Holy Lord. She looked good and truly debauched. As she glanced back at the door, her stomach rolled again with unease. This was foreign territory indeed. She was actually thinking like a woman as she wondered what was going on in Grady's head out there.

She wondered what he thought of her now and how awkward it was going to be when she finally left the bathroom. She knew she'd been wrong...but he hadn't stopped her. In fact, the second time had been entirely his doing...his sweet, slow, almost-loving doing.

B.J. grinned. *The second time.* Imagine that. They'd had sex two consecutive times in a row.

Thinking things couldn't be as bad as she'd originally surmised, she hurried to the shower, turned on the water, and cleaned herself quickly. All the while, she almost expected Grady, the sexually repressed nymphomaniac who'd just gone twice in a row, to pop in and join her for some kinky, yet satisfying, shower play. But he didn't enter the bathroom.

Once she'd rinsed herself clean, she hurried out of the tub and slung a towel around her body, wrapping it up under her armpits and tucking the end between her tender breasts. She hadn't brought any clothes into the lavatory, so she went to the door and eased it open, wondering if he'd be dressed or not.

But when B.J. ducked her head into her hotel room, all traces of Grady Rawlings were gone. The only thing to let her know she hadn't imagined everything was the soreness between her legs and the hot rash of beard burn on her neck, not to mention the pile of her damp clothes strewn across the floor.

Straightening, she stepped fully into the room and ignored the ball of disappointment that thumped into the base of her stomach. Of course, she was relieved too, she assured herself. If he was upset or remorseful, she didn't particularly want to face him and look into his accusing eyes.

But the disappearing act kind of stung. It told her without a doubt their encounter had been a mistake.

B.J. nodded to herself, mentally repeating that

it had indeed been a stupid, careless blunder as she slumped toward the bed. Not bothering to put on clothes, she dropped the towel and crawled under the covers.

Curling into a tight ball, she lay there. She shouldn't have left him out here alone. Or better yet, she shouldn't have pushed him into any of this tonight. She should've just shut up and let it all alone. Damn it, she shouldn't have been so rude, and she certainly shouldn't have kissed him.

But she had. She'd done it all.

He was probably in his room, feeling as guilty as hell. He hadn't planned on ever being with another woman again. Something inside her told her he hadn't. Not that it mattered. She'd destroyed his plans and felt like a piece of crap for it.

"What a complete mess," she announced to the quiet room.

Then, unable to help it, she burst into tears.

"God, what's wrong with me?" she muttered.

B.J. Gilmore, the tomboy of Tommy Creek, Texas, never cried. But, tonight, she did. She let the tears flow as she bawled herself to sleep.

Chapter Five

Grady crawled out of bed before dawn. All night, he kept jerking awake every half hour, haunted by erotic images, until he finally grew fed up with trying to sleep and shoved the sheets off his burning skin. He took a shower. As the water sluiced over his shoulders and through his hair, steaming the air around him, he closed his eyes, rested a hand against the shower wall, and bowed his head. Deciding this had to be about the most confusing moment of his life, he let out a long breath and lifted his face to the spray.

From one perspective, he wanted to hate B.J. Gilmore. She had no right to pressure him into doing anything he didn't want to do, something he hadn't been prepared to do. This was his life. He decided when he was ready to move on and when he wasn't.

Damn some hot-headed tomboy who thought he needed a little prodding.

On the other hand, he wanted to return to her room, lock them both inside, and continue where they'd left off. She'd been right about one thing. Going without sex for too long couldn't be healthy...*hadn't* been healthy. It'd turned him into a maniac, an utter savage. He just wanted to tie her to the nearest bed and keep her there for two weeks straight. He wanted to pound and rut until she passed out from orgasm overdose. The things he had in mind would make it so she'd never walk right again.

God.

Rippling with need, his dick lengthened and his

balls tightened. His body wanted more of B.J. Gilmore, and it didn't care what he had to do to get her.

Yet decency told him he should apologize. His mother hadn't raised him to be the type of man who kicked up a woman's skirt twice in a row without protection and then ditched out on her at the first opportunity. He was better than that. A gentleman.

Guilt clogged his throat, and he swallowed, trying to work it loose.

Truth be told, he wouldn't have survived if he'd stayed in her room. His nerves were rent to hell, and every particle of his being felt scattered and disorganized. He didn't know who he was or how to be. He just knew he had to get as far away from her as possible.

In his entire life, he'd only been with one woman. He'd dated Amy for three years until they'd had sex on the night of their junior prom. At that point, it was a given they'd eventually marry. So, he'd never thought he'd be with anyone else. She'd been "the one." He'd assumed he'd never have another for the rest of his life. But he'd had B.J., the very woman his dead wife had helped raise.

He'd always thought of her as the mouthy little Gilmore tomboy whose mama had died in a car accident when she was only three. B.J. was a tough hard-ass who didn't take crap from anyone. Grady had never looked at her in a sexual light before, not until he'd glanced at her in the elevator and seen her nipples poking through her wet shirt, making him want to warm them with his breath. Of course, she'd been talking to him about sex, so at that point it was the only thing on his mind. But Grady was thirty-two years old, for Christ's sake. He should've had more restraint. The mere sight of a woman's tits definitely shouldn't have pushed him over the edge.

Yet it had.

And now, here he was...confused. There was shame, sure. He'd just been with a woman who wasn't his wife—whom he never intended to make his wife—and he'd liked it. It went against every single old-fashioned moral fiber he possessed.

Then there was anger. If she'd only left him alone, he wouldn't have touched a hair on her head the entire trip, and none of his morals would be compromised. God, why hadn't she just left him the hell alone?

The guilt for ditching out on her afterward ate at him the most, but the longing thumping through his bloodstream didn't help in the least. His libido craved her again. Like a junkie going through withdrawal, his body felt edgy and impatient, needing more...now.

He didn't want to want her. He wasn't ready for this pulsing, gut-eating kind of necessity. He still loved Amy. He wanted to be with Amy. He wanted to make love with *her*, not some rude, irritating wannabe man.

But Amy was gone, and he felt lost and so conflicted, the water turned cold in his shower before he realized how long he'd been standing there.

Cursing under his breath, he shut off the stream and pushed the shower door open to reach for a towel.

One thing was certain. He needed to apologize. It didn't matter how much he blamed B.J. for their encounter, he'd fully participated. And leaving her alone afterward was inexcusable.

He'd say something on the plane.

But damn...he certainly didn't relish the idea of being stuck alone with her on a tiny aircraft the entire way back to Tommy Creek...not when she'd be close enough he could smell her or, God help him, lean over and taste her.

****

B.J. arrived at the rented hangar half an hour before their rendezvous. Blood thrummed through her veins as she neared her plane. Today, she wanted to fly fast. She needed to vent, and her skywagon was just the tool in which to do that.

She'd had her Cessna TU206 for five years now. The Gilmore family business already had three planes between them. But ever since she was six years old and her father had taken her up on a crop-dusting job, she'd wanted one to call her own. Pop let her think she was commandeering the throttle, and she'd been a goner. It'd taken her sixteen years to finally get approved for the loan to buy her own.

The money she'd borrowed for her twenty-year-old Cessna exceeded the mortgage on her house, but B.J. thought it was worth it. Her single-engine aircraft did everything she needed it to do. It was an SUV of the air. She used it for aerial photography on occasion, cargo-hauling at other times, and least frequently she transported up to four passengers or flew for skydiving lessons and jumps. She figured it'd pay itself off in another ten years if business kept on as it was.

Thankful it was a bright, sunny day, she pushed her mirrored sunglasses into place, making sure they were snugly settled before she patted the side of her Cessna in welcome. Nothing short of the hand of God was going to make her take those shades off either. Under the reflective lenses, her eyes were puffy and red.

Her hair was up in a ponytail—big shocker there—and she wore a black tank top with blue jeans. It definitely didn't scream, *come and get me, big boy*, but when she glanced up and saw Grady watching her as he approached, she felt as if she were wearing the slinkiest, hottest piece of lingerie on the planet. He wanted her. It was spelled out in his clear blue eyes as his gaze slowly traveled down her body and meandered its way back up again.

Shock and animal awareness collided hard in her gut. She still couldn't believe he'd actually showed. It wasn't like there would be any commercial flights landing in their small countryside airstrip anytime in the next millennium, but she'd wondered if he'd just rent a car or something and drive home. She'd in no way thought he'd torture himself by riding back with her in a small enclosed space for nearly a whole hour.

But here he was at eight o'clock sharp, staring at her like he wanted her for breakfast.

She sucked in a breath and tried to keep it cool, though questions stirred inside her. Did that hungry look mean he'd forgiven her? Did his presence mean he wasn't mad? Could she hope all was okay between them?

When their gazes met, he paused, his eyes frosting slightly. She sighed. Okay, so maybe everything wasn't entirely kosher. Turning away quickly, she opened the clamshell cargo door.

"Come on, B.J.," she muttered to herself as she tossed her bag haphazardly into the belly of her plane. "You're the queen of casual. You treat everyone the same. Just imagine he's everyone else and not Grady Rawlings."

Yeah, imagine she hadn't spent a third of the night pissing the hell out of him, another third of the night screwing his brains out, and then the last third of the night sobbing like there was no tomorrow because of him. Sure. No problem.

She sucked in a breath and turned back. He'd drawn close enough for her to see the tired yet wary lines around his eyes and mouth. He looked about as ready for another confrontation with her as she felt about apologizing to him, which pretty much meant neither of them would be doing any talking for the next hour.

"Ready?" she asked.

He nodded and opened his mouth. No words came out.

Her stomach did a flip-flop, but she amazed herself by keeping it cool. Arching a brow, she asked, "Yeah?"

He closed his mouth, shook his head, and then glanced away, obviously horrified with himself for chickening out.

"Then let's head out," she answered brusquely. "I just finished my inspection."

Not bothering to touch his luggage this morning, she deserted him and made her way to the cockpit. Behind her, the cargo doors shut and seconds later, Grady slipped into the seat next to hers. A wave of déjà vu hit. Hadn't they already played this game before? Uncomfortable silence. Awkward attempts at conversation. Stolen glances.

Except this time around, B.J. knew what he looked like naked.

She didn't think she could do it. There was no way she could act like nothing had happened. On the other hand, there was no way she could talk to him about what happened either. And there didn't seem to be any kind of happy medium.

Briefly she wondered what he'd do if she politely said, *Hey, would you please step out of the Cessna and find your own way home? I can't take the sexual tension and all this guilt I'm feeling.*

B.J. shook her head and started the plane.

Okay, so they were obviously going to go with the whole memory-loss plan and pretend neither of them could recall attacking each other less than eight hours ago and ripping the clothes off their bodies.

"Here goes nothing," she muttered under her breath.

From the corner of her eyes, she saw him turn

his head her way as if he'd heard her speak but hadn't caught the words. When he didn't comment, she blocked him and proceeded to get them in the air.

Five minutes later, they'd climbed as far into the sky as she was going to go, and B.J. pushed the limits of their speed. But it didn't help. As much as she loved going fast, today it didn't seem to give her the rush she craved. Instead, she kept staring at Grady's knee from the corner of her eye. His thigh was incased in tight Wranglers, and she wondered if she reached over and set her hand on it, if it'd still be as hard as she remembered it being last night.

God, she really needed to get her mind away from that. If she was going to do anything about their evening together, she should be giving an apology instead of partaking in a little air action. This was so not the day to join the mile-high club.

She had an awful feeling if she tried to eat crow, though, and own up to her mistake of pushing him into the sack—er, against the door, as was the case—then she'd somehow turn the tables around and demand to know why he'd ditched out on her just when things were getting good.

Okay, so she knew why, and she didn't blame him a lick. That didn't mean it didn't hurt.

Gritting her teeth, she commanded herself to stop thinking about it altogether. There wasn't going to be any kind of resolution if she tried to bring up the topic, not that she wanted to anyway. So, ignoring the tension was going to have to be her best bet. But, hell, there was no way she could ignore it, especially when he shifted in his seat and stirred the air around them, rustling up his scent so her body responded and the insides of her thighs tingled.

B.J. couldn't do it any longer. She glanced over. "Want to learn a couple of things about flying?" she blurted out, not even realizing what she was going to ask.

He lifted his face. His blue eyes showed surprise, but other than that, she couldn't read anything. The nerves in her guts knotted and then tightened painfully. She ripped her gaze away.

"The basic concept is pretty simple," she started in, ignoring his lack of response and the growing ball in her stomach. She needed to get her mind off...well, you know. And nothing could grab B.J.'s attention like talking planes.

So, she talked planes.

"There're four forces at work when flying. Lift, weight, thrust and drag."

Oh, God. Did she just say thrust?

"To take off, your thrust, uh, has to be more powerful than your drag and your lift has to be more powerful than your weight. To land, it's vice versa. Drag dominates thrust and weight dominates lift."

When he didn't say a word in reply, she shrugged and continued. No way was she going to drive herself nuts, just sitting there, letting her thoughts take over. So she blubbered on.

"Weight and drag are natural forces. You see, weight is merely gravity trying to yank the plane back to earth, and drag is like the wind on your face when you're running. It's air pushing against you when you're trying to go forward. Therefore thrust and lift are fashioned by the plane mechanically to get it up and going."

And here came *thrust* and *get it up* in the same sentence. Jesus.

"The propeller makes up our thrust to...to work against the drag and keep us heading forward, and lift happens when air blows above and below the wings, helping us go up and down."

Grady remained stonily quiet; she didn't have a clue whether he was listening to her prattle or not. There was no way she was going to glance over again though. Her hormones had nearly fried themselves out the last time she'd snuck a peek.

"So, once you've got your lift and thrust overpowering weight and drag," she droned on, sounding more like an encyclopedia than herself, "you're in the air. Now once we're sky bound, we deal with pitch, roll and yaw to keep the plane going in the direction we want."

Lifting her hand to demonstrate, B.J. held her hand flat, palm facing down.

"Pitch is moving the nose of the plane up and down." She lifted her fingertips higher than her wrist. "Roll steadies the wings." She moved her thumb higher than her pinkie and then rotated back to dip her thumb lower than her pinkie. "And yaw," she finished, "is controlled by moving the rudder to change the direction of the plane left and right." She kept her palm flat and twisted her hand at her wrist, moving the tips of her fingers to the left and then to the right.

"So, what're all those meters for?" Grady asked, surprising the spit out of her when he pointed to the gauges in front of her.

For a moment, she was too startled to speak. But Holy Lord, the man was actually listening to her boring lesson. She quickly licked her lips and dove headfirst back into the tutorial.

"This here's called the instrument panel. And this..." She motioned to six round gauges in front of her. "...is the basic T arrangement. The attitude indicator is always the top center gauge."

"Attitude indicator?"

B.J. grinned and risked an ornery grin his way. "Yeah, it tells us if the plane's in a bad mood or not."

When he just stared at her, she rolled her eyes. "Okay, so it really shows the plane's pitch and bank. It tells us if the wings are even and where our nose is according to the horizon.

"Here," she offered. "Let me just roll us a little to the side, and you can watch the change on the indicator."

When she tipped them over toward the right, Grady immediately snaked his hand out and latched his fingers around the edge of his seat.

B.J. cleared her throat. "Sorry about that," she offered and leveled the plane back to rights.

Grady remained stiffly quiet.

"Anyway," she went on, rubbing at the back of her neck, "to the right of the attitude indicator is the altimeter. Right now, it's adjusted to measure feet above sea level. And to the left of the attitude indicator is the airspeed indicator, comparable to a speedometer in a truck. See this white band here? That's the normal speed for operating when you're landing and the flaps are open. The green range is for normal operation without the flaps all the way out. And yellow is for smooth air operation, only you don't make any abrupt control movements when you're going that fast."

B.J. sucked in a breath she hadn't realized she'd been holding. "Then there's this small little red line," she concluded.

As she pointed at it, she glanced Grady's way. "Never redline it," she told him seriously.

The red line showed the maximum airspeed and was never to be exceeded for any reason. B.J. liked to fly in the caution zone under the yellow band, pushing her limits. But she'd never redlined it before. Certainly not like she'd done last night in the hotel when she'd pushed a certain someone beyond his limits. What had resulted was a complete malfunction of a total gentleman. Redlining a plane was a lot like the explosion that had happened to Grady when she'd pushed him past his yellow zone.

"So, where's the gas gauge?" he asked before she could finish explaining the basic T arrangement.

"Oh, it's right—" As her finger landed on the gauge, she paused and frowned. "What the hell?"

Instantly alert, Grady whirled from inspecting the panel to studying her face. "What?"

"We're low on gas."

"What?" he said again, a little more anxious this time.

"We shouldn't be this low," she murmured to herself. "I filled up before we left yesterday, and a single tank should be able to get us—damn," she muttered, clicking the mike of her headphones to a different frequency.

It took her nearly a minute to make contact, but finally her father's voice called out, "B.J., what's the problem?"

"I need to talk to Leroy," she responded. "*Now.*"

Once again, a white-knuckled segment of time passed in uncomfortable silence. B.J. could almost see her father bustling from the tower and yelling at his brother to get his butt into gear. He knew full well she wouldn't be contacting base yet unless there were problems. Pop was probably having a coronary right now, wondering what was wrong with her.

As they waited, the tension nearly poured off her passenger in waves. B.J. was thankful he was keeping quiet, though. She didn't want to explain what she thought the problem was. She didn't want to look him in the eye and tell him they might not make it home.

Finally, Leroy's static-filled voice growled through the speakers. "What?"

"Hey, Bub," she greeted casually. "Remember when I asked you if you changed that fuel line, because I thought it looked a little ragged?"

"Oh, yeah. Forgot."

Her blood congealed in her veins. "You forgot? But you said you'd already switched it."

"I was going to, but…"

"But *what*, damn it?"

Leroy only muttered a lame, "Sorry."

B.J. clenched her teeth. "Leroy, when I get home, I'm going to kick your butt to New York and back." *If* she made it home.

She glanced over and caught Grady's face. His features had turned ashen, his upper lip beaded in sweat.

"Just sit tight," she said in a grim voice.

"Anything I can do?"

Before she could tell him no, Jebediah Gilmore's voice came back on the line. "B.J., what's the situation?"

For a second, she couldn't answer. The engine shuddered; Grady sucked in an audible breath while she cursed.

This was all wrong. There hadn't been any puddles leaking from the plane when she'd done her pre-flight inspection this morning. No torn hoses. No sign of trouble. The line must've finally come loose *after* they'd already gone wheels up. Damn it.

"We're leaking gas like a sieve," she told her father after she spent a moment steadying the wings. "We were three-quarters full when we headed out of Houston, but now it's less than three-quarters empty."

"How far away are you?" Pop asked calmly.

B.J. glanced toward Grady. "Halfway there, maybe."

For a minute, her dad didn't answer. They were all doing the math in their heads, all realizing she'd be short making it home a quarter of a tank.

"Okay," Jeb's voice responded. "Just take 'er easy. Keep me updated."

"Will do," B.J. answered.

Once it was just Grady and B.J. again, he finally said, "Is there an airstrip nearby where we can land?"

She shook her head numbly. Not in this part of the state. "We can either head back or keep on toward home."

"Which is closer?"

"Probably Houston. But it'll take a lot of gas to get us turned back around."

"So, we'll keep on toward Tommy Creek," he stated more than asked.

B.J. nodded. After a tense moment, she finally glanced over. "If worse comes to worse, we'll run out of fuel and have to dead stick somewhere."

He nodded. "What does that mean?"

"It means we'll have to land somewhere without engine power..." Maybe like in an open field somewhere.

Though he'd already been pale enough, Grady's face drained of the rest of its grayish tinge. "That's possible?"

"Hell, yeah."

He glanced toward her, his blue eyes full of hope. "And you've done it before?"

She swallowed. "Uh...no. Sorry." Wincing, she knew she should've joined in when Buck and Leroy had that dead stick landing competition a few years back.

Grady's head bobbed again. He was taking this awfully well. For all the trouble she'd caused him in the last twenty-four hours, the man should be cussing her up one side and down the other.

"I'm sorry," she said again, feeling the apology from the bottom of her heart. "About everything."

Sorry she'd pushed him into cheating on his dead wife and then for maybe killing him today in her plane.

Grady didn't answer. He just looked out the window at the earth he no doubt didn't want to crash into. "I shouldn't have left," he said and swung his head around slowly to pin her with an intense look.

"I shouldn't have left your room without..."

Good Lord, he was going to apologize to *her*? After all the things she'd put him through—was still putting him through—he actually thought he'd done something wrong.

Though it did B.J.'s heart good to hear him say such, it only caused her own guilt to multiply.

She shook her head and lifted her hand to shut him up. "Don't worry about it." She definitely didn't want to talk about this right now. If she was going to die in a few minutes, she'd rather just take it all to the grave with her.

But Grady was obviously more into the deathbed confession thing than she. "I was wrong," he insisted. "I was raised better than to—"

"Look," she cut in. "We can talk about it on the ground."

"But—"

"I'll land us safe and sound, Slim. Don't go thinking this is it. All right? Neither of us is going to die today."

He didn't answer, and she glanced over at him. "We're not going to crash." When she noticed he wasn't strapped in, she scowled. "Put your damn seatbelt on."

He blinked. "I thought you said it wouldn't make any difference."

B.J. sighed. "It was a joke, Rawlings. Can't you take a joke?"

Grabbing the protective strap, he muttered under his breath, "Next time you want to tell a joke, try knock, knock or why did the chicken cross the road."

She heard him, but decided to act like she hadn't. "If we have to make a hard landing, that harness just might save your life and keep you from being jostled around and getting the shit beat out of you."

Grady clicked the belt into place and then tightened the straps for good measure.

"If you'd feel safer, you can get into a seat in the back," she offered.

"What about you?"

She was about to come back with a sarcastic crack about who'd fly the plane if she cowered in the back with him, but then the engine cut out momentarily, and she clenched her teeth as the stick became harder to control.

"I'll be fine." She held on tight as the engine stopped, sputtered, and then roared to life again.

Grady didn't move away from her side, and she didn't want to think about how much that reassured her.

"How are we on gas?" he asked.

"Lower," was her vague answer.

He looked too pale. She didn't like scaring him, so, having pity, she reached over and squeezed his hand. He squeezed back and wasn't going to let go. B.J. would've thought his fingers would be freezing, but they were warm and comforting, and she wanted to hang on forever.

But..."Okay, I need my hand back now," she finally admitted.

He immediately let go, and she wrapped her fingers around the throttle.

The next half hour held some of the most nerve-wracking minutes of her life. The engine kept coughing and wheezing, not getting the gas it needed, and the gauge level kept sinking closer and closer to empty. Her father got back on the radio and started asking for updates more frequently. As B.J. calmly relayed how the steering was getting choppier, she wished Pop would shut up so she didn't have to say aloud what was going on, letting Grady know how bad things were getting.

When their hangar finally came into view and

she could read the large black letters spelling "T. Creek" painted on the silver tin roof, she'd never been so relieved.

"We're going to make it," she said and grinned at Grady...just as the engine died.

The only sound that followed was the free wind, whistling through the cracks of the aircraft.

His eyes went wide. "Oh, my God."

"No, it's okay," she assured, her voice calm as she held the throttle, nice and steady. "It's okay. I've got it. I'm not going to let anything happen to you. We're still going to make it."

He managed a nod but looked green around the gills. Not that she blamed him. He probably wouldn't believe her until they actually touched ground.

It wasn't the smoothest landing she'd ever made, but with shaking hands and no help from her plane, she thought she did damn fine. By the time they stopped skipping down the runway and were slowed to a stop, Grady had his seatbelt off and looked like he was going to leap from the plane and kiss the tarmac. But he stayed rooted to his seat, both hands wrapped firmly around the edge of his thighs as if they might have to be surgically removed.

B.J. tugged off her headphones and undid her safety harness. "You okay?"

He nodded. "Yeah. You?"

"I'm good," she said, then let out a whoop of triumph. "God *damn*!" She leapt across the cockpit and right into his lap. Grady jerked in surprise as she threw her arms around his neck and gave him a brief but hard victory kiss on the mouth.

When she pulled away, she grinned and let out a breath. "Was that great, or what? Oh yeah! It feels good to be alive."

Ignoring the stunned look on his face, she shimmied off him and threw open the door, already hopping out.

Her father and all three brothers barreled toward her. As soon as her two feet hit the runway, she hurried to meet them, aiming straight for Leroy.

"You could've gotten us killed, you jackass," she snarled, her fists already clenching.

"What?" he said. "You landed just fine."

Growling, she wound her arm back and decked him full in the mouth, causing his head to snap back.

He cursed and covered his face with both hands. Red immediately seeped through the cracks between his fingers.

Feeling no remorse, B.J. raged, "Next time you're not going to do something I ask you to, tell me so I can goddamn do it myself."

"Next time, just do it yourself." Leroy muttered, wiping blood out of his nose. He took a step toward her, his own hand balling. B.J. widened her stance and braced herself, in the mood to fight.

But Rudy caught her around the waist and pulled her away just as Buck put a hand on Leroy's chest and stopped him midstep.

"Cut it out, you two," Pop bellowed.

"She hit me first," Leroy said, scowling around Buck's shoulder at her.

"And you deserved it," Pop stated, getting a defiant sneer for his comment.

B.J. was about to smart back something else to set Leroy off even more when she finally noticed Grady exiting the plane with his bag in tow.

She paused and turned. Still pale as all get out, he hobbled past them. Her innards lurched with guilt.

"You sure you're okay?" she said, moving toward him.

"I'm fine," he said and held up a hand as if to ward her off.

"Grady." Pop stepped forward, yanking off his ball cap and holding it to his chest. "On behalf of the Gilmore plane service, I apologize for all this trouble. If you'll just follow me to the hangar, I'll write you out a refund right now."

B.J. gulped, suddenly remembering he was a customer, and she'd just gravely mistreated her customer. Damn, he could sue her if he wanted, and not just for almost getting him killed, but probably for sexual harassment too. Shit.

But Grady shook his head. "No...just...just send it through the mail."

He began to turn away when Leroy opened his dumb mouth. "Hey, you ain't going to sue us now, are you?"

B.J. tensed and held her breath. She noticed her brothers and father doing the same.

Grady glanced around to glare at Leroy, and she was sure that was it. They were going out of business from one lawsuit. But Grady's eyes flickered her way, silently studying her. "No, I'm not going to sue you. I just want to be left alone."

He pivoted and strode away. Still feeling crappy for the way she'd treated him, B.J.'s shoulders deflated. This just wasn't his week. And it was all her fault. Realizing the best thing she could do for him was leave him alone, she stood back helplessly and watched him leave.

Chapter Six

Grady waited two weeks after that near-fatal flight home before he visited the cemetery. With him, he brought a handful of Amy's favorite flowers.

He'd played the Houston trip over in his mind a thousand times. There were so many things he could've done differently, *should've* done differently. He wasn't proud of himself, and he wasn't satisfied with how things had turned out. B.J. might've pressured him into doing something he hadn't felt ready for, but he'd done it under his own free will and even instigated a good portion of it. He didn't need to feel any kind of anger toward her for that.

But he did.

Then she'd turned around and saved his life the next morning, keeping her head under pressure and landing them safely. If she'd kissed him a second longer after landing, he would've overcome his shock and kissed her back. Hell, he probably would've taken her right there in the cockpit. And it wouldn't have had anything to do with gratitude either.

"I guess you already know what I did," he said without preamble, setting the irises at the base of his wife's marker and kneeling down to sit on the grass beside the bouquet.

He gave a small laugh as he looked at his hands. "Yeah, you always knew what I did, usually before I was even going to do it." Grinning, he lifted his face and stared at the name of his wife on the gravestone. "Remember when I proposed? You were holding out your hand for the ring before I'd even gotten down on one knee."

Grady smiled for a good three seconds before his face fell and his muscles tensed in misery. Dropping his gaze from the name that always caused him heartache, he caught sight of a weed and pulled it up. Amy didn't deserve weeds growing over her dead body.

"The funny thing is," he confessed as he reached for another, "I didn't feel guilty. Not during, anyway."

Tossing the weed away from Amy's plot, he lifted his face toward the bright day and squinted at the sunlight. For some reason, he wondered if B.J. was up there somewhere, cruising through the clouds in that death trap of hers. God, he hoped she'd fixed the fuel line.

Jerking his gaze guiltily from the sky, he turned back to Amy's name.

"I always thought it'd feel different than this. I thought, I don't know...I just assumed I'd think of you the whole time...that'd I have to close my eyes and pretend it was your lips I was kissing, your body I was touching."

He shook his head and lowered his gaze, ashamed. "But I didn't even remember you. Not till afterward." Letting out a long sigh, he closed his eyes and confessed, "And that's when the guilt finally came.

"I know I didn't betray you," he said after a moment of silence. "You'd want me to move on. And I know you'd even approve of the woman. You always liked..." He couldn't say her name aloud, so he settled with, "*her*. But, God, I don't know, Amy."

Pausing, he wondered why he was confessing all this to someone who couldn't hear him. Probably because she *couldn't* hear him, he decided.

"I feel bad because I didn't picture you at all through any of it. I didn't think of how you—hell, I wasn't thinking at all. And that's not me. You know that's not me. As soon as she touched me, my mind just shut down. I lost control of myself like I'd never lost control before. I just...I had to have her...right then."

He winced when he whispered, "That never happened with you. I think that's what bothers me most. I experienced something strong and intense with someone else and...it should've been you."

He cradled his head in his hands. "I'm not sure what I'm trying to say. I guess, I'm sorry. I'm all tore up because I felt something...something amazing, and it wasn't because of you. You had nothing to do with it. Well, okay, it all started because we were fighting about you, but...as soon as the clothes came off, you were completely erased from my mind. I was so mad and desperate I would've done anything to get inside her. And I can't even say it was just about sex. It was *her*.

"I hate to admit this, but if you'd walked into the room at that moment, I still would've wanted her."

He was quiet for a moment. Then he said, "That's what has me feeling so crappy. I wanted a person...a specific woman, not just some warm body to fill the space you left. For the first time in two and half years, it wasn't about you.

"Yeah. If you were here now, you'd be giving me a lecture, I know. You'd be happy I made a big step with moving on...and you'd be mad because I haven't called her."

He shut his eyes and rested his back against the gravestone. "I know I should call or go see her...or something. I'm not a one-night stand kind of person, and I'm not going to be. But damn it, Amy, I'm scared to death. That woman intimidates me. She makes me want things, feel things...things I never felt or wanted with you. I lose my head when I'm around her, and I don't know how to deal with that. You always let me be my logical self, go my slow, methodical pace. She doesn't. I can't talk to her or look at her. I'm just...I'm not ready yet."

Nothing answered his troubled report but a light breeze that sifted through his hair. He smiled lightly, keeping his eyes closed, and imagined it was Amy's fingers. But then he frowned. He couldn't remember what his wife's touch felt like. Instead, he remembered a brown-haired wildcat who cursed like a sailor when she came apart in his arms. Frowning, he fisted his hands in the grass and wished for things that could never happen.

He wanted his wife back. He wanted his safe, comfortable, predictable Amy. He wanted to shred her tombstone with his bare hands and dig out her body so he could grab her by the shoulders and shake her back to life if for no other reason than to just talk to her.

He and Amy had been inseparable since their freshman year of high school when they'd first started dating. Not only had the woman become his wife and lover, but she was the best friend he'd ever had. They'd talked about and shared everything.

If Amy were here, she'd know what to do concerning B.J. She'd be honest and tell him how to handle everything. But then, if Amy were here and still alive, there'd be no issue with the tomboy to resolve.

That thought caused his breath to hitch in his chest.

As much as he regretted ever being with smart-mouthed B.J. Gilmore, he still relished those few minutes they'd shared in her hotel room. At the twinge of guilt rippling through him, he lifted his hand to the center of his chest and rubbed, because the pain was actually physical. The agony ate at him, and he couldn't deny the truth.

No matter how much he missed his wife and wanted her back, deep down, he was secretly glad she'd been out of the way so he could experience a taste of B.J., because nothing had ever been as good as sliding inside her. Those few minutes she'd wrapped her legs around him had been hotter than all the years he'd spent with Amy.

Lowering his head, he buried his face in his hands and shuddered. "I'm so sorry."

****

Three weeks after sleeping with Grady, B.J. still felt awful about what she'd done. She figured she should do something to show her regret, make it up to him somehow. But she'd already apologized, and that was a record for her. Besides, she never saw the man much anyway. Maybe she should just leave it alone and forget it had happened...except she would dream about their time together and wake in the middle of the night, aching.

She'd flop on her back and curse at the ceiling. There definitely had to be something wrong with her if she got off on making good men like Grady Rawlings suffer.

So, she tried to ignore the situation and act like it wasn't happening. That didn't work either. Though they lived in the same small community, they usually didn't spot hide nor hair of each other for months at a time. But B.J. knew she was cursed when she saw him three times in that third week. The first instance, she'd seen him retreating as she'd stepped from the post office. He'd hightailed it out of there like he'd seen her inside and was escaping before they could cross paths.

Since he was trying the whole evade-and-ignore remedy, she did the identical thing back to him the second time around. She'd been about to go into the hardware store to order new parts for her airplane when she saw him standing at the checkout counter, getting something for his oil rigs, no doubt. Screeching to a halt, she immediately changed course and darted around a corner, lurking there until she saw him leave the store and cross the street.

The third time, however, she wasn't so lucky and couldn't avoid a...collision of sorts. She was in the diner, chowing down on some breakfast, when she caught sight of him through the window striding toward the entrance. Eyes going wide, she deserted her bacon and eggs and flew out of her stall. He was almost to the café, and there was no way she could leave without bumping into him, so she ducked around the corner, fully intent on hiding in the hallway to the bathrooms until he left.

She knew exactly when he entered, because the air in the building changed. Not only did the bell above the door ding announcing a new arrival, but all talk fell dead, and even the clinking of silverware paused.

Sal, the waitress, was finally kind enough to say, "Well, howdy there, Grady. What can I get you today?"

B.J. made a growling face, wanting to defend him. No wonder the poor guy had reverted into himself, turning all quiet and solitary. Everyone treated him like a freak. *Don't go near that Grady Rawlings. Widowhood might be contagious.*

She frowned and then clenched her teeth when she heard him go and order a full meal. *Damn,* she mouthed. She'd have to hide until he was done. Sal would probably clear her breakfast away and complain about her dining and dashing.

But B.J. didn't care. She was prepared to stay right where she was for as long as it took. Until Ralphie Smardo ruined it all.

The brainless doofus opened his big trap and started talking. He'd come into the café about the same time as her, and he'd gone to sit at the counter with a couple of other bachelors. And as soon as he sat down, he immediately started complaining about his old lady.

The boy was all bent out of shape because he and Nan were having trouble in the bedroom. According to him, she was bored, claiming he wasn't fun and adventuresome.

"Now, I can be just as adventurous as the next guy," he whined.

From her hiding spot, B.J. rolled her eyes. If Ralphie's form of adventuresome was grunting out, "Hold onto somethin'," for foreplay then, sure, he was one wild boy.

"Why, just a couple years ago, B.J. and I…"

In the hallway, B.J. froze and felt the blood drain from her head. *What the hell?* Why was he mentioning her name in the middle of his sexual exploits? If he splurged a single detail about their *one* time together, she was going to murder him slowly and painfully.

Straining to hear what he was going to blab about her, she jumped when he hollered, "Hey, B.J.!"

She closed her eyes and then covered them for good measure.

"Where'd she go?" she heard Ralphie say. "I coulda swore she came in here the same time I did."

B.J. shook her head sadly. Yep, she was going to kill him.

"I think she headed toward the john a few minutes ago," Sal answered.

B.J. sank further into the shadows of the hall. But it didn't help, because suddenly there was Ralphie poking his big, dumb head around the corner.

"Hey, B.J.," he hollered.

"What?" she snapped and gritted her teeth as she moved out of the hallway, brushing past him and storming back to her booth where, thank God, her breakfast still sat waiting.

Grady was at the bar with a coffee cup steaming in front of him. He turned slightly and regarded her with a shuttered gaze. She paused as their eyes met.

She wondered what he was thinking of her, realizing she'd been with Ralphie. As shame filled her, she turned away and slid into her seat. She commenced to ignore him and tried to ignore Ralphie too, but the idiotic man just kept on.

He fell into the seat across from hers. "You remember when we went skinny dipping that one night, right?"

B.J. had just picked up her fork, but at his words she stopped in her tracks, the utensil paused halfway between her mouth and plate.

"What the hell," she said.

"Now tell me that wasn't fun and adventurous, huh?" he encouraged with a goofy grin.

She could only gape in disbelief.

"Ralphie," she sputtered. "You...you stupid *oaf*! Nan's going to skin you alive if you go announcing to everyone in the goddamn diner you went skinny dipping with someone else."

Ralphie blinked in confusion. "But...but that happened way before me and her got together. Hell, it was years ago."

"So why did you even—"

She broke off, unable to believe the dumbass. How dare he announce to the entire place she'd had a weak moment and gotten kinky with him once? And with Grady present too. Not that she cared what Grady thought, but damn it, she did care. She didn't want him to think she was... Lord, she didn't care. Let him think what he wanted. It didn't matter.

"Jesus, Ralphie," she snapped and threw down her fork. After getting to her feet, she dug into her wallet and tossed down a load of bills. "Don't go bragging about someone else and expect Nan to be fine with that. I don't care if it was five years ago or five days ago."

Ralphie looked worried now. "Y-you really think she'll be upset?" He bumbled to his feet as well, crowding her with an anxious look.

B.J. lifted an eyebrow and set her hands on her hips. "Did you take lessons to be a moron, or does it just come naturally?"

She pushed by him and stormed angrily from the diner.

****

It only took Ralphie an hour to show up at the hangar. B.J. had her Cessna sitting out in the sun where she had a side hood lifted to expose the engine. After almost crashing, she'd been going through and checking everything. After replacing the torn gas line, she'd installed a few other items needing replaced. Stuff she'd been thinking about fixing someday was suddenly top priority, and B.J. was giving her skywagon the spit and polish overhaul.

Ralphie pulled his truck alongside her plane, his forearm hanging out the opened window and his big, dopey face drooped in mute apology. In the bed of his truck were the four tires she'd won in the poker game that suddenly felt like years ago.

"B.J.," he said solemnly as he cut the engine and exited the truck.

She slipped a grease rag from her back pocket and wiped off her hands as she followed him to his tailgate. Once he had it opened, he turned to her and tightened his face with regret.

"I'm real sorry," he said, kicking at a pebble on the ground. "'Bout what I did at the café. I shouldn't of—"

"Hell, it's no big deal," she grumbled, giving up her dirty hands for hopeless and stuffing the rag back into her pocket. "I was just in a mood. You didn't do anything wrong."

Ralphie didn't answer. He merely lifted his face, squinted at her since the sun was in his eyes and said, "Well, I'm sorry anyhow. I had no call to start that kind of tale about us. True or not."

He kicked at the rock again. "I shoulda known better. And you were right. Nan's already done heard about it and thinks I cheated on her."

"Well," B.J. answered. She didn't want to be mean and say, *that's what you get for opening your pie hole, you big idiot,* but she was tempted.

"Anyhow, I brought you them tires you won." He motioned lamely toward them with limp fingers.

B.J. nodded and stared at the set for a second. "Thanks," she said. Then with a sigh, she hopped into the bed and started to roll them out.

Ralphie lurched into action to give her a hand. "I went ahead and kept the wheels on," he explained. "In case you want them too."

"They didn't get bent when Rick Hopper wrecked?" she asked, surprised.

Ralphie scratched at his chin. "Don't seem to be."

"Well, then...thanks." He must be damn sorry if he was going to give her the wheels too. That, or his problems with Nan were dour.

Once the set was rolled out and piled on the ground, Ralphie wiped sweat out of his eyes and glanced around. "Where's your truck? I'll get started putting these on right now."

B.J. felt herself soften, unable to make him suffer anymore. "I'll see to that," she said. "You didn't even have to do this much, Ralphie. Thanks."

He nodded morosely.

"And..." She stalled for a moment before offering the next suggestion, "if you want, I'll call Nan and try to smooth things out with her. Let her know she has nothing to worry about from me."

Ralphie jerked his face up, his cow eyes hopeful. "Really?"

"Yeah, really. Now get out of here before someone spots your rig and reports back to her, saying we're doing the dirty mambo in the back of my plane as we speak."

Eyes flaring with panic, Ralphie jumped toward his truck. "Damn, I hadn't thought of that."

B.J. wasn't surprised.

He shimmied himself behind the wheel and slammed his door. After starting the engine, he glanced at her once with worry. "You swear you're going to call her?"

She rolled her eyes. "Smardo, just get outta here already. I got it under control."

"Thanks, B.J." He lifted his hand in farewell even as he put the engine into gear. Starting to roll away, he called, "You're a real pal."

B.J. sighed as she watched him book it out of there. The poor man was pitiful, absolutely hopeless. Setting her hands on her hips, she studied the pile of tires and couldn't help but grin. At least she'd gotten something profitable out of the deal.

Wiping sweat off her forehead with the back of her hand, she got to work, first lugging each tire back to the hangar, then piling them in the corner.

She might be slender, but B.J. wasn't a puny stick by any means. By the time she returned to her plane to retrieve the last tire, though, she'd run full out of steam. Sweat pouring, stomach rolling, she dropped the tire by her feet and held it still as it bounced and tried to roll away.

Bent over, she sucked air through her gritted teeth and willed the nausea to pass. It didn't, only working steadily up her throat and making her think she was going to urp all over the tarmac. Heat reflected off the glossy black surface, and suddenly, she wondered if she was going to pass out instead.

Closing her eyes, she counted to ten until both the dizziness and queasy stomach settled. Then she straightened and groaned as she lifted the tire again and hauled it in to rest with the others. She was so wiped out, she didn't have the energy to return to her plane.

Slumping toward the corner office, she tried to remember what she'd eaten for breakfast. When she recalled the whole diner visit and how she'd completely deserted her bacon and eggs because of Grady and Ralphie, she sighed.

There was her problem right there. She was starving. Hot and starving.

Once inside the stifling office, B.J. moved immediately to the water cooler and poured herself a drink. She went and stood in front of the single oscillating fan as she guzzled. When only a swallow was left, she upended the rest of the cup over her head and delighted in the cool wetness trickling down her face and neck.

"Ahh." She sighed, closing her eyes and spreading her arms wide until the hot air from the fan lifted the back of her shirt and dried her sweaty skin. "Much better."

Crumbling the paper cup, she tossed it in the trash and started for the phone. After looking up the number, she dialed Nan's house.

Chapter Seven

"You got a lot of nerve calling me," Nan Lundy answered the phone three rings later.

At the sound of the woman's righteous indignation, B.J. sighed. Yep, she had her work cut out for her here. "Nan, listen—"

"No, you listen to me, hussy. I don't care how much you want my Ralphie—"

"Oh, please. I don't want—"

"You can't have him, y'hear? That's *my* man, so keep your damn paws off."

"*Your* man?" B.J. snorted. "I thought you said he was boring?"

"I... I didn't mean it that way."

"Well, now, maybe you did," B.J. said, changing her tune. Nan wasn't going to listen to a word she said unless she played her cards right. So B.J. held her breath and said, "If you don't appreciate *your* man the way you should, I just might snag him when you're not looking."

Even as she spoke, she wrinkled her nose at the very idea.

Nan gasped. "Why, you dirty little—"

"I think I can show Smardo a real good time," B.J. went on, cringing at the lie and trying not to gag before continuing. "He did just fine a few years ago when we went swimming in Eden's Watering Hole. So, I guess I wouldn't much mind hooking up with him again."

"In your dreams, Gilmore."

"If you keep telling him it's over between the two of you, it might just be in my reality." Her

81

stomach gave a lurch of pure revulsion, and she swallowed back rising bile.

"It's...it's not over between Ralphie and me." Nan sounded desperate. Worried. "What're you talking about? What did he tell you?"

B.J. grinned, but managed to sound spiteful when she answered, "He said you wouldn't talk to him. Said you think he's cheating on you, and you have no faith in him."

"I never said—"

"So, the way I see it, he's fair game."

"He is *not!*" Nan fairly screamed. "You stay away from him. He's mine."

"Then claim him as yours and quit giving him the silent treatment, or I will steal him, Lundy. You just watch me."

When Nan slammed the phone in her ear, B.J. smiled.

"Score!" she called and fisted a hand to pump the air with it. "That ought to do the trick." Satisfied with the way she'd handled the call, she brushed her palms against her thighs.

Not that she understood what Nan wanted with a big lug like Smardo anyway. Nor did she see how Nan was in any way worried B.J. would want to steal him. Bluck. The whole idea of ever kissing Ralphie again put a nasty taste in her mouth. In fact, it made her feel sick to her stomach all over again.

Realizing she wasn't going to hold the puke at bay any longer, she lunged toward the bathroom, pushed up the seat of the toilet and bent over it, losing everything she'd eaten since yesterday. Her roiling gut hurt so bad, she fell to her knees and clutched the sides of the porcelain god, not even worried about how nasty the floor was or how many times her brothers and Pop had no doubt missed their aim.

Sweat beaded her brow and upper lip by the time her stomach had wrung itself empty. Groaning, she closed her eyes and flushed, spitting out the sulfuric taste of rotten egg in her mouth. She staggered to her feet, reaching for the wall when dizziness assailed her.

Lord have mercy, she felt gross. She wanted to go home and take a nice long shower, then change into her jammies and sleep for the next week.

But as she stepped from the bathroom, wiping dust and grit from the back of her clammy neck, she spotted her father seated at the office desk with his feet propped up, resting on a pile of papers. She paused and warily eyed the way he ran his finger over his bushy mustache.

"Pop," she greeted.

"You just ill in there?" he asked, nodding his head toward the bathroom.

"Yep," she answered. She didn't want him to know the thought of sleeping with Ralphie Smardo made her literally sick to her stomach, so she added, "Heat's really getting to me today."

She moved to the water cooler and poured herself another drink. As she downed a third cupful, she glanced at him, apprehensive about the fact he was studying her with the strangest expression.

"What?" she asked, though she was pretty sure she knew what he was thinking.

B.J. was a healthy girl. She was never under the weather. She couldn't remember the last time she'd gotten puny enough to yak. This was a strange occurrence, sure, but it really was a sweltering day. Heat did strange things to people when it was as hot and dry as today and they'd skipped breakfast. She'd just pushed herself a little too hard. That was all.

"I was going to ask if you wanted to fly a freight load to Fort Worth, but—"

"I can do it," she broke in. "Where're the goods?"

Pop eyed her untrustingly for a moment. "You sure?"

"I'm good to go, Pop. You want me to get a doctor's slip saying I'm healthy or what? I told you I was fine."

"Don't go gettin' your panties in a bunch. I'm still your pappy, and that gives me the right to worry about you iffin' I want to."

B.J. would've rolled her eyes, but the look in her father's gaze made her refrain. A bitter taste of regret filled her mouth. She wondered—not for the first time—if Jeb Gilmore had wanted a more girly girl for a daughter. From the rumors she'd heard, her mother had been one of those frilly types who liked lots of lace and ruffles. She wondered if Pop would be happier if he could see more of Dellie Gilmore in her.

Clearing her throat and straightening her shoulders, she held back from being too much like herself and politely said, "I'm feeling better than I did a few minutes ago. Whatever was in my system is out now. I'm sure I'm back to one hundred percent."

Still studying her with those watery brown eyes of his, Pop picked up a Dixie cup and spit some of his tobacco into it. "The freight's sitting in the southwest corner on two pallets. Make sure Buck helps you load it. They want it delivered by noon tomorrow."

B.J. nodded solemnly. "I'll have it there this evening," she answered and started from the office to get back to work.

****

Straddling the neck of a broken oil well's pump jack, Grady fumbled with a piece of baling wire he was using to twine around two hunks of steel to hold them together. Slick with his own sweat, his grip kept slipping. It played havoc on his patience.

His father had been steadily teaching him the

rules of trade in order for Grady to one day take over the family business. Since he was the oldest and the only sibling out if his brother and two sisters even interested in oil, it was a given the company would be his some day

Rawlings Oil was the only petroleum field around Tommy Creek. They'd been in business since his grandfather Granger Rawlings had discovered a bubbling crude on his cattle ranch nearly fifty years ago. Since then, the entire herd had been sold, and the range was now covered with nodding donkey oil wells instead of cow patties.

Employing a good portion of the county, Rawlings Oil supplied jobs and commerce for hundreds of area residents. Rawlings was a big name in these parts, and being a Rawlings came with a load of responsibility.

Since the new guy Grady had hired on to help repair faulty equipment was afraid of heights, Grady found himself shimmying up the side of a steaming hot piece of grease-coated metal to fix a minor repair.

Since Amy's death, he'd relished days like these, full of hard, manual labor. Focusing on his job and piling a bigger workload onto his shoulders had been something to keep his mind off...things. So he'd dived headfirst into finding the grimiest, hardest tasks for himself. But today, he couldn't concentrate. His mind kept retreating back to the diner.

All he'd wanted was a quick breakfast and a cup of coffee. But no...he'd just had to listen to Ralph Smardo start a fight with B.J. Gilmore.

Skinny dipping.

Grady couldn't picture it. Not that he wanted to picture it. But he couldn't stop thinking about it. She'd gone goddamned skinny dipping with Ralphie, The Junkyard, Smardo. Clenching his teeth, Grady grabbed a hold of both ends of the wire and gave a violent twist.

He told himself he shouldn't be jealous. He shouldn't even care. Ralph said it'd been years ago, so they'd probably had their fling when he was still married to Amy. But, damn it, the feeling of helpless rage still pounded through his blood. The thought of B.J. with anyone else made him want to break something.

That made no sense at all. He didn't have any kind of claim on her. Hell, he hadn't even talked to her since Houston. She could've been with a dozen guys in that time and she'd have every right to them. He'd deserted her in the hotel room, and he hadn't talked to her once since—excluding that whole near-death experience on her plane. Then, he'd gone out of his way to avoid her when he'd seen her out and about.

In anyone's book, that would signify the end for them.

Yet he still dreamed about her. He remembered what she smelled like, how her skin felt against his. He wanted the very essence of her coated to his mouth so every time he licked his lips, he could taste her.

If only he hadn't gone to the damn diner for breakfast.

As he lost his grip on the wire once again, a bead of sweat dripped into his eyes. Growling out a curse, he slammed the palm of his hand against the metal neck on which he sat. "Damn it."

"Need some help?"

Grady jumped clear out of his skin and twisted around. He hadn't heard the truck pull up, but there was his father, approaching with a slow, loose-legged stride.

"I got it," he muttered and used his dirt-caked sleeve to wipe at his face.

"Here, take my gloves," Tucker Rawlings said

from the ground where he'd stopped just below where Grady was working.

"I just took mine off," Grady answered. "I can't get a hold of anything with them in the way. But my hands are so slick, I can't get a good grip now, either. And I lost my pliers somewhere in the north field about an hour ago."

"I got an extra pair in my truck," Tucker offered.

As his dad started back to his rig, Grady began to mutter under his breath. The day had been going just fine until he'd decided to stop at the diner on his way to work. "I should've just starved," he muttered to himself.

"What's that?"

Giving another startled lurch, Grady realized his father had returned. "Nothing," he mumbled.

Tucker winced against the sunlight and studied him for a moment. "You doing okay today?"

Not quite meeting Tucker's gaze, Grady answered, "I'm fine. Why?"

"You seem...distracted."

Grady ignored him a minute as he once again tried to twist the two pieces together with his thumb and forefinger. "I'm fine," he hissed and then cursed again as his thumb slid off and the sharp end of the wire stabbed him in the palm.

"I'm fine," he snapped once again when Tucker made a move to climb the side of the oil well and check his wound. His father stopped in his tracks and scowled.

"You're bleeding. I can see it from here."

"It's nothing."

"Take the pliers, will you?" Tucker held them up.

Grady wrapped one arm around the neck of the pump and stretched down to grasp the tool. When his fingers wrapped around it, he said, "Thanks."

Tucker nodded quietly and shoved his hands

into his pockets as he watched Grady deftly make a twisty tie out of the thick metal cord.

"Want to come to supper tonight?"

Grady nearly winced as he shook his head. "No, thanks. I..." He faltered when he couldn't think up an excuse why except that he just didn't want to. So he settled with another, "No, thanks."

His father looked a little too sympathetic for his comfort, and he wanted to escape...fast. Finishing his task, he handed the pliers back and wiped his hands on his jeans before he started to shimmy his way back toward earth. After descending four feet, he let go of the beam and jumped down the rest of the way.

"Your mother was saying just this morning how she hasn't seen you in a while," Tucker said, hovering until both of Grady's feet were firmly planted on the ground.

Letting out a breath, Grady leaned over and started collecting all the spare parts and tools he had accumulated around the base of the pump jack.

"I'll stop by and say hi on my way home," he relented.

But that was it. He wouldn't stay for a meal and allow both his parents to gang up on him as they tried to get a bead on how he was really dealing with his life these days.

"Don't worry about me, Dad. I'm not digressing again. I don't need to see a doctor, and I don't need any kind of medication. There's no depression and no more insomnia. I'm fine." Actually, he'd probably prefer the insomnia to the dreams he'd been having about a certain big-mouthed tomboy.

Everything gathered, he lifted his toolbox and started for his truck.

"I know you don't like my pity, Grady," Tucker said, falling into step beside him. "But you're my son, and I can't stand to see you this way."

Grady closed his eyes and fisted his hands around the handle of the toolbox, wondering if B.J. had been right in Houston. Did he bring on everyone's sympathy by acting so pitiful? "There's nothing to be done about it, though," he muttered. Sometimes, he just couldn't stop hurting.

"Yeah, well...doesn't mean I have to like it," Tucker answered. "If there's ever anything you need from me or your mother, we'll be there—"

"I know," Grady cut in with a reluctant smile. He stopped and turned to face his father. "I know you'd die for me, if you had to. But you can't live for me, Dad. I have to figure out how to do that myself."

"That's why this sucks so much," Tucker relented as his shoulders slumped. "Because I *can't* live your life for you, can I? I can't get you past this rough patch. God. This has to be the worst part of parenthood."

Grady wouldn't know. His child had been born dead, cut out of his wife with a knife.

He busied himself by setting his equipment in the bed of his truck. "I saw him, you know."

Tucker frowned. "Saw who?"

"Bennett." His son.

His dad sucked in a breath but didn't respond. Grady stared into the bed of the truck, assailed by memories.

"He was bloody and still, curled in the fetal position. The doctor and nurses were so busy trying to work on him and Amy, I don't think they realized I was still in there, watching the cesarean." Grady lifted his face and glanced over his shoulder at his dad. "He had a really thick head of hair...just like Tanner." Though they would've only been cousins, the two boys probably would've looked like twins.

Tucker wiped at his face and quietly said, "God, Grady. I was wrong. I haven't lived through the worst part of parenthood, have I?"

Grady sent him a sad smile. He shook his head, thinking he shouldn't have said anything. But he couldn't seem to forget that flight to Houston when B.J. Gilmore had talked about Amy. When she'd told the story about Amy baking Leroy's porn, he hadn't felt like someone was cutting him in half. It made him wonder if maybe he was going to get through this after all.

But seeing his father's sympathetic glance told him otherwise. The despair came rushing back, clogging his windpipe and making it hard to breathe. He couldn't understand why he'd been able to share an Amy-story with B.J., a woman he wasn't all that close to, and he couldn't bear to mention his son to his own father.

Maybe it was because B.J. hadn't looked at him with pity or tried to find a way to fix his misery. Instead, she'd opted to remember a happy time, and she'd actually made him smile over the recollection. Grady hadn't smiled from hearing Amy's name since the day she'd died. But somehow B.J. had given him joy from a simple memory.

He wondered briefly if that was why it'd been so good to be inside her. She was the first person in two and a half years to look at him and see a man...not a widower.

In the blink of an eye, all the bitterness and anger he'd been feeling for the tomboy evaporated. Suddenly, he was very glad she'd prodded him into her hotel room.

****

B.J. was late to work the next morning. Not that there was any kind of set schedule around the Gilmore Hangar, but she usually showed up before eight. This morning, though, she slept in for some reason. Stranger yet, she'd gone to bed early the night before. When she'd finally opened her eyes, she hadn't felt like moving. Thinking she was probably getting a nasty summer flu, she pushed herself up and took a long, hot shower until she worked out the soreness in her muscles.

But as soon as she started the coffee for breakfast, her stomach rejected the smell. So, she dumped out what she'd brewed and fixed herself a couple pieces of dry toast.

On the drive to work, she frowned, wondering why she didn't have a sore throat. Experimentally, she coughed and then pressed her fingers to her larynx, but her windpipe wasn't even raw. Then she sniffed through her nose and frowned. None of her nasal passages were congested. It was just her stomach going to town with a nasty cramp fest and a strange dizzy feeling, making her continually lightheaded. She wasn't achy like she usually got when she was sick, but she sure felt tired.

It made no sense. What was even more confusing, she started to recover by the time she hit the airport. Shaking her head in bemusement, B.J. parked her truck and started for the hangar. She veered toward the office so she could check the day's schedule. She had a few aerial pictures she wanted to take, but other than that, she didn't remember any particular runs that had to be made.

The second she opened the office door, however, where her father was already seated behind the desk, the smell of freshly brewed coffee hit her like a twister attacking a trailer park. The aroma went straight to her gut and started the uneasy feeling all over again.

Covering her mouth, she pushed inside and plowed her way to the bathroom. Five minutes later, she exited on unsteady feet and glared at the coffee machine as she headed toward the water cooler.

"Weren't you scrawny yesterday too?"

B.J. nodded and guzzled water, mopping at her face when some spilled over the brim and dribbled down her chin.

"Well, you pregnant or something?" Pop asked.

B.J. stopped drinking, lowered the cup, and stared at her father. A sudden vision filled her of Grady levered above her, straining as he said, "I want slow." Her mind had been so busy on trying to speed him up, she hadn't even worried about protection.

"Damn, Pop," she murmured, running a hand over her suddenly clammy face. "I hadn't even thought of that."

He scowled and pulled a can of chew from his back pocket. "Well. You been with a feller?" he asked as he flipped the lid and pinched out a finger full of tobacco.

She nodded, not able to meet his gaze as she silently answered.

"Use rubbers?"

B.J. gave a slight shake of the head. She risked a brief glance his way and watched him tuck the chew in his cheek and then wipe his hands on his pants.

"Well," he said and sighed as if he was too old for this. Frowning disapprovingly, he started in. "What'd I always tell you about protection, girl?"

"I know, Pop," B.J. muttered in absolute mortification. But, hell. It had been years since she'd gotten any lectures on sex from her father. He'd never had any prejudices about her being female. He'd line her up with her brothers and give her the same exact speech on safe sex he gave the boys.

"I know," she repeated quietly and closed her eyes. "I just...this was different."

He made a sound that said he'd heard that line before and didn't buy it. "Was it that Smardo boy then?"

"*What*?!" B.J. burst out. Her eyes flew open, and she whipped her head up to stare at him in horror.

"God, no. What in the world made you think—"

The facts struck her, and her mouth dropped open. Feeling her face heat, she glanced away and wiped at her mouth. "Guess you heard about that little scene with him in the diner yesterday morning, huh?"

"Guess I did," Jeb answered.

She could feel him trying to crawl into her brain and figure out who might be responsible for a possible pregnancy, but B.J. wasn't about to tell him anything. Not yet. She wanted to make sure it was true first.

"If it wasn't Smardo, then who're we talking about here?"

B.J. refused to speak. She refused to even think of the person they were talking about. Not yet...not until she had all the facts. She'd already caused Grady Rawlings to suffer enough in the past month. She wasn't going to throw his name around until she was certain. And probably not even then.

"Well, then...tell me or don't tell me. It don't matter none," Jeb said with suddenly tired-looking eyes. "You still got a situation here to deal with. So, I'd say you best get yourself checked out and see if there's a bun in there or not."

Chapter Eight

Two days later, B.J. sat in the doctor's office, numb and dazed. The twenty-seven-year-old tomboy of Tommy Creek, Texas was pregnant.

"I'm going to give you a list of over-the-counter prenatal vitamins," Dr. Carl told her. He was the only gynecologist for a hundred miles, so B.J. had scheduled an appointment with him. Now she wished she'd just taken one of those home pregnancy things, because hearing a professional's word on the subject made this feel way too real and unavoidable.

"What I want you to do is choose one brand and start taking it immediately. Your body needs all sorts of nutrients it didn't before, and your remaining healthy is of the upmost importance. Now, don't forget to schedule an appointment with Lara at the front desk for next month before you leave. And here's a couple pamphlets you need to read through."

Too stunned to argue with the man, B.J. nodded, slipped the pile of papers from his hand with limp fingers, and walked like a zombie toward the secretary's desk.

Dr. Carl's receptionist, Lara Alberts, was a middle-aged woman who liked to stick her long nose in other people's business. When B.J. approached her, she stumbled a step, realizing Lara was going to discover her condition. Shit.

"Well, hey there, B.J.," Lara greeted. "I didn't realize it was time for your yearly already. I thought you visited more around the end of the..." Her words died off as she opened B.J.'s file and read the reason for her visit. "Oh my!" she gasped and raised wide, curious eyes. "You're...you're..." Her gaze fell to B.J.'s stomach.

"I'm ready to check out," B.J. growled, glowering as she plopped her checkbook on the counter. "What's the co-pay?"

Lara fumbled for a minute, glancing at her with wide, curious eyes every few seconds as she looked up the amount.

Yes, it's a goddamned supernatural phenomenon. Someone knocked up B.J. Gilmore. What a freaking wonder. The world must be coming to an end.

But B.J. kept her trap shut and settled for a healthy glare. Lara, thank God, didn't pry for more details, though she did try to talk about the weather as they hashed out a date for B.J.'s next appointment. Not in the mood for any kind of chitchat, B.J. merely booked it out of there as soon at Lara handed her a card bearing the date of her check up.

She walked to her truck in a trance.

Pregnant.

It didn't seem real. What in the hell was she going to do with a baby? It was like Santa Claus moving to the Bahamas, Nashville turning rock and roll, the White House hosting the worldwide mud wrestling competition. It just didn't happen.

B.J. didn't know anything about kids. She'd been one a long time ago, but that had sucked, end of story. She saw her brother's daughter every couple of weeks, but his girl was the spitting image of her mother, begging and whining all the time until her parents gave her what she wanted.

Shuddering in horror, B.J. hoped like hell she didn't have a kid like Buck's brat. She closed her eyes and rested her head against the steering wheel, trying to picture a little brown-eyed girl with her hair and Grady's—

An image of Grady flashed through her mind.

Grady. Oh, God. Grady.

Remembering him, she sat up straight, her eyes flying wide open. "Holy shit."

This was his kid too. Grady was going to be a daddy...again. Suddenly, she felt like curling into a ball and weeping—yet another sign of how pregnant she really was. Her hormones were already whacked out of control.

But, damn it, how was this going to affect Grady? He'd be devastated. He'd already lost two children before they'd ever been born. Amy had miscarried halfway through one pregnancy before she'd died in the delivery room with her second.

Amy had wanted a baby so bad. Even B.J.'d heard about all the trips to the fertility doctor she'd taken to get pregnant. And then she hadn't been able to stay that way without having problems. Grady and Amy's attempt to start a family had been a long, tortuous battle, ending in tragedy.

The fact that his one act of indiscretion with another woman had ended with a conception was going to be a bitter pill for him to swallow. He probably already felt like he'd committed adultery on Amy, and now the ultimate horror had happened. He was going to have a baby with another woman. God, why didn't B.J. just go and spit on Amy's grave while she was at it?

She didn't want to be the one to tell him. She wasn't a coward by any means. In fact, she never backed away from a good confrontation. But she did *not* want to see his face when he found out. It might send him over the edge. She feared he was already having a hard enough time dealing with the fact he'd had sex with someone who wasn't his wife. She didn't want to pile a kid on him as well.

It wasn't fair. Everything was wrong. Amy

should still be alive. She should be the happy mother of a whole brood by now. And Grady should be with her, not shackled to B.J., of all people, because she'd pressured him into one hot, unforgettable encounter.

Biting the inside of her lip, she tried to think up a way to escape this. Maybe she could flee the country and go live on a beach in Cancun. Yeah, she and her baby could be surfer bums. They could open a bar in the sand—like in the movie *Cocktail*—and drink margaritas every night of the week. Right. Except the whole baby and bar mix was taboo. Shit.

Or...or...hey, she could convince Grady it wasn't his. Now, there was an idea. Since Ralphie had been spouting off about skinny dipping, Grady probably already thought she had a pretty active sex life. She could say she'd been seeing some other guy in the next county over.

She'd have to lie about the date of conception as well and claim it was undercooked when it came out early. Or maybe she could make up an affair before their time together, which would make the kid overcooked. Either way, it didn't matter. The lie would be totally worth it to keep him from this kind of trauma. He'd buy her story because he'd want to. He wouldn't want to worry about raising a child who wasn't Amy's.

On the other hand, she'd be keeping him from his baby if she did that. And Grady Rawlings was one responsible fellow. He'd want the truth, and he'd insist on doing something about it. If he made a mistake, he lived up to it. He'd have to be a part of the baby's life and would want at least partial custody.

God, but wouldn't that be fun working through a custody battle with a high and mighty Rawlings? Not only was Grady going to hate her, but every member of the community would too for messing with the sacred Rawlings family. With his surname being hallowed in these parts, it was even more of a horror he'd been chosen as the next leader of the Rawlings Dynasty. Who wouldn't think she'd trapped him into parenthood for a shot at his money?

B.J. groaned and rubbed at the aching spot in the center of her forehead. She had to tell him, no matter how awful it was going to be. There was no other logical, moral-minded choice. The big question was, *how* was she going to do it?

Hey, Slim, I'm pregnant. So...have a nice day.

Or, maybe...

Remember that one night in Houston when I attacked you and we did it without a condom? Twice. Yeah, well...oops.

Shit.

There was no easy way to break the news.

****

Grady knew B.J. was trying to reach him. He'd seen her name flash across his caller ID twice now. And he'd been home both times. On her first call, he'd been too stunned to answer.

Well, maybe stunned wasn't quite the right word. Yeah, at first there was shock. Why in the hell would she call him? By rights she should think he was a bastard because he hadn't contacted her. But then the tingling apprehension set in. She was on the phone, and if he picked up, he'd hear her voice. If he heard her voice, he had a feeling he'd probably wind up in bed with her before the night was over.

Knowing that was exactly what his body craved, he wondered if that was really what he wanted. It still felt too soon. He didn't like rushing his decisions, and this especially was something he needed to think through...completely. Starting an affair with B.J. Gilmore would be complicated on all sorts of levels. But from the way his blood hummed through his body at the mere knowledge she was seeking him out, patience and deliberation suddenly didn't seem like such a great virtue.

Before he could make the decision to talk to her or not, his answering machine picked up. Amy's voice clicked on, telling the caller to leave a message, and B.J. disconnected, which was probably for the best because hearing Amy when he'd been all gung ho for a taste of B.J.'s voice had filled him with a guilty bee, buzzing through his system with stinging awareness.

He wasn't sure why he'd never bothered to change the old message. It was macabre to keep a dead woman's voice like that. But deep inside, he just couldn't relinquish what little he had left of his wife. He'd never hear her again if he destroyed the recording.

Grady hadn't given a damn what anyone else had thought about it until B.J. tried to call. Wondering if she considered him pathetic, he brushed his fingers over the phone where a recording of Amy's words lay trapped for all eternity. The quandary of whether to delete her greeting washed over him briefly before he finally decided against it and turned away.

The next night, however, when the phone rang again, Grady's muscles tightened with tension, and he hurried to the caller ID to see if it was B.J. It wasn't like he never got phone calls. His family was constantly ringing him for all types of reasons. But instinctively, he knew it was her.

When he saw her name appear on the screen, he answered the phone without thinking, not wanting her to hear Amy's message again. But as he pressed it to his ear, he realized, oh hell, now he had to talk to her.

The greeting he gave sounded brusque and rude, even to his own ears, and he winced, hoping he hadn't scared her off. But when he heard the click on the other end, his heart gave a violent shove against his ribcage. Shit. He *had* scared her off.

He closed his eyes and tried to decide if this was a good thing or not. As he ran his fingers through his hair with one hand, his thumb hovered over the call-back button. When he wondered what he'd say if she actually answered, he blew out a breath and set the receiver back in its cradle.

The next night, he found himself waiting by the phone. Yeah, he was stretched out in his La-Z-Boy, sipping iced tea and watching NASCAR, but he brought the dang receiver into the living room with him and sat it in his lap. So, when it actually rang, he fumbled for the talk button and answered before a name could even flash across the caller ID. When it turned out to be his sister from Reno, he nearly snapped her head off for checking in to see how he was.

He was in an irritable mood by morning. He cut himself shaving, burnt his tongue on his morning coffee, and stubbed his toe on the side of his bed.

Since he had meetings that day with investors, he couldn't go grunge and wear his comfortable field clothes. He'd just shrugged on a pinstriped shirt and was raiding his closet for a matching tie when he heard someone pull into his drive. Grabbing the first tie he saw, he moved toward the window to glance out the shades.

The sight of B.J.'s Dodge had him sucking in a breath. For a second, he could only stare. She was here. Good God, she was *here*. His skin prickled with a sudden anticipation. When he realized he'd turned as hard as a stone just knowing he was going to see her in less than thirty seconds, he yanked the tails of his shirt back out of his slacks to hide his response.

Then he checked the mirror, cursed, and pulled a toilet paper square off his chin. Taking the stairs two at a time, he hurried to the first floor. But as soon as he approached the entrance, he heard her diesel engine rev. Frowning in confusion, he moved the screen door and stared out as she backed down the drive. Not sure what to think, he wiped his chin with his hand.

What puzzled him the most was why she kept making these attempts to get a hold of him, only to chicken out before making contact.

And then it struck him. She was as uneasy as he was. Though it was hard to picture the steely-nerved tomboy with any kind of weakness, he had to admit the idea calmed him considerably. If she possessed the same fears and doubts he did, then another dimension had just been stacked to their relationship. That like-mindedness gave them a connection Grady couldn't ignore.

It also placed the ball in his court. She'd put in her three tries; now it was his turn to make an effort. But the idea of going to her filled him with indecision all over again. Pursuing her would make this all too real. Thinking about being serious with B.J. Gilmore had been nerve-wracking enough. But actually doing something was a whole other story.

He knew where to find her. Ten to one, she'd be at the hangar, working on that old plane of hers. But he didn't move.

This was foreign territory. Months before he'd asked Amy out for the first time, he'd been prodded by family and friends galore. It'd been expected. And when he'd finally approached her, he'd already known she'd say yes.

With B.J., none of that applied. Nothing was certain, and the only guarantee he'd have was craziness, absolute chaos, which was totally not him. It'd probably be like that every time with her too. A relationship with B.J. wouldn't be safe and comfortable and predictable. And he was everything that was safe and comfortable and predictable.

Imagining himself otherwise just didn't...fit.

But it felt strange sleeping with a woman and then not talking to her again. Sex had always been a special, bonding event for him. He hadn't slept with Amy only because he'd wanted sex. He'd also wanted to show her how much he loved her. But again, that hadn't been the case with B.J.

He wasn't used to sex without emotions being involved. He'd liked the importance of coupling as a means of showing his affection. And no matter how mad he was at B.J. for practically pushing him into being with her, he couldn't hate her or block the desire budding in him.

The link he felt wasn't just going to go away. Didn't mean he had to make his move today, though. B.J. had waited at least twenty-four hours between each of her attempts. So, Grady decided to let the matter sit until this evening, when he wouldn't have a meeting to plan.

Eight hours later, everything changed.

He stopped by the gas station on the way home and, as he filled up at the pump, he heard two guys outside the front doors, gossiping. Grady wasn't the type to listen in on rumors. But when he heard the name B.J. Gilmore mentioned, he lifted his head and glanced over.

"Yeah, I heard," one guy said to the other, shaking his head in dismay. "I still don't know whether or not to believe it, though."

His buddy chuckled. "Well, we'll know soon enough when she starts growing a pooch or not."

Grady frowned, not comprehending their lingo.

Then the first guy added, "I just want to know who supposedly knocked her up. I didn't know she was seeing anyone? Hell, I didn't even think Gilmore was interested in men."

"What? You didn't hear about what happened at the diner last week with Junkyard Smardo?" the second man responded.

As he proceeded to spill the gory details of Ralphie announcing how he'd gone skinny dipping with the biggest tomboy in the county, Grady stared sightlessly at the two men. His ears buzzed so he didn't hear the gas pump click off, signaling his tank was full. His fingers merely gripped reflectively around the handle, and gas kept gushing until it spewed out the side of his truck and sprayed his pant leg.

Grady dropped the nozzle and leaped back a step, staring at the dripping mess.

"Shit."

By the time he'd pulled himself back together enough to return the station's gas hose to its resting place and head toward the station to pay, the two men had decided Ralphie was their top suspect as the baby's daddy.

"Can you just imagine a little Junkyard Smardo running around? Big ears, buck teeth and double chin."

"Hopefully, it turns out looking like B.J. I'm still convinced she's got a body that just won't stop under all those man clothes."

Brushing past the men, Grady hurried inside to finish his business. He had to talk to B.J...now. Realizing that was probably the reason she'd been trying to get a hold of him, he couldn't help but feel a little stung by the fact she hadn't wanted to see him personally, she'd merely wanted to deliver an update.

She was pregnant.

God, he hadn't even considered that possibility. It'd taken so much work for Amy to conceive, he'd been under the impression a lot more than one time was needed to get the job done. But one night with B.J. definitely wasn't one night with Amy on any level.

Grady returned to his truck. He even started the engine and put the gearshift into drive, but he kept his foot on the brake, unable to move.

This wasn't fair. Amy, who'd wanted children her entire life, had died trying to get the baby she desired. For years, he'd felt like a failure because he'd been unable to grant her deepest wish. Yet now, after one stupid try, he'd planted a child in B.J., and there was no way in hell she'd been desperate to become a little mama.

He felt like hell. How could he so easily impregnate one woman, a woman he hardly knew, but he couldn't manage to come through for his wife who'd been the absolute love of his life?

Taking his foot off the brake, Grady pressed the gas. He had to talk to B.J. He had to know how she could do this to him. He didn't want to be a father. He didn't want to look down and see a bloody little corpse ever again.

Why couldn't she have just left him alone in Houston, damn it?

Since B.J. lived in a small two-bedroom bungalow farmhouse hardly two miles from the filling station, Grady pulled into her drive only minutes later. Her truck was sitting out front, telling him she was home. As he parked behind it and slid out of his cab, he took a long, calming breath.

Realizing he was probably going to hate this encounter, he slowed his step but still reached her porch all too soon.

When he knocked on her door, he heard her call, "It's open."

Grady stepped inside. As soon as he'd gained entrance, he stopped and let the door quietly fall shut at his back. Her living room was small but tidy. It looked like a neat bachelor pad. The furniture was old, ugly and mismatched but appeared incredibly comfortable. The colors were neutral, nothing flashy or feminine. She had posters on the wall of four-wheelers and airplanes. And the television was on, turned to NASCAR.

B.J. entered from a doorway on the left. She was barefoot, dressed in an old pair of faded blue jeans with holes ripped in the knees. She had on an equally old T-shirt with a beer logo on the front, and her wet hair was pulled back into its usual ponytail. She carried a bag of microwave popcorn and tugged it open as she strolled in from the kitchen.

The voice of the gossipmonger from the filling station filled Grady's head. *I'm still convinced she's got a body that just won't stop under all those man clothes.* He knew just how true those words were. Lithe form, long legs, tightly packed muscles, soft curves, breasts that more than filled his hands. His mouth watered.

When she saw him, she jerked to a stop. "What are *you* doing here?"

His first thought had nothing to do with children. The first—and pretty much the only—declaration to enter his head was, *Mine.*

Chapter Nine

"You wanted to see me?" Grady asked, clearing his throat and returning to his senses.

B.J.'s eyes widened, and she shook her head. "N-no."

Grady's jaw went hard. "You called twice and stopped by once this morning," he reminded. "What was it you needed to tell me?"

Her head once again swung back and forth, "I don't...nothing," she insisted.

He bit back a sigh. The woman was an awful liar. It did nothing to ease his growing anger.

"So, the gossip around town isn't true then?"

B.J. frowned. "I don't listen to the gossip around town, so I don't know what you're talking about."

He lifted a brow and sent her an arch look. "That so? You have *no* idea what I'm talking about, huh?"

"I just said I didn't," she snapped a little too defensively; her stance went from cowering to attack-mode.

"Well, I heard about five minutes ago that someone had knocked up B.J. Gilmore."

That finally evoked the response he'd expected. Her face drained of color and she dropped her bag of popcorn, spilling kernels around her bare feet.

"Who told you that?"

Grady folded his arms and stared hard. "I overheard Gabe Watson telling Ulrick Pullson about it at Herb's Quick Stop. Both of *them* already knew."

"*Who?*" she demanded, and then she shook her head furiously. "Oh my God, I can't believe this. How could anyone know? I just found out myself Tuesday when I went to Dr. Carl's office and got the damn test taken. I mean, okay, so Pop suspected, but there's no way my own father would start a rumor..."

"Dr. Carl's office?" Grady repeated, his lungs constricting.

Dr. Carl had been Amy's doctor too. Just knowing B.J. was going to go to the same man who'd been standing over his wife when she died made him break out in a cold sweat.

Then reality intruded, and he frowned. "Doesn't Lara Alberts work in Dr. Carl's office?"

B.J. gasped. "That *bitch*! I ought to get her fired for breaking doctor patient privileges."

"I don't know," he murmured. "I'm kind of glad she's the queen of gossip, since that was obviously the only way I was going to find out about this...because you sure as hell weren't going to tell me. Were you?"

B.J. suddenly looked like a little kid who'd been found painting the bathroom walls with toothpaste as she braced herself for the angry lecture she probably thought would follow. Her face was pale and her eyes scared, nothing like the confident, no-cares-in-the-world B.J. Gilmore he'd always thought she was.

"I...I just wasn't sure *how* to say it," she answered quietly. "I mean, was there any way to break it to you easily?"

Grady opened his mouth, but B.J. hurried to add, "One thing was sure, I definitely wasn't going to tell anyone *else* until you knew."

She stopped suddenly as if just realizing something. Then she scowled and pressed her hands to her hips, snapping, "Wait a second. What even makes you think this is *your* kid?"

She'd already given it away, but his answer was a quiet, heartfelt, "Because I'm not that lucky."

B.J. looked like she was going to cry, and he felt like a heel for saying such a thing. He wasn't typically a rude man. But B.J. wasn't the type to break down and bawl when her feelings were hurt either. So why did the two of them together seem to bring out the worst in each other?

God, he wanted to scrub his face with his hands and mutter, "What a disaster," but he didn't want to hurt her any further. She already looked like she was on the edge and might crumble any second. He sighed then and really did scrub his face with his hands.

"I guess we'll need to get married," he announced, sounding none too pleased.

"What?" she yelped. "Oh, no. Hell, no. I'm not getting married. I'm not marrying *anyone*."

Again, Grady sighed. "B.J., there's a child to consider."

"So?" she retorted, taking a good three steps in reverse and holding up her hands to ward him off. "Single parents raise kids all the time. It's not a big deal."

"Well, I want *my* child to have two parents," he said slowly, holding back his impatience. "Living in one house."

"Hey, you can want all you like in one hand and shit in the other. See which one fills up faster, okay, Slim, because I'm *not* getting married."

"Will you just be reasonable?"

"Reasonable?" she shouted. "You're the one losing it. Do you know how freaking disastrous it would be for us to get freaking married? God, Grady. Do I look like June Cleaver to you? I'm telling you, it would not work."

Grady studied her for a moment before he spoke with complete assuredness in his voice. "We're getting married."

****

B.J. couldn't believe her ears. The man had lost his mind. He'd gone insane.

But marriage?

Could he mention anything crazier? Probably, but marriage was as far as her imagination could span at the moment. She was just too...befuddled to think much of anything. Befuddled and maybe a little scared, because the notion of tying herself to Grady Rawlings for the rest of eternity was...well, she couldn't even allow her brain to go there. But the idea made her shiver from the inside out—and not because she was cold...or disgusted.

"I came over here," he was saying, "prepared to cuss you up one wall and down the other—"

"Well, I really wish you'd get to that instead," she interrupted. "And quit blathering on about marriage." The word caused her to shudder again.

Pretending he hadn't heard her, he continued, "But now that I'm thinking about it, it doesn't seem so awful. I mean, Amy wanted me to be a father. She died trying to make that happen. What if this is her way of getting her wish?"

B.J. didn't want to argue with such a hopeful statement. What she really wanted was to curl into a ball and weep. That was probably why she sounded so sympathetic when she said, "But what if I miscarry like she did?"

He went still at the question, and she bit her lip. She almost couldn't go on, as touchy a subject as this was, but she had a point to prove, and she meant to do it no matter how much it hurt him, though hurting him just might kill her.

"What then, huh, smart guy? Suddenly there's no baby, and we're still married. Think about *that*. It's the stupidest thing in the world to get married just because of a child. If you really want to be involved in this kid's life, we'll work out some custody issues. You can have as much daddy time as you want. But that's it."

He was shaking his head before she even finished talking. "I want more."

"There is no more. I mean...what...what about *love*?"

He sent her sharp look. "What about it?"

"We don't love each other," she blurted out desperately. "How can you expect a marriage to last if the people getting hitched don't even love each other? Jesus, it's hard enough when they do."

"Love isn't any kind of guarantee. I loved Amy and we didn't last, now did we?"

"But...she died."

"What's your point? Death, divorce, it doesn't matter. I'm not with her anymore. Love doesn't mean forever."

B.J. didn't have a comeback. She merely stared at him mutinously. She wasn't going to give in, though, and realizing it, Grady sighed in irritation.

"To tell you the truth," he said quietly, "I'd just as soon *not* be in love the next go-round."

"Gee, thanks," the words blurted out of her before she could stop them. But really. Ouch. No matter how tough she acted, hearing him say he didn't want to ever love her stung like a son of a bitch, and there was no way she could've hidden her knee-jerk reaction of wincing.

His lips parted with the realization he'd actually hurt her feelings, and the apology in his eyes made her humiliation complete. She looked away.

"I didn't mean—" he started, but she lifted her hand to stop him.

"I know what you meant. Don't sweat it."

"No," he said. "You don't know. You don't know at all. That's just it. I can't...I won't ever let any woman...I mean, if I did, it could be Amy all over again. Don't you see? If I left myself open, someone else could leave me, or die, or whatever, and there'd be one more huge, gaping hole split open right through the middle of me. So I'm just going to pass on the whole love thing from now on, because I could certainly do without that kind of heartbreak for the rest of my life."

"Damn it," B.J. muttered, scowling at him to hide the guilt of letting her own emotions take over when this was really about him and his misery. "Don't go saying sad crap like that when I'm trying to disagree with you. I'm not going to back down, Slim. You're wrong about this, and you're just making me feel like I kicked a sick dog. So cut it out."

"I'm not wrong," he insisted.

"We're not getting married, end of story. Will you wake up and face the new millennium?"

"I don't care if it's old fashioned. A child needs a sturdy foundation. There's too many mixed families out there with too many messed up kids."

She snorted. "Well, it's going to have me for a mom, so I'd say it's already screwed there. Sorry, bud."

Grady blinked, looking surprised she could say such a thing. "I think you just might surprise yourself on that count."

Her mouth fell open. "What? Are you on drugs? What the hell makes you think I'm in any way *motherly*?"

Grady stepped suddenly closer to her. When he lifted his hand to set it on the side of her neck, she knew he had to feel her pulse leap under his fingers. Her eyes widened and her lips parted, letting out a surprised puff of air.

"I want to marry you, B.J.," he murmured, his face drawing closer to hers. "Why don't you want to marry me?"

Though his achingly sweet tone melted everything inside her like butter over hot pancakes,

B.J. balled her hands into fists. She wished she could sneer something scathing like, *Gee, maybe because this whole marriage idea has nothing to do with me and everything to do with your own sense of morality.* But she couldn't utter the words.

Strange. She kept finding more and more she was unable to say aloud lately, which was very unlike her. But the truth was, if he really cared about her or the baby, he'd—

Grady's fingers curled, and he ran his knuckles over her jaw, watching his own hand caress her as if it was the most intriguing sight in the world.

B.J. stopped breathing even as she warned, "Don't crowd me, Slim," and grabbed his hand, pulling it from her cheek. But, oh wow, that felt good. She didn't remember to let go of him, and her fingers cradled his warm, thick wrist, wanting to pull it back to her and press his palm against her aching breasts. "You can't sweet talk me into this."

He had the gall to look amused. "I assure you, it never once crossed my mind I could sweet talk the ultimate hard-ass, B.J. Gilmore, into doing anything."

When he tilted his head as if he was going to kiss her, she swallowed and tightened her grip on his wrist like that would stop the procession of his lips.

Meeting his gaze with a stony expression, she said, "You can't seduce me into it either."

He looked startled by the idea. But a moment later, his gaze settled on her lips. He sucked in a breath when she flicked out her tongue nervously to wet them. He was going to kiss her anyway, damn it. This wasn't good. If he got her on her back, she'd probably agree to anything he wanted, probably even let him coax her into his ridiculous idea of marriage.

B.J. braced herself, preparing to rebuff his

advance and knowing she'd fail.

But he threw her off track when he quietly admitted, "I can't stop thinking about Houston."

Her thighs trembled, and her nipples tightened. God, but she couldn't stop thinking about it either.

"We were good together," he breathed, tilting his face even closer until their foreheads were centimeters from touching. "And don't try to disagree with me. I'll know you're lying. You liked it just as much as I did."

"S-so?" she uttered in a suddenly shaky voice. "Good sex does not—"

"It'd be a nice little side benefit, though, wouldn't it?" His mouth was close enough it brushed hers with every few words he spoke.

"Just imagine it." His warm breath caressed her face. "Any time you wanted it, there I'd be. You could wake up on a lazy Saturday morning, roll toward me, and take me any way you wanted."

She swallowed, helpless but to imagine it.

"I miss that about being married," he said, tugging free of her hold on his wrist so he could bring his fingers back to her face. Tracing the bottom curve of her lip, he continued. "I miss knowing someone was beside me to touch and kiss whenever I wanted. But knowing it'd be you would be even more..."

He didn't finish the sentence, but he didn't have to. Closing her eyes, B.J. lifted her face in surrender. Grady took her offered lips greedily, drinking the taste of her, straight off her tongue. Groaning, he moved his fingers up into her hair, holding her head steady as he ate at her mouth.

It'd been over a month since they'd been together. But she could still recall the exact texture of his fingers on her. His familiar smell invaded her nostrils, dragging her under and sweeping her into a quickly rising flood of passion. His hands were hot and sure as he stripped off her shirt in one swift move and cupped her breasts.

"Ouch, ouch, ouch," she cried, going stiff in his arms, yet tightening her grip on him and holding on for dear life. "They're tender."

"Sorry," he rasped.

She thought he'd leave the swollen members alone. But telling him they were ultra sensitive only seemed to make him more interested. Gentling his touch, he pushed down the cups and gathered the twins in his hands, massaging with a skill that made her suck in a breath and arch against him.

"Oh, wow," she breathed out. "Ahhhhhh."

She closed her eyes as he kneaded and leaned down to suck one peak into his mouth. And she quickly learned tender breasts not only made them easily hurt but just as easily pleasured. Gritting her teeth, she belted out a stream of curses, thinking if he didn't get inside her soon, she was going to go off without him.

Seeming to read her mind, Grady picked her up and carried her to the couch. In a frenzy to unbutton her jeans, he growled out a frustrated groan.

"I need more hands," he muttered. "I want to touch you everywhere, all at once."

As her pants came undone under his harried ministrations, he paused to place a hot, scorching palm over her stomach, right over their baby. The move jolted her and zapped her back to reality, reminding her how sex would be a really bad idea right now. Too much was still unresolved.

"Stop," she panted, covering his hands with her shaking fingers.

Grady lifted his face but kept his fingers on their unborn child. His eyes had dilated, and the heat she saw in them about made her forget their problems and drag him down to finish what he'd started. It was a little overwhelming to see just how

114

much he desired her. They weren't in Houston now. She hadn't liquored him up first and coerced him into doing the unspeakable. This was pure, hot need in its rawest form, coming at her from a man she'd never thought would willingly want her. But...

"This isn't going to resolve anything," she said, taking a deep breath.

She wouldn't stop him if he pressed the matter. In fact, with the slightest cajoling, she'd probably beg him for more until they were both naked and sweaty and depleted from rippling orgasms. But he seemed to realize the timing was wrong too.

Blowing out a breath, he lifted his hands from her and scooted to the other end of the couch. After rearranging his zipper to relieve some of the pressure behind it, he slouched down into the cushions and cradled his head.

B.J. pushed her bra back into place, biting her lip when rough cloth abraded her pouting nipples. Then she went and retrieved her shirt. She noticed he wouldn't look at her until she slipped the top on and was smoothing it down over her hips.

"I won't marry you," she said.

His gaze was unreadable. He studied her a moment and then nodded. "I think we should at least tell our families together."

B.J. arched an eyebrow. "Tell them what? That we're *not* getting married?"

"That you're pregnant," he corrected, sending her a scowl for her lame attempt at sarcasm. "Unless...you've already told yours. But from the way you talked, I assumed you hadn't told anyone yet."

She shook her head. "No. I haven't."

"Okay." He nodded. "Then we should do that together."

"All right," she muttered reluctantly. But that was definitely going to be one chore she wanted to put off.

When she glanced at him, though, and saw the expectant look in his eyes, she winced. "What? Right *now*?"

He scowled. "When exactly did you plan on telling them? *After* the baby's born?"

She shrugged a little guiltily. "I don't know. But putting it off for as long as possible did sound like a good plan."

Grady sighed. "We can't put it off now we know the word's spreading. Our families need to learn from us...especially your side."

"My side!? Why especially my side?"

"Probably because my folks wouldn't think twice if they heard you were pregnant. They wouldn't know it's mine. But it's pretty obvious the baby is yours...so, it's more urgent to tell your side."

She sighed out a sound of disgust. "God... Fine, let's get this over with then."

****

Since Grady won the argument over telling their families together and right away, he let her drive when she insisted.

Leroy and Jeb were still at the hangar, working when she and Grady arrived. Buck was gone, no doubt home with his bitchy wife and bratty daughter.

And Rudy was absent as well, more than likely at some bar, getting drunk off his ass.

Stopping in the doorway, B.J. could feel Grady stumble to a halt beside her. From the corner of her eye, she saw him glance at her curiously, probably worried she was going to chicken out.

But that wasn't what she did.

He wanted her to make the announcement. So, she'd announce.

Cupping her hands around her mouth, she hollered into the huge tin building. "Hey!" she yelled, her voice echoing back to her.

Pop turned, and Leroy set down the blowtorch he was getting ready to use.

"If anyone cares to know. We're having a baby."

Chapter Ten

With that said, B.J. turned to stalk off. Grady remained in the wide entrance, staring after her. A clanging of metal sounded from Leroy's direction, probably him dropping the blowtorch.

B.J. finally glanced back and, yep, her brother was scurrying to pick up his fallen equipment.

"You coming?" she asked Grady.

But the voice of her father shouted out, "Get your tail back here."

B.J. muttered a curse, closed her eyes, and turned in Pop's direction. Grady fell into step beside her. It shocked her just how comforted she was by his automatic show of support. Grady Rawlings might be a quiet, reserved person, giving off the impression he was shy. But he had backbone. He didn't back down from certain duties, even ones that made *her* want to run for the hills.

"You're pulling our leg, ain't ya?" Leroy said, laughing as he glanced from her to Grady. "I mean, you two..." He shook his head and slapped at his knee. "Brat, you couldn't get a Rawlings to notice you if you stripped naked and—"

"Enough," Jeb growled and jabbed at his son to shut him up. Then he propped his hands on his hips and glared disapprovingly between B.J. and Grady. "So...when's the wedding?"

Grady looked expectantly at her. "That's what I'd like to know."

B.J. threw her hands in the air. "We're *not* getting married."

"You...you mean it's true?" Leroy sputtered.

Spinning to aim an incredulous look at B.J., he said, "How in the sam hell did you get *Grady Rawlings* to—"

"Will you shut the hell up," she snapped, mainly because Grady was taking a threatening step toward him, which her idiotic brother didn't even notice.

"I want to know why there's not going to be a wedding," Jeb growled.

"Pop, that's really none of your concern."

"No, I want to hear this reason too," Grady said, crossing his arms over his chest and cocking her an arch look.

B.J. growled. Damn. She knew she probably hadn't heard the last of his marriage-talk nonsense, but she never would've guessed he'd so sneakily enlist the help of her own father.

"Don't you start with me again," she groused. "We already went over this. There's no reason we should marry. I told you, you can have as much Daddy time as you want. You can—"

"That's not the same, and you know it."

"You're being ridiculous." She raised her voice. "We are not getting hitched after one measly night in a hotel room."

"B.J.," he said under his breath, risking a quick glance toward her dad, clearly not receptive to the fact Pop was listening to their every word. "Will you just listen to me? I—"

"Hell, no. I'm not going to stand here and listen to you rant and rave like a psycho. We're not getting married, and that's that."

"Guess you two are still working out the date," Pop cut in. He eyed Grady thoughtfully before sighing. "I suppose there's worse out there that could've knocked up my little girl."

For the first time since entering the hangar, Grady looked contrite.

B.J. decided she didn't like the hold Grady

Rawlings had on her, because she felt the urge to say she'd marry him just to wipe that miserable look of shame off his face. No, she'd never liked seeing anything suffer, but that trait seemed magnified ten-fold with this man.

"Can we leave now?" she asked abruptly, more uncomfortable with the situation than she ever would've admitted. In fact, she'd probably just turn tail and stalk out of there if the obstinate man who'd knocked her up hadn't insisted on them riding together.

He nodded once and then focused his attention on her dad. "There *will* be a wedding," he assured him.

"Woo-wee, little sister," Leroy hooted. "You sure hog-tied him around your little finger, didn't ya? Who'd a thunk it? You must got a golden—"

"That's enough," Grady growled, effectively making her annoying brother swallow his tongue.

When he glanced at her with an impatient, restrained anger, she knew it was way past time to skedaddle. She nodded, feeling a hard plop in the base of her stomach. Felt kind of strange watching someone defend her.

Together, they turned toward the exit.

****

B.J. had never been inside the main Rawlings homestead before. The thousands of times she'd passed the mansion, she'd always wondered what it was like. Today, she finally found out.

As Grady knocked on the front door, a lump of pure fear settled in the base of her stomach. Telling Pop she was knocked up was one thing. Informing the fancy Rawlings was completely different. Shoving her clammy hands into her back pockets, she waited behind Grady and forced herself to stand still. The urge to turn and flee was pretty strong though.

As the door started to open, she held her breath. She actually expected a maid or butler or something to answer, but when Tara Rose Rawlings herself peeked her head out the door, B.J. almost groaned. Damn. The Rawlings were home.

"Grady," his mother exclaimed, her eyes brightening instantly.

"Mom," he murmured respectfully as she reached out to hug him.

"What a delightful surprise." She hooked her arm with his to draw him forward. "Come in, come in."

As he moved, she finally noticed B.J. lurking behind him. "Oh! I'm so sorry. I didn't see you there." When Grady stepped inside and to the left to let B.J. in, the two women fell to a stop and studied each other cautiously.

Tara Rose's smile froze. After blinking back a blank look, she asked, "It's D.J., right? D.J. Gilmore?"

"B.J.," Grady corrected.

A hint of pink highlighted the tops of his mother's cheeks. Still smiling at B.J., she spoke through gritted teeth to her son. "That's what I said."

"You said D.J."

His mother finally turned from B.J. to pin her oldest with an annoyed look. "No, I said B...not D. Don't question your mother."

That was when the most amazing thing happened. Grady grinned.

Both Tara Rose and B.J. gaped.

"Yes, ma'am," he murmured, all the while smirking from ear to ear.

B.J. was still thinking he had the most enticingly ornery look ever when Tara Rose cleared her throat. "Well, let's not stand in the foyer all day. Come into the parlor."

Said the spider to the fly.

B.J. shivered but followed mother and son into the next room, where they all three stood, awkwardly staring at each other as if expecting someone else to break the silence. Tara Rose kept sending curious little glances B.J.'s way, and B.J. was trying to get Grady's attention by glaring at him, silently urging him to talk. But he seemed intent at rubbing at a scuff on his shoe with the heel of the other boot.

Finally, he glanced around. "Where's Dad?"

"He received a call and had to check something in the south field."

Grady grew alert. "Everything okay?"

"I'm sure it is." Tara Rose pushed his concern aside with the sweep of her hand. "He's always getting calls. I'm just glad it wasn't three in the morning this time."

She grinned B.J.'s way, probably trying to share an inside joke to make her feel included in the conversation.

But the tense smile B.J. returned had the older woman glancing away and sending her son a questioning look that asked, *What the heck is going on?* It was clear she had no idea why her son would come to call, bringing the "Gilmore girl" with him.

"Anyway," Tara Rose said, clearing her throat. "Ah..." She glanced around the room as if she had no idea what to do with herself. "Oh! Why don't you two have a seat? I'll get us some refreshments."

Looking eager to leave, she scurried toward the exit.

B.J. hoped Grady would decline for the both of them. But he obeyed his mother's suggestion and started toward a cushioned high-back chair. She would've called the other woman back and told her she needn't bother with trying to entertain them, but she already knew if she tried to talk, nothing would come out except a dry croak.

As soon as his mother disappeared around the corner, B.J. whirled toward Grady, who'd plopped into the chair already. She didn't want any "refreshments." She wanted to drop the news like a stink bomb and get the H-E-double hockey sticks out of there before she caught a whiff of the rotten hang time.

But when she spotted the crushed look on his face, she paused.

"I didn't realize he received so many after-hour calls," he murmured to himself. "I never get a call from work."

The unspoken question, *Why don't I ever get a call?*, lingered in the air between them. B.J. suddenly remembered the nasty words she'd said in Houston. *You make everyone in town uncomfortable whenever you're around because you freeze the living folks out like they should all feel sorry they're still alive and your wife isn't.*

He lifted his eyes then, and he looked at her as if he were remembering that exact same line. She opened her mouth to apologize for being such a butt that night, for hurting him like she had. But a rough male voice spoke from behind them.

"Well, well. Be still my heart. If it ain't that little Gilmore gal."

B.J. spun around and sucked in a delighted breath. "Now there's the love of my life," she said and surged forward.

Grady's grandfather, Granger Rawlings, had to be over eighty years old if he was a day. He'd lived in the Rawlings mansion since the moment he'd it built nearly fifty years ago. In a wheelchair now, he'd lost one arm and half a leg in an explosion on the oil field years ago. But she'd always adored the gruff old man. And he returned the affection one hundred percent.

Where other children had shied away from the intimidating oil tycoon, B.J. had been drawn to him. She still remembered the first time she'd ever seen him. It had been at one of Tommy Creek's annual homecoming festivals. Since the Rawlings had sponsored the event, the entire family had gathered around a booth where they passed out free drinks to the townsfolk. B.J. had walked right up to Granger and tugged on his sleeve to get his attention.

"Who stole your arm and leg, mister?" she'd wanted to know.

Instead of snapping at her for the rude question, he'd thrown back his head and hooted with glee. Then, slapping at his good knee, he'd urged her to climb onto his lap and commenced to tell her the story of exactly how he'd lost his missing appendages. She'd found the old timer's gory account so fascinating, she'd gone back to him every time she'd seen him after that—at Fourth of July picnics, Christmas parades, and Spring dances—crawling into his grandfatherly lap and demanding another story. The man had never failed to entertain her with some type of tall tale.

Knowing she'd disappoint him if she did otherwise, B.J. plopped down on Granger's lap now and pressed a loud, sloppy kiss to his wrinkled cheek. He grinned approvingly and tugged at the back of her ponytail. She might've gained a good fifty pounds since the first time she'd sat on his knee, but neither of them cared.

"Where you been, darling?" he asked. "I haven't seen you in years."

Slinging an accommodating arm around his neck, she continued to grin into his dancing blue eyes, which she realized were the same hue as Grady's. "Well, hell, I thought you were long dead by now, old man."

Granger laughed and smacked her leg in a light,

playful gesture. "Missy, I'm way too young to croak yet." The smile on his face made him look twenty years younger than he had to be. He winked. "Besides, I can't go anywhere until you finally agree to marry me."

"Marry you?" B.J. said in surprise. God, what was up with these Rawlings men all of the sudden? None of them would shut up about getting hitched. "Why in the world would I want to marry an ancient, lecherous coot like you?"

Really getting into the flirtatious mood, Granger leaned closer and said, "Give me five minutes alone away from my grandson over there, and I'll show you why."

B.J. couldn't help but laugh, all the while thinking it must run in the family. She was just as drawn to Grady as she'd always been to Granger.

Glancing Grady's way, she was curious to see how he was taking all this interaction. But he merely sat slumped back in his chair, looking amused. Arching her a look, he asked, "Want me to go?"

"Do you mind terribly?" she asked, leaning toward Granger and resting her cheek on his forehead.

But before he could comment, his mother came bustling into the room with a silver serving tray full of cups and saucers and a coffee pot. The smell of Folgers hit B.J. almost instantly. Slapping a hand over her mouth, she surged off Granger's lap and stared wide-eyed at Tara Rose.

"Do you have a bathroom?" The words rushed from her mouth as her stomach rebelled.

"Er...of course...it's down the hall to the..." She never even finished the sentence, because B.J. had already turned and fled.

****

"Is she okay?"

125

Grady turned his gaze away from the doorway where B.J. had beat a hasty retreat and glanced at his mother. "Uh..." was all he could manage to say.

"Looked like she was going to upchuck to me," his grandfather said, wheeling closer to where his daughter-in-law was setting down the tray on the coffee table in front of Grady. "Leaped up like the smell of that coffee didn't agree with her."

Tara Rose frowned and glanced down at her refreshment. "Hmm," she said, giving the coffee pot a strange look. "How odd. I've never seen anyone have an aversion to the smell of—"

Breaking off in mid-sentence, she lifted her face and pinned an accusing look at her son. He could tell immediately when the truth dawned. Shifting uncomfortably in his chair, he stared back, unable to wipe the guilt off his face. As her face drained of color, Tara Rose glanced toward the abandoned doorway.

"I heard the strangest rumor yesterday at the beauty shop," she murmured.

"What's that?" Granger asked, reaching forward to help himself to a cup of coffee.

Tara Rose frowned at her father-in-law. "Dad!" she hissed. "I didn't bring out enough for you too."

"Well, it's not like *she's* going to drink any if the very smell makes her hurl." He glanced at Grady. "What? She pregnant or something?"

As Tara Rose sucked in a breath and spun toward him to hear the answer, she covered her gaping mouth with two hands.

Grady sank further into his seat. "Is that what you heard at the beauty shop yesterday?"

She nodded. All he could see over her fingers was her large brown eyes.

Grady hissed out a curse. "Well, doesn't that just beat all. My own mother found out before I did."

"Oh, God," Tara Rose said in a small voice.

"What're you two talking about?" Granger wanted to know. He glanced up from where he was stirring in a healthy spoonful of sugar. He studied Tara Rose and then turned to Grady. Pausing, he lifted his bushy eyebrows. "Holy hell. Are *you* the one responsible for her condition?"

Grady scratched at the back of his neck and winced. "How long till Dad gets home?"

"Could be hours," Granger boomed. "Now, quit holding out on us, boy. That your baby in her or not?"

Grady nodded once and quietly murmured, "It's mine."

"Oh. Oh, my Lord," Tara Rose whispered and sank into a seat, staring glazy-eyed at the wall.

Granger grinned. "Well, boy, howdy," he cheered, smacking Grady's hip. "I always knew you had good taste in the ladies, kid. But you topped the cake with this one. That Gilmore girl's a fine woman. Good breeding stock. Why, the two of you will have strong, healthy babies. Damn, boy..."

He beamed as he continued to pummel Grady's thigh like he was giving a congratulatory slap on the back. "What a way to carry on the line. I couldn't have picked out anything better for you if I'd chosen her myself. B.J.'s a sturdy one. Got nice, wide, child-bearing hips and—"

"Dad!" Tara Rose hissed in a strangled voice.

Grady lifted his face in time to see B.J. standing frozen in the doorway, her face drawn and pale.

"Oh, good," she said as a bead of sweat trickled down the side of her face. "I missed the big announcement."

Then her eyes rolled into the back of her head, and she passed out cold.

Chapter Eleven

"Now, why are you driving my truck again?"

Grady held in a deep sigh. But then he glanced at B.J. in the passenger seat, and the frustrated weariness dissolved instantly. She still looked pale. Too pale.

"How's the head?" he asked, reaching out to once again feel the bump she'd accrued from landing noggin-first on his mother's hardwood floor.

She quickly lifted her hand to the spot before he could touch it, sinking her finger into the thick mass and wincing.

"It's fine."

Dropping his fingers, Grady's eyes drifted over her hair before once again returning his gaze to the road. He couldn't recall ever seeing her hair down before. It was surprising how long and...pretty it was. The brown hue was a rich chocolate with golden hints of natural highlights. The locks were more straight than curly, providing a healthy bounce to them that tumbled over her shoulder and made him want to bury his nose in her neck and have all that long, silky hair coat his face.

"Still have a headache?" he asked, forcing his attention back to the road as he realized he hadn't even seen her hair down the night they'd slept together. But he'd certainly been quick about pulling the ponytail holder from her skull so he could feel for a bump when she'd passed out nearly twenty minutes ago.

B.J. muttered, "It's not so bad I can't drive my own freaking truck."

Grady ignored the comment, all the while trying to forget the fear that had pounded through him when he'd seen her wilt to the floor like a stage actress in some dramatic Shakespearean performance. Only this had been real...way too real. Still upset he hadn't been able to make it to her in time to catch her, Grady winced as the thump her skull had made when she hit the floor continued to echo through his ear canal.

"Oh, my God," his mother gasped as Grady fell to his knees in front of the collapsed B.J.

"B.J.?" he rasped, irrationally afraid she'd already passed on to the next world. He scooped her into his arms, gently cradling her head and feeling around for blood and brain-tissue.

"She okay?" his grandfather asked as he drove his motorized wheelchair up behind Grady and stopped next to Tara Rose, who was standing with both hands covering her chest.

The injured party herself answered. "What the hell am I doing on the floor?"

Grady thought he was going to take his own turn on the floor and pass out from relief. B.J. cursed as he found the tender spot on her scalp. Instinctively, she swatted his hand away. But he'd already felt for himself the skin had not been split open. There was a decent-sized goose egg growing, but that seemed to be the extent of the damage.

"Are you okay?" he asked, immediately reaching out to help her when she tried to sit up.

"Just dandy," she muttered, wincing and then swaying as soon as she was upright.

Grady reached out to steady her, tightly wrapping his hand around her shoulder. Even after she caught her bearings, he continued to hold onto her, grateful she was at least conscious. Worry pounded through him, he couldn't seem to breathe right.

"What happened?" she asked, glancing past him at his mother and grandfather.

"You passed out cold, kiddo," Granger said. "Took the prettiest little nose dive to floor I've ever seen."

B.J. snorted. "Really? I guess all that practice in front of the mirror paid off then?"

Tara Rose sputtered out a surprised laugh at her sarcastic comment, and Granger threw back his head and hooted, slapping gleefully at his good knee. Grady couldn't understand how they could make jokes. Just because she was up and talking didn't mean she was okay. There could be a concussion, internal bleeding...Amy had been alert right up to the minute she'd died.

B.J. started to rise. Since he still had a hold on her shoulder, he tightened his grip, tempted to push her back down until he was convinced she was fine. But from the determined look in her eye, he knew she'd struggle against him if he held her against her will. To avoid hurting her, he helped her up.

"Are you sure you're okay?" Tara Rose asked, hopping forward to take B.J.'s other arm. He was glad his mother had asked since he'd wanted to. But his vocal chords were still frozen with fear. If anything happened to her—

"I'm good," B.J. said, giving both Grady and his mother a confused scowl as they each latched onto an arm and didn't let go. The blasted, independent woman honestly didn't think she needed help. But she soon learned otherwise when she set her feet under her.

"Ooooo..." she said, wincing and latching a hand around her stomach. "Coffee."

She turned as if to head back toward the bathroom but swayed dizzily in the process. Grady tightened his grip to steady her. But she didn't seem to like his restraint.

"Gonna puke," she said, her voice sounding alarmingly frail.

Tara Rose bounded into action, grabbing a nearby trashcan and handing it to him. B.J. caught sight of it, snatched it to her chest and buried her face in the opening. As her stomach revolted, she started to slide to her knees. Grady assisted the descent to keep her from falling face first. Then, since he'd been the one to rip the ponytail holder out, he gathered her brown locks into his hand and held her hair out of her face.

"Get that coffee out of here," he snapped, glancing at his mother with a scowl.

She leapt to comply. Snagging the cup from her father-in-law's hand just as he was lifting it to his mouth for a sip, she tossed it onto the silver serving tray and lifted the entire thing in one swoop. Then she was gone, leaving only a trace of the rich decaffeinated brew behind.

"Bluck," B.J. muttered when she came up for air. "That was nasty."

"Here's some water," a breathless Tara Rose said as she reentered the parlor, baring a huge glass of ice water.

"God bless you," B.J. gasped and reached for the cup.

Grady stayed crouched next to her as she guzzled. He rested his forearms on his bent knees and looked up at his mother, concern flush on his face. She bit her bottom lip and winced, shaking her head as if to say such behavior from a pregnant woman didn't seem normal.

And that was when he decided he wanted to talk to a professional, right then. "I'm taking her to the doctor." He removed the empty glass from B.J.'s hand.

She frowned. "Why? I don't need to see him for a bump on the head."

Ignoring her, Grady grasped her elbow, "Up," he said.

"Ugg...here we go again," she groaned as she started to rise. B.J. spread her arms out as if to steady herself, already bracing for the dizziness. When she didn't sway once, she straightened with a relieved smile.

"Well," she said, turning toward Grady. "That wasn't so bad. See, I'm better already."

But he wasn't convinced. Glancing toward his mother, he said, "You'll let Dad know?"

She rolled her eyes. "Of course. And everyone else in the family as well."

"Thanks." He took both of B.J.'s shoulders and steered her toward the door. "Let's go."

"But..." She resisted his hold and turned back to his mother. "I just made a mess all over—"

"Don't even worry about it," Tara Rose assured her, using her foot to push the trashcan way from B.J.'s grasp. "Just go with Grady so he can make sure you're okay."

She gave B.J. a speaking look, and something passed between them, some kind of telepathic woman talk he'd never been able to understand. Then B.J. glanced at him. When she nodded and stopped resisting, he gritted his teeth.

He didn't want her to agree only to appease his fears, but at this point he didn't even care... He had to know if she was going to be okay. There was no way he could live through killing another woman by making her pregnant, no way he could stand there and watch the life drain out of her after giving birth to his dead baby. He would never do that again.

As he glanced across the cab of her truck at her now, the anxiety was still causing his blood to course though his body in almost dizzying waves.

She groaned and closed her eyes. "I can't believe I yakked all over your mother's floor."

"You yakked in a wastebasket," he corrected.

"She must hate me right now." As she spoke, she scooped her hair up with both hands and refastened the locks with her holder.

"The trashcan was lined with a plastic bag," he argued logically. "It won't take anything at all to clean."

She glanced over and sent him a dry look. "I wasn't talking about the trashcan."

He snapped his mouth shut. After a moment, he answered, "You know, I think she'd be a lot more forgiving if you married me and made an honest man out of me."

B.J. rolled her eyes but didn't bother to answer. As he pulled into the drive of a ranch-style brown house, she sat up and blinked.

"Where are we? I thought you were taking me to the hospital?"

Before Grady could answer, she caught sight of the man in the yard, pushing himself to his feet where he'd been kneeling in a flowerbed.

She gasped. "Oh, my God. Grady, you took me to Dr. Carl's *house*? We can't just barge in on him when he's home, relax—"

"He won't mind."

At the confident note of assurance in his voice, B.J. arched her brows, impressed. "Well," she said. "I always knew the Rawlings name held a lot of sway in these parts, but—"

"He better see me whenever I want," Grady growled from between gritted teeth. "The man was holding a bloody knife in his hand and standing over my wife when she died."

As B.J.'s mouth dropped open, he glanced away. He didn't blame Dr. Carl for Amy's death. He knew the doctor had done everything in his power to save her. But neither would he ever forget the stunned look on the man's face as he gaped at the heart monitor blaring out one long, continuous beep.

"I didn't even think," B.J. said. "Of course, he would've been her doctor too, wouldn't he?" Her face went pale as she glanced at him. "God. If you want me to find another OB/GYN—"

"There is no other baby doctor around here," he muttered and pushed his way out of the truck. He nodded a greeting to Dr. Carl, who was already striding forward to meet him.

"Grady," he said, stretching out his hand. "This is quite a surprise. What brings you by?"

After giving the older man a brief handshake, Grady reached into the cab of the truck and tugged B.J. out through the driver's side. "She just passed out and hit her head. Hard."

The doctor blinked at B.J. and then whirled back to Grady. He didn't have a medical degree for nothing. From the utter shock in his expression, he caught on immediately. *Grady* had impregnated B.J. Gilmore.

"Oh," he whooshed out the word and then seemed to return to reality. "Well then, B.J. Why don't you step up onto the porch for minute?"

As he took her elbow and drew her forward, B.J. said, "I'm fine, Doc. Really. Noggin's a little sore, but that's to be expected."

Grady trailed them with restless impatience. A little sore his ass. "Her skull hit a wood floor so hard I swear it bounced."

Ignoring B.J.'s scowl at Grady, Dr. Carl said, "Why don't we just have a seat up here." He pulled a black steel swiveling stool out from the tall round table under his covered porch and patted the seat. "I'll have a look for myself."

"She threw up too," Grady said. "Two times. I've never seen anyone vomit as much as she did."

The doctor nodded and disappeared inside the house.

"Tattletale," B.J. muttered.

Glancing up in time to catch her sticking out her tongue, then folding her arms over her chest and turning away from him, Grady should've been amused. Instead, a vision of Amy laid out in her casket—only an empty, lifeless shell—hit him hard and fast. He couldn't picture B.J. dead. She was too lively, spirited, animated. Like Grandpa Granger, she was meant to grow old and sassy, zipping around in a wheelchair and flirting with the younger generation.

She could not die.

Grady was tempted to grab her and yank her to him, kissing her till she lost her irritation, kissing her while she was still so alive and healthy. But Dr. Carl saved him from making a fool of himself, returning with a stethoscope and a handful of other medical goodies.

The doctor studied B.J.'s pupils before he checked her blood pressure and took her temperature. "Nausea is perfectly common among pregnant woman." He plucked the stethoscope plugs from his ears and turned toward Grady.

Grady merely shook his head. "Amy had a queasy stomach a few times when she was pregnant, but she never threw up," he insisted, "in either pregnancy. And she certainly never passed out."

When the doctor sent him a sad, sympathetic smile, he ground his teeth. God, he hated this. He hated the helpless fear, and he hated everyone feeling so damn sorry for him.

"Amy was a different case entirely. Each woman goes through her own unique symptoms. B.J. has none of the complications your wife did."

Grady merely scowled. His eyes slid to the woman sitting on the stool. With her legs dangling over the side, she looked like a child, waiting for the pediatrician to plant a "Good Job" sticker on her

135

shirt. It made his stomach knot with tension. The thought of losing her the way he'd lost Amy made him physically ill. And the fact he was just now realizing this caused his skin to tighten about two sizes too small for his body.

He didn't want her to die. He didn't want their child to die. He wanted them both to stay healthy. And that insight scared the living hell out of him.

"This gal here has about the most ideal equipment for a pregnant woman I've seen in a long time," Dr. Carl praised, setting a hand on B.J.'s shoulder as he sent Grady an intense, reassuring smile. "Everything I've checked is normal and healthy, and I foresee no problems at all in the upcoming months. You have nothing to worry about, Grady."

Realizing he'd gone off the deep end with panic, Grady nodded. But he couldn't help but linger close to B.J. as she hopped off the stool just in case she hit another dizzy spell. Thanking the doctor, she shook the old man's hand and immediately turned to him.

"Satisfied now?" she asked.

Though she managed to put a pinch of annoyance in her voice, like being forced through this ordeal aggravated her to no end, he still heard the softness in her tone. The irritating woman was more concerned about his mental wellbeing than her own physical health.

Lowering his gaze, he nodded and mumbled, "Let's go."

Chapter Twelve

B.J. glanced down at her wristwatch as her younger brother stumbled into the hangar. It was nearly noon, and she'd asked him to come in at nine to help her take some aerial pictures.

"Don't even start," he groused as he pushed past her, smelling like a stale brewery. "I'll be out and ready to go in a few minutes."

"Whatever," B.J. said on a shrug. "I've already waited three damn hours on you. What's a few more minutes." She'd been enjoying the race on television anyway. "Just don't start the coffeepot."

Rudy paused and scowled over his shoulder. "Why the hell not?"

"What? Are you the only person in the county who hasn't heard?" She rolled her eyes as she patted her belly. "I'll be yakking all over you in the plane if I get one whiff of coffee."

Her brother blinked. "Yeah, I heard about the baby. But...the smell of coffee really makes you sick jus 'cause you got a bun in the oven?"

"Apparently. I stocked the fridge with cola if you need a caffeine fix."

"Yeah? Thanks." He turned away and started off.

B.J. returned her attention to the NASCAR race, thanking God Rudy hadn't freaked out over her condition. Ever since yesterday when she and Grady had gone public with their news, she'd been treated like an alien with two heads. She suddenly understood why he'd withdrawn into himself after Amy had died. It sucked to have everyone staring and talking about you wherever you went.

The snap and fizz of an aluminum can opening behind her told her Rudy had returned. Without looking up from the screen, she said, "Twenty bucks says Gordon wipes out on that last turn there before the race is up."

Rudy stopped at her side, took a five-second long chug, guzzling loudly as he swallowed. Then he wiped his mouth with the back of his free hand and burped. "You're on."

"Hell, I'll give you twenty bucks just to tell me who really knocked you up. Rawlings or Smardo?"

B.J. growled and closed her eyes. "Leroy." He'd been popping over every couple of hours to annoy her. "I swear to God, if you don't shut up about that, I'm going to give you another bloody nose."

Rudy snorted.

Leroy ignored her threat. "Twenty bucks," he coaxed, waving a bill in front of her face. Though he tried to move it fast enough she couldn't tell what denomination it was, she knew it was a single dollar.

Rolling her eyes, she shoved his hand out of her sight. "Get out of my face, asshole, and stop asking me stupid questions."

"I thought it was a pretty good question myself."

At the new voice, all three Gilmore siblings froze and then turned in unison. B.J. felt rather than saw her two brothers slink a respectful step back when they found themselves in the presence of Grady's father, Mr. Rawlings Oil himself. B.J. had to admit her legs quivered a little with intimidation, but she made sure she didn't change her stance any: cocked hip, arms crossed, and expression bored.

Giving Tucker Rawlings a single nod, she asked, "Can we help you with something?"

He flickered a single, meaningful glance toward her brothers.

"Uh, I'll just go start the pre-flight inspection

before we take off," Rudy said.

Leroy added, "Yeah, I'll help."

The two stumbled over each other in their haste to flee.

B.J. watched them go. Cowards. *Thanks a lot, guys,* she wanted to call after them. *Abandon your own sister to the big bad wolf.* But instead she stood her ground and faced off with Tucker Rawlings alone.

"Well, I guess I should've expected to see you sooner or later," she said.

Instead of answering, Tucker glanced toward the television just in time to catch Jeff Gordon nosedive into the very wall B.J. had predicted he would. She'd never felt so sick about winning twenty bucks in her life.

"You like to gamble, do you, B.J.?" Grady's father asked, letting her know he'd been standing behind her long enough to catch her wager with Rudy.

She didn't answer. But he obviously didn't expect her to because he continued talking. His eyes met hers, so brilliantly blue, for a moment she felt like she was looking at his son. "What say the two of us make our own wager?"

Her tension was so great, she couldn't even sweat. "'Bout what?"

One corner of Rawlings's mouth curved up as he sent her an amused look. "'Bout my son, of course."

B.J. shuddered out a breath, knowing this conversation was somehow going to leave her damaged. Seriously damaged. "What about him?"

Instead of responding, he turned away to watch Rudy and Leroy walk around her Cessna. "That airplane's yours, right?" he asked and glanced back over his shoulder at her.

She gave a brief nod, uneasy about his interest in her baby.

"You owe, what, thirty-three grand on it, don't you?"

B.J.'s stomach dropped. It felt like someone had just pushed her over the edge of the Grand Canyon, and she dangled there in space for a split second before falling. But what the—

He'd nosed into her debts? Into her plane? What did he want with her plane? Why would he bring her plane into this?

Realizing this conversation had just taken a turn she knew was headed down a doomed path, she stood steady. Petrified, but steady. "It's thirty-two and half," she corrected, feigning all the courage and bravado she didn't feel.

"Actually, it's thirty-two thousand, six hundred twenty-three dollars and eighty-eight cents if I paid it off today."

"If *you* paid it off?" she repeated.

"Okay," he revised on a shrug. "Not if. When." He reached back to his hip pocket and produced a thick envelope. "The deed to your Cessna. I just paid it off."

B.J.'s vision blurred. For a moment, her equilibrium shorted out. She had no idea if she was vertical or not. She must've swayed, reached out her hand for support, or something because the next word out of Tucker's mouth was, "B.J.?" He sounded concerned. Steady fingers dug into her bicep, grounding her.

She blinked him back into focus and brushed his hand away. "I'm fine." Turning away so he couldn't see her face that had no doubt lost its color, she repeated, "I'm fine." But in the next breath, she rasped, "Oh, my God. You bought my plane."

Spotting the pile of tires she'd won off Ralphie, she plopped down on top of the stack and looked up at Grady's father. "What...what do you want from me?"

He took his time answering her. After blowing out a long, steady breath, he said, "Grady's bound and determined to marry you to set this thing with the baby right."

B.J. snorted. "Well, I already told him no, so you don't have to worry none there."

Tucker gave a slight, amused smile. "You don't understand. After everything my boy's been through in the past three years, I'm just as bound and determined to see he *gets* everything he wants." His gaze slid to her, his unfinished sentence lingering thick in the air... *And he wants you.*

B.J. shivered and sucked in a stuttered breath. "So, uh...you bought my plane so I *would* marry him? Wow. That's not what I expected."

Tucker laughed softly. "It's a little more involved than that."

B.J.'s hopes sunk. "Of course it is."

"If you thought was I going to pay you off and try to run you out of town, you weren't too far off," Tucker admitted. "That was my initial reaction. But...Grady's been different lately. He actually mentioned...this week he talked some about what happened to Amy."

B.J. felt a lump grow in her throat, wondering if Grady felt as guilty as she did about cheating on Amy like they had. God, of course he did. She lowered her head, ashamed.

"I've waited two and half years for him to open up to me, to say something, *anything*. And now finally..." Tucker shook his head. "I didn't catch on to what had changed with him until Tara Rose told me about your visit yesterday. Suddenly, I realized it wasn't *what* had changed him. It was who."

"So, what're you saying?" B.J. asked, her voice gone hoarse.

"I'm saying he wants to marry you, so that's what you're going to do. And you'll stay with him for as long as he needs you around. Then, when he grows tired of you, *that's* when I expect you to take your plane and get out of Tommy Creek."

B.J. cocked an eyebrow. "What if he never grows tired of me?"

"Well, now, that's where you can lay money on your bet. You keep him happy until the baby's born, and I get some proof it's his child, then you can have the deed to your plane, free and clear. Call it a wedding present. If not..." He shrugged. "Take your plane and leave town, shipping the baby back when it's born."

B.J. froze. "Excuse me? Did you just say, 'ship the baby back'?"

Tucker Rawlings nailed her with an inflexible look. "It's the baby he really wants."

Feeling sick to her stomach, B.J. resisted the urge to cover her belly, instinctively wanting to protect the child inside.

Okay, yeah, she'd been avoiding the whole I'm-going-to-be-a-mommy issue. Just thinking about having a kid, utterly dependent on her, made her feel queasy and panicked. But to actually give the baby up? That thought had never even crossed her mind.

"What if I can't prove the kid's Grady's?" she asked, suddenly so desperate she needed Tucker Rawlings to feel a bit of uncertainty as well.

He sent her a hard smile. "Oh, Grady's not going to learn about the paternity test. That's for my own peace of mind. He's not ever going to learn about this little conversation we're having either..." He paused, sending her a meaningful look. "Is he?"

Her insides flamed with anger because Tucker Rawlings had her right where he wanted her; she stared at him with a stubbornly stiff jaw. "Do I look like a tattletale to you?"

He nodded, reassured. "So...if you marry him,

142

sign a prenuptial agreement of course, and keep him happy until the baby's born, I'll give you the plane, free and clear. You marry him, sign the same prenup, and he realizes what a mistake he's made, you hand over the baby and take out for parts unknown...with your plane. Either way, the Cessna's yours, B.J. I gotta say, that doesn't sound like such a bad deal on your end."

She gave a short nod. No, it didn't sound like a bad deal. Except for that part about abandoning her own child...oh, and the being-held-under-Tucker-Rawlings-control thing. That sucked eggs.

The whole agreement made her want to throw something—preferably something sharp and deadly—right at Tucker Rawlings' head.

Remaining as cool and collected as she could, she asked, "And if I say no deal? To hell with you and to hell with my plane; you can keep it. What're you going to do then, Mr. Almighty?"

His eyes sparked with challenge, and B.J. had a very bad feeling she'd just asked the exact wrong question.

"Oh, I still have an ace up my sleeve."

Though she kept her body still and didn't shrink from the victorious gleam in his eyes, she wanted to cringe so bad, already dreading something more awful than she could comprehend. "An ace in what form?"

"From what I hear, you run a good bluff. You can act like you don't care what happens to your plane all you like, B.J. And, hell." He gave a shrug. "As old and worn out as it is, maybe you don't care. But can you act so blasé about your family?"

An uneasy chill raced up the back of her spine. "What about my family?"

"Seems my family might owe your family's plane service a lawsuit for nearly killing my boy on that trip home from Houston."

All the air vacated B.J.'s lungs. "Just what the hell are you going to sue us for? Grady wasn't hurt. None of his possessions were damaged or lost. And he was given a full refund for the scare."

"Ah, but he *was* spooked, wasn't he. You made him fear for his life...probably caused lasting emotional damage."

"Oh, Jesus. Gimme a break." B.J. rolled her eyes, even as her stomach rolled with unease. But dear God. If the Gilmore Plane Service got a bad rep from the Rawlings family, no one in Tommy Creek would ever do business with them again...hint of a lawsuit or not. No one displeased the Rawlings.

"So, what do you say, B.J.? Do we have a deal?"

She shook her head. "I gotta think about this."

He gave a short nod. "You do that. And remember...breathe a word of any of this conversation to Grady, and all deals are off."

****

B.J.'s phone was ringing as she stepped inside her back door. She groaned. If it was Tucker Rawlings, she was going to hang up on him. She'd had enough of Grady's father for one day. He'd ruined her entire afternoon as it was.

Expecting to hear his voice and dreading it, she dropped the mail and lunchbox she'd carried in with her onto the kitchen table and scurried to the phone.

"Hello."

"Hello. B.J.?" a hesitant female voice asked.

B.J. frowned. Who was this? "Yep. Sure is."

"Oh. Well, good. This is Jo Ellen. Jo Ellen Gerhardt."

Pausing in her perusal of the mail, B.J. lifted her face. Oh, dear God. Here we go again. If it wasn't the father, it was the daughter. But, Jesus, if Jo Ellen planned to give B.J. a piece of her mind for getting herself knocked up by Grady, then she was going about it in way too polite a voice.

"Okay," B.J. said. And?

She could imagine what kind of threats and name-calling Grady's sister was going to start tossing around.

"Mama called last night and told us the happy news...about the baby."

"Yeah?"

Dropping the cable bill in her hand, B.J. squinted blankly across the room and wondered what her caller's main objection was. She seriously doubted the woman wanted to congratulate her. Thinking Grady's sister could only have nefarious plans just like her dad, B.J. braced for the outpouring.

"Well, I was just wondering if you'd like to come over for a little while," Jo Ellen said. "To, you know, girl chat."

Girl chat? B.J. winced at the word before the main subject of the question struck her. Jo Ellen was inviting her over?

Okay, so maybe she wanted to cuss her out in person.

"Are you busy for the next hour or two?" Jo Ellen sounded almost hesitant.

Well, hell. A whole hour's worth of name-calling? Grady's sister must have some doozies. She could already imagine the typical insults. Gold digger, hoochie mama, bitch, slut, whore. But damn, a whole hour's worth?

"I guess I've got some time," she muttered on a sigh. Might as well get this over with now.

"Great," Jo Ellen gave the perky reply. "I'll see you in a few minutes."

As she hung up, B.J. glanced down at her clothing. She'd been outside in the heat all day under a grimy plane engine. She should probably take a shower and change first. But, hell. Who honestly dressed up for a dressing down? Shrugging, she wiped her palms on her pants and headed back out the door.

****

Five minutes later, she stood at the Gerhardt's, ringing the bell. In these parts, everyone knew where everyone else lived. In fact, B.J. could remember who'd lived in this particular house before Jo Ellen and her husband had bought it two years ago when they'd married. It was a modest-sized place, but clean and well taken care of. Jo Ellen was a Rawlings who'd actually married down on the social chain.

Come to think of it, Grady had done the same thing when he'd hooked up with Amy. In fact, Amy's father still worked for Rawlings Oil in the office as a peon paper-pusher. Then again, the Rawlings family were the top dogs in this area. They couldn't help but marry down. Emma Leigh, Jo Ellen's twin sister, had to move all the way to Reno to find someone as rich as her to marry.

While B.J. was still wondering if Grady's sister was going to accuse her of being an opportunistic social climber, the front door opened before she could knock.

"B.J.!" Jo Ellen said with a pleasant greeting smile, managing to sound surprised as if she hadn't been expecting company. "That was quick."

As Grady's sister held open her front door and stepped aside, B.J. entered a pristine living room that belonged on the cover of one of those home decorating magazines. Glancing down at her boots, she hoped to high heaven she hadn't stepped in anything gooey lately.

"I made some pastries," Jo Ellen said as she pushed the door shut, imprisoning B.J. in the house with her. "The kitchen's this way."

She started off, and B.J. was helpless but to follow.

Jo Ellen Rawlings-Gerhardt was pageant-queen pretty. With her petite build and flawless complexion, she certainly didn't look like a farmer's wife. But B.J. couldn't fault the woman her choice in men. Cooper Gerhardt was as masculine as Jo Ellen was feminine. He had one of those body-builder physiques with a golden Adonis's head pasted on his hunky, muscular shoulders.

Though Jo Ellen had short hair, it was styled to perfection. It was dark brown just like every other member of her family's, but she had hers frosted with thick blonde highlights and sprayed into a neat, fashionable pose. B.J. had to keep herself from reaching up to make sure her ponytail wasn't hanging limp. She hadn't touched her mane since that morning after taking a shower.

The kitchen was as immaculate as the front room. With sparkling white cabinets and counters, it looked brand new and extra clean.

In the depth of her brain, she wondered if Amy had been such a good housekeeper too. B.J. guessed she had. She used to give off that aura of perfection just like Jo Ellen did.

"I made cinnamon rolls." Jo Ellen opened the oven and pulled out a pan where she'd been warming them. As she turned to find B.J. fallen to a stop, she grinned. "When I was pregnant, I was utterly ravenous for sweets. I couldn't get enough of them."

She held out the tray of still-warm rolls. B.J. stared at them, heard her stomach growl for a taste and cautiously lifted her face to the woman offering them, expecting some kind of ulterior motive behind such a kind act, like maybe as soon as she reached for a roll, the floor would open under her and she'd fall into the dungeon below.

Jo Ellen frowned, obviously curious as to why her guest wasn't immediately snatching a roll. Not wanting to offend, B.J. shrugged and followed her stomach's advice, scooping up one and bringing it to her mouth.

Grady's sister beamed in approval. "Mama told me how much coffee turned your stomach, so I bought some juice. That'll be good for the baby."

When she poured a glass full of apple cider and nudged it encouragingly in front of B.J., B.J. paused and eyed it warily. Suddenly, the entire visit felt like one big trap.

Lifting her gaze, she said, "If you're oozing all this kindness in order to make me feel like slime for putting your brother through nine months of worry-ridden hell, then you're doing a damn fine job."

Jo Ellen smiled as she picked up her own cinnamon roll and nibbled off an end. "Well, thank you," she said, as if complimented. "But, no, that wasn't my intent."

"Then...?" B.J. pressed, giving her an impatient look.

Jo Ellen sighed, sat down her roll and picked up a napkin to dab at the corners of her mouth. "B.J.," she said patiently. "This baby you're having is going to be my son's first cousin, my son's *only* cousin within a hundred miles. So I think it's pertinent we get to know each other. Besides, you're going to need a lot of help in the next few months to come, and I don't want you to be left out in the dark."

"Help?" B.J. asked blankly.

Jo Ellen's face softened. "Honey," she said, reaching out to lay a gentle hand on top of B.J.'s. "Do you have any idea what you're getting yourself into? You're going to have a baby. *A baby.*"

B.J. blanched. "Oh, God," she said. Why did Jo Ellen have to go and remind her? She'd been doing so good at avoiding that little detail.

"The way I see it, you're probably clueless about how to deal with this."

"I am," B.J. admitted, feeling suddenly sick. She sat down the cinnamon roll. "I really, really am."

"You have no mother or sisters or even a grandmother to give you any kind of tips or advice. I mean, sure, there's your sister-in-law, Phyllis..."

Thinking of going to Buck's wife for any kind of assistance made B.J. wince. Hell no, she'd rather talk to Leroy about PMS cramps.

Jo Ellen grinned. "That's what I thought. Ergo, I've decided to take you under my wing, so to speak. So...if you have any questions, concerns, or—"

"Am I going to have to pee this often the entire pregnancy?" B.J. asked immediately.

Jo Ellen threw back her head and laughed. "You have no idea," she affirmed. "And it only gets worse too. I swear, Tanner was tap-dancing on my bladder through my third trimester."

B.J. was wondering if she'd look like a moron if she asked what a third trimester was when a sharp infant cry came through the baby monitor sitting on the counter by the pan of cinnamon rolls. She gave a jerk of surprise.

Grady's sister, however, softened. "And speak of the little angel himself," she said. Starting for the door, she motioned for B.J. to follow. "Come meet my son."

B.J. frowned, leery. If Jo Ellen ended up changing a diaper in front of her, she was probably going to hurl the few bites of cinnamon roll she'd managed to swallow.

When they reached the nursery, B.J. stopped short. The dim room smelled like baby powder, and that was the only thing she recognized. She might as well have stepped onto Mars. Everything past the door's threshold was completely foreign. Gaping at the pale blue walls lined with nursery rhyme borders, she didn't pay much attention to Jo Ellen crooning at the wiggling bundle in the crib.

Holy hell, did she need to buy all this crap for one itty bitty little baby? This was going to cost her a fortune, not to mention the fact she had no idea what any of it was or what she was supposed to do with it. Maybe Tucker Rawlings had a point. She wasn't cut out to be a mother. The kid would get along better if she just left it with Grady and took off.

Her stomach burned at the thought, and she pressed her hand to it, to her baby.

"B.J.," Jo Ellen murmured as she picked up the swaddled infant. "This is Tanner. Tanner, meet your new Aunt B.J."

At being referred to as an aunt, B.J. swung around and paused, coming face to face with a bright-eyed little boy who was staring up at her from his mother's arms. He looked so calm and serious until she made eye contact. Then he broke into a smile and waved both arms in excited baby-greeting.

Charmed by the little critter, B.J. grinned back and took a step toward mother and son. Unable to help herself, she reached out, and the boy immediately did the same, latching his entire fist around her index finger.

Something hard and inherent moved inside her. Good lord. She was supposed to raise one of these things? It was as exciting as it was scary.

"Grady said he had a lot of hair," she murmured in awe. "But he didn't mention the curls."

Jo Ellen lifted her face, stunned. "Grady talked to you about Tanner?"

Shrugging briefly, B.J. glanced up. "He only mentioned the hair," she said. When the other woman looked completely bowled over, she frowned, confused, and dropped the infant's fingers. "Why?"

"I thought..." Jo Ellen shook her head and wiped a single tear from her eye. "I'm sorry. It's...I've never seen him hold Tanner. He'll barely even look at him."

Not sure what to say, B.J. fumbled for a moment before she offered, "Well, I'm sure it's hard for him after...you know, after what happened." Wondering if he'd be able to hold his own child once it was born, she sat her palm over her stomach and swallowed hard.

Jo Ellen must've sensed her worry. Forcing a smile, she thrust her son forward. "Do you want to hold him?"

B.J. immediately backed away. "What? Oh. No. No, I don't think... No thanks," she said. "I don't want to break him or anything."

Jo Ellen's smile faltered. "B.J.," she said, her voice going stern with disapproval. "You *need* to get used to this before yours is born. You don't want to be scared of holding your own child, do you?"

"Uh..." Was this a trick question? Of course she didn't want to be scared of her own kid, but...damn, did she have to start practicing now? She had nine months to get it down.

"Here," Jo Ellen said, taking matters into her own hands. "Sit in the rocker, and I'll slip him into your arms."

Wanting to refuse but not sure how, B.J. found herself shuffling reluctantly toward the rocking chair.

"Are you sure about this?" she asked.

Jo Ellen rolled her eyes. "Trust me. You'll be fine. The main thing to worry about is supporting his head. Other than that, just don't drop him, and you're home free.

"Now," she added once B.J. had eased into the chair, "cradle your arms like you're holding an imaginary baby."

B.J. did so, feeling like an absolute moron.

"Perfect," Jo Ellen congratulated with a smile. She leaned down to settle the child in B.J.'s arms and added, "Just make yourself comfortable, and he'll be comfortable too."

Yeah right, B.J. wanted to mutter. She felt *real* comfortable.

"You got his head supported?" she asked anxiously as the sweet-smelling little body was laid in her grasp.

"Yes, he's fine," Jo Ellen whispered, letting go and taking a step back.

It took B.J. a good five seconds to look down. When she finally lowered her face, Tanner Gerhardt looked back up at her with a pair of wide, curious eyes. Their gazes met, and he once again broke into a grin.

"Oh," she whispered, falling completely in love. "Oh, wow."

Jo Ellen moved to stand beside them and lean over her shoulder to make eyes at her son as well. "I know," she said. "It's even more amazing when it's your own."

B.J. unconsciously started to rock slowly back and forth.

"I'm not sure why he woke up," Jo Ellen murmured. "But he could probably nap for another half hour if you want to put him back to sleep."

"Okay. How do I do that?" B.J. asked, pumped and eager for her next baby lesson.

"Well, I have some sedatives, or we could just bonk him over the head with a hammer. Take your pick."

B.J. whipped her head up in time to catch Jo Ellen rolling her eyes. "Just keep rocking him," she said. "He'll probably drop off in a few minutes."

Glancing down at the baby, B.J. was surprised to see his lids flutter drowsily.

"See, there he goes," Jo Ellen added. She set a hand on B.J.'s shoulder. "I'm going to take those cinnamon rolls off the pan and put them on a plate.

Call if you need anything."

B.J. nodded but didn't bother to look up. She barely even heard the quiet pad of Jo Ellen's feet as she exited the room; she was too busy studying the features of the baby's perfect little face. Experimentally, she reached out and twined one of his blond curly locks around her finger. The fine hair had to be the softest she'd ever touched.

Still in a state of petrified shock, she felt herself grin. She'd visited Buck's house a few times after his daughter had been born. But on all those occasions, his baby had done nothing but wail. It was startling to see they were sometimes quiet too. Hell, she might be able to put up with the crying if she had some of these precious, cuddly moments.

Suddenly it didn't matter what the Rawlings took away from her and did to her family—no way on earth could she give up her baby. She wanted a child, her own child, to look up at her with big, curious eyes just like Tanner Gerhardt was.

Sensing someone in the doorway, B.J. lifted her head. "I think he's asleep," she said. But it wasn't Jo Ellen returning. Instead, it was Cooper, Jo Ellen's husband. He leaned in the doorway, munching on a cinnamon roll, watching her coo at his son with a raised eyebrow.

"Hey, Coop," she whispered as she sent him a smile in greeting. "I hope you don't mind. I'm going to practice on your kid until mine comes along."

Cooper slipped into the room and neared the rocking chair to look down at his sleeping son. "Just don't break him," he said quietly, obviously having already talked to Jo Ellen.

B.J. flipped him off but quickly lowered her hand and glanced down to make sure the baby was still sleeping and hadn't seen the gesture. Cooper chuckled softly and crouched to his haunches so he could lay a soft kiss on his son's hair. B.J. watched

Cooper lovingly nuzzle his nose against the infant's cheek.

"Remember when we fooled around once?" she said, suddenly recalling a long-ago event she hadn't even thought of in years.

Cooper choked on the cinnamon roll in his mouth and tripped in his haste to stand upright.

"Jesus, B.J.!" he yelped, jerking a few steps away. "What the hell?"

"Shh," she hissed. "Don't wake the baby."

"Well, what in God's name are you doing mentioning that?" he hissed back. "It happened a *long* time ago. And my wife is in the other room, for God's sake."

She nodded. "I know. I just wanted to say I'm glad we didn't do anything more...you know. That's all."

Coop nodded as well and stared at her like she'd lost her mind. "Okay," he answered. "I'm glad too."

B.J. smiled. "I really like Jo Ellen. And I'd hate to feel awkward around her for some mistake *we'd* made twenty centuries ago."

Coop couldn't respond this time. He just nodded, unable to make eye contact.

"She's the one, isn't she?" she pressed.

"What?" he asked, looking confused and then glancing anxiously toward the door.

"The woman you were all depressed about that night. It was Jo Ellen, wasn't it?"

"Oh. Ah...yeah. It was her."

"Well, I'm glad everything worked out for you two," B.J. said. "You got a sweet wife and a really good kid here."

"Thanks," Coop replied, "...I think. Just don't go mentioning that night again, okay?"

B.J. winked, and Coop suddenly seemed like he was in a hurry to leave.

But when he reached the doorway, he stopped

and glanced back. Cocking his head to the side, he studied her thoughtfully.

"What?" she demanded. "Am I doing something wrong?" She looked down at the baby in worry.

Cooper smiled as he shook his head. "No. Tanner's fine. I just realized... You're actually a soft touch, aren't you?"

She frowned. "Excuse me?"

"That night," Cooper said. "You were only trying to cheer me up. You came over to me in the bar because you said I looked sad."

"So?" B.J. answered.

"Well...that makes me think the same thing happened with Ralphie Smardo. I can see you saying yes to him just to boost his ego."

"Oh, God," she moaned, closing her eyes. "Does everybody know about *that*?"

He nodded solemnly. "About the skinny dipping? I'm afraid so. Your little diner scene is quickly becoming legendary."

B.J. rolled her eyes. "I never should've let that little slime ball touch me."

Cooper shrugged. "But you did," he murmured, "because you felt bad for him."

She scowled. "He kept whining about never getting a woman. I just wanted to shut him up."

"Uh huh," Cooper said, knowingly. "So you gave him some sympathy sex. Just like you did Grady."

B.J. stopped and opened her mouth as she frowned at Cooper. But no words came out.

Cooper chuckled. "Don't you dare tell me you don't feel bad for him. Hell, everyone in the county feels sorry for Jo Ellen's brother. He's been through hell; you only have to look at his face to see that."

"You are so wrong, Gerhardt," she insisted. "I don't do sympathy sex."

Cooper's return look said otherwise, but he murmured, "If you say so."

Chapter Thirteen

"Sympathy sex?"

B.J.'s mouth fell open. She hadn't been home from Jo Ellen's but an hour before Grady came knocking. She'd had time to shower and shave her legs and feel refreshed for an evening of lazing around the house and eating a frozen dinner. But Mr. Rawlings had other ideas.

As soon as she opened the door to him, those two dreaded, accusing words came out. They didn't exactly register in her brain though. She was too busy staring at him and thinking how absolutely beautiful he was. His father's visit and sister's phone call immediately forgotten, all she saw was a man who made her heart pound hard and her breathing turn choppy.

"You're into sympathy sex?" he repeated.

Groaning out a curse, B.J. gritted her teeth. "I'm going to kill Cooper for opening his pie hole." Then, frowning as Grady pushed past her to enter the living room, she muttered, "Sure. Come on in."

"Why Cooper?" he asked, turning to send her a questioning look. "Cooper's not the one who told me. Jo Ellen is."

B.J. gasped. "Oh, my God! Jo Ellen heard us talking?" She lifted her hand to her suddenly aching temple. Damn. There went the only female friend she'd ever had. And she'd been anxious to ask Jo Ellen more pregnancy questions.

Wincing, she asked, "Is she totally pissed at me?"

He frowned in confusion. "Why would *she* be

pissed?"

"Because of what Cooper and I did—" she started to blurt out before she realized Grady obviously hadn't heard the whole story. "Wait a second," she said, setting her hands on her hips. "What exactly did she say to you?"

"She said you only slept with men you felt sorry for. Cooper was *not* mentioned in that list." But from the way he closed his eyes and shook his head sadly, he'd already added Gerhardt to the register. "Please, God," he muttered. "Don't tell me you slept with my brother-in-law."

"No!" she said. "Definitely not." When he gave her a probing stare, she shifted uncomfortably, crossed her arms over her chest and scowled. "Besides, he wasn't your brother-in-law at the time."

"Oh, my God. You slept with Cooper?"

"No," she yelled back. "He stopped before it went too far."

Grady paused. "*He* stopped?" When she gave a miserable nod, he pierced her with a look and set his hands on his hips. "And just how far did you two go before *he* stopped?"

B.J. let out a dramatically long sigh and tried to stop blushing. "Not that it's any of your business because it happened way back when you were still married to Amy, but we barely got our shirts off," she admitted on a mumble.

Grady didn't look happy about thinking of her with a shirtless Cooper. "That's it?"

She nodded. "This was right before he and Jo Ellen hooked up. And he was all bummed out because he thought he was never going to see her again. So, he couldn't go through with it...with me."

"Ah. So, it was sympathy sex with him too, huh?"

She glared. "I do not do sympathy sex! I mean, come on. Have you ever seen Cooper Gerhardt shirtless? Pity was the last thing on my mind, I assure you."

"Uh huh," he said, not believing her. "And I'm sure Junkyard Smardo is simply irresistible with his shirt off, isn't he?"

B.J. couldn't help it. She winced. Ick. Ralphie had just been plain scary without his clothes on. She had to be thankful it'd been fairly dark, or his pasty white skin and beer belly would've chased her away long before they'd started.

Clamping her mouth shut, she refused to incriminate herself any further.

"And what about me?" he asked in a low voice, stepping ominously closer. "What was it about me you were so unable to resist? The way I brooded into my beer throughout supper? Or maybe it was how I ignored you and tried to avoid all conversation."

B.J.'s lips parted in surprise.

He was hurt. She blinked, unable to believe it. He honestly thought she'd only slept with him to ease his miserable life. And, clearly, that didn't sit well with him. He hadn't wanted any kind of pity or sympathy. He'd wanted honest-to-goodness lust.

Not sure how to tell him her pity had gone out the window the second her mouth had touched his, she sighed.

"You seen a mirror recently, Slim?" she asked. "Because you're not exactly hurtin' in the looks department either."

Humming in appreciation, she blatantly skimmed her eyes up his trim jeans and tucked-in shirt to his tanned throat and striking face. Oh, yeah, he wasn't lacking at all.

"Smell good too," she added, moving even closer until her nose was only inches from his neck, where she took a big whiff, almost groaning when she inhaled his irresistible male scent.

The heat coming off his body was intoxicating.

B.J. shivered in delight. "I don't mind the way your hands felt on me either," she whispered into his ear.

She lifted her fingers to his hair and was about to tell him she liked the texture when he caught her wrist. She gasped in surprise and met his steely stare.

"I remember Amy talking about how you used to take in stray dogs and patch them up." His nostrils flared as he spoke, telling her their proximity affected him even though he held himself back. "I'm not some lame bird with a broken wing, B.J."

No, he was a man, a flesh and blood, virile man who wanted something from her besides pity. Well, B.J. decided she could oblige...with pleasure.

"Thank God," she purred, rubbing against him. "Because right now I want some hard, fast sex, no strings attached, no emotions involved...just body to body, mouth to mouth..." She murmured the last few words against his lips and didn't finish the sentiment before his tongue was scraping over her teeth.

His hands skimmed her body once before he grasped the hem of her shirt and pulled it over her head. She stripped off his pants. More articles of clothing followed as they stumbled toward a hallway.

"Where's your room?" Grady asked, wrapping his arms around her waist and hauling her off her feet.

Dazed by the explosion of need roaring through her and the desperation with which she wanted it quenched, she pointed out a door. He pushed it open with his foot and carried her all the way to the bed.

Sitting her on the mattress, he followed until they were facing each other. As she peeled off his shirt, he focused his attention on her breasts.

"Are they still tender?"

She could only nod. He took care removing her

bra. When she still winced, he whispered his regret and bent his head to spread a few apologetic kisses over the swollen flesh. B.J. forgave him immediately, especially when he sucked a throbbing bud into his mouth.

Warm, caressing fingers skimmed down her skin and hovered over her stomach a moment before pressing gently as if greeting the baby inside.

"Passed out any today?" he asked, glancing up at her with concern.

B.J. shook her head and lifted her hand to his hair.

"Vomited?" he wondered.

Her hand dropped as she sent him an irritated scowl. "No, doctor," she said impatiently. "I have *not* passed out or hurled once today. Do you want to take my temperature next?"

He grinned. "Only if you think you can handle my thermometer?"

Mouth dropping, B.J. could only gape at him for a moment. Then she sputtered, "Oh, my God. Did I hear wrong, or did the golden boy of Tommy Creek, Texas just make a dirty, suggestive comment?"

"Golden boy?" he echoed in surprise. Shaking his head, bemused, he leaned over her, causing her to lie back on the bed. "Let me convince you just how wrong you are."

Giving her a hard, demanding kiss, he set his hands on her knees and pushed them apart. B.J. was ready. She wanted to feel his thick probing head at her entrance more than she wanted her next breath. And when she did, she breathed out a sigh of relief. Finally. He pushed his way deeper into her.

But suddenly, he stopped and pulled out. B.J. tightened her thighs around him in protest, but he merely shook his head. "Not yet," he told her. "I refuse to rush this."

"Rushing sounds fine to me," she argued.

But he had other ideas.

Murmuring coaxing words she couldn't even understand, he slipped his fingers down to toy with her, and his mouth evoked pleasure from her skin. He kissed her throat and breasts, working his way across her stomach. B.J. tensed, expecting and craving the feel of his tongue between her legs. But he didn't go any further than her belly button.

After dipping a finger inside to test her moisture, Grady straightened above her, bracing his arms on the mattress at either side of her head. He gazed into her eyes, going frustratingly slow as he started to enter her again as if purposely tormenting her.

Once he was seated fully, he stroked out once and pushed immediately back in to the hilt. B.J. cursed and dug her nails into his shoulders.

"You like?" he asked.

Biting her lip to swallow down a cry of desire, she rasped, "You know I do."

He pulled all the way out. "Then marry me," he whispered against her throat. "And you can have it whenever you want."

B.J. jerked in surprise. She couldn't believe he could think of anything but getting back inside her. It was insulting to realize his mind was still functioning enough to think about his ridiculous plans for marriage. Plus the M-word brought up a picture of his father and all the blackmail and wagering he'd begun mere hours ago. For some reason, that nastiness felt wrong popping into her mind while she was with Grady, poor Grady who was innocent and blissfully unaware of what kind of deals and schemes his family was trying to make on his behalf. No way was she going to let any of that touch him.

"No," she heard herself growl.

Rolling onto her stomach away from him, she

crawled across the mattress and grabbed her bra. He came up behind her and caught her wrist, shaking it once until the piece of cloth dropped from her grasp. Then, pinning her hand to the bed, he attempted to push his way inside her from behind.

"Marry me," he said again.

"Damn it, Grady," she sobbed and tried to crawl off the bed. "Don't do this right now. I said no strings."

"But what if I got depressed in the middle of the night," he asked, his voice light and teasing, though it carried a hard underlying edge. "I'd need your sympathetic touch."

"Will you shut up?" she snapped, trying to close her legs and buck him off. "I didn't give you a pity fu—"

He cut her words off with his mouth on the back of her neck and his hand on her breast. She tried to pull away, but he caught her around the waist and entered her completely.

She gasped and arched her back, forgetting everything but him—moving with him in sync to his rhythm and loving him with everything she had.

"Later, then," he growled and grabbed her pelvis, pumping furiously.

B.J. squirmed and pushed back against him, wanting it harder and faster. Needing more than he could reach from his position, she fumbled a moment and pressed her own fingers against herself, trapping the sensitive bud between her thumb and the base of his pumping penis. In moments, she let out a groan of release, and he followed almost immediately.

Once the last shudder racked her, she collapsed on her stomach and rested her face in the pillow. He settled his weight on top of her, spooning her into the mattress. She marveled at the feel of his warm flesh matted to hers.

Unable to keep her deepest, darkest secret inside a moment longer, she whispered, "I can't believe you'd even suggest I'd ever sleep with you out of pity. I think I wanted to have sex with you since I was twelve and saw you making out with Amy on my living room couch."

She closed her eyes and waited for the fallout and accusations. She'd wanted her babysitter's boyfriend. She'd wanted a married man. She'd wanted Amy's man. To her, that was grounds for a stoning.

But Grady merely set his hand on her shoulder and kissed her hair. He didn't say anything, and she thanked God for that. She wouldn't have been able to bear it if he had.

Tears seeped from her lashes because she knew she didn't deserve his easy forgiveness. Amy had been like a big sister to her, sometimes even a stand-in mother, and B.J. had lusted after her property.

And now...now she was falling for that same woman's man.

****

B.J. woke in a river of sensuous pleasure. Already boneless from their previous encounter only hours before, she could only lay there as Grady's rough fingers glided gently down her stomach and across her hip. It wasn't morning yet, but still late in the night. Grady had yet to go home, and she could only thank her lucky stars as he kissed her shoulder and slowly combed her nether hair with his fingers.

The lights in the room were still blazing because they had both fallen asleep soon after making love. Yawning, she turned her head and met a pair of vivid blue eyes watching her. Letting out a contented sigh, she arched her hips and felt her thighs spread to allow him more room to explore.

"Feel nice?" he asked as he nipped her earlobe.

B.J. couldn't answer. She could only feel, so she

moaned out an affirmative.

"Then just imagine it," he said, dotting kisses along her jaw and down her throat. All the while, his fingers played between her thighs, and his bare legs moved restlessly against hers. "If we were married, we could do this all the time...anytime."

She shook her head from side to side. "Don't start that again, Grady. Please. We're not going to..."

She gasped before finishing the words because he pushed his index finger inside her. Then he removed it fully, and she groaned in agony from the loss of his filling presence. Moving on to other areas, he rubbed his slick finger across the nub just above her opening. B.J. hissed out a breath and fisted her hands around a wad of sheets.

Grady sat up suddenly so he could watch his own handiwork. He stared intently for a second before glancing up.

"You touched yourself right here earlier," he said. "When I was inside you."

B.J. damn near went cross-eyed as he massaged that very area. "Did I?" she managed to rasp.

He nodded and licked his lips as he watched his fingers work. "I'd never seen a woman do that before." Sending her a boyishly fascinated grin, he added, "I liked it."

"Is that a hint?" she asked and rolled her eyes. Reaching down, she batted his hand away and took up the task for herself. Her hips arched all the way off the bed when she went straight to the spot wanting the most attention.

"Holy God," Grady choked out and grew even more avidly alert. Starting to really get into his voyeuristic venture, he positioned his legs so his feet were stretched out up by her face and propped his elbow on the mattress next to her hip as he leaned in close to see every detail clearly.

Growing suddenly reticent, B.J. felt her face

heat. "Are you just going to watch?"

He nodded, his eyes glued to the progress of her fingers. "Don't stop," he commanded, his voice strained.

B.J. grinned as he studied her the entire time. He looked so entranced, she got off on the hot gleam in his eyes almost as much as she did from the pressure of her own fingers. When he finally looked up and met her gaze, she climaxed.

As her heart rate started to settle, he looked ready to pounce, but he merely stared at the notch between her opened thighs.

"What are you waiting for, Slim?' she asked, amused. "A handwritten invitation? I don't get any readier than this."

He licked his lips, looking hungry like he wanted to eat her whole. His eyes darted toward hers and then back down. "Can I..." He paused as if debating whether or not to ask. Then he cleared his throat and glanced up. "Can I taste you?"

B.J. honestly hadn't thought the night could get any more erotic. She'd come hard and long and felt sure she was done till the next full moon. Someone stick a fork in her. But at his seemingly shy question, a pulse of pure desire beat its way up her thighs and fried the nerve endings in every erogenous zone on her body.

"Well, hell," she said, opening for him. "If I'd a known you wanted to go down on me, I would've let *you* finish me off."

He looked uncertain for a moment, then said, "I probably couldn't have given you an orgasm anyway. I've never...you know, done this before."

B.J.'s mouth dropped and then she shook her head. "Well, you cheap bastard," she said and laughed outright. "I bet all the girls you've been with don't miss you at all."

He frowned slightly. "Amy would never let me,"

he said defensively. "She thought the whole idea was..." He shrugged. "Dirty...unsanitary. She didn't think she'd be able to kiss me again if I went anywhere near there."

His words fell off as he glanced at that tempting spot on B.J.

"So, what about the other women?" she couldn't help but ask.

He sent her a strange frown. "Other women?"

The hairs on the back of B.J.'s neck spiked with apprehension. Needing to appease her own unease, she pressed, "You know, the other women you've been with."

He shook his head. "I started dating Amy when I was fourteen," he reminded her. "We never once broke up, and...well, you already know you're the only one since she died."

"Oh...my God," B.J. murmured, feeling utterly dumbfounded. She sat up as if to escape the realization. This was *not* what she wanted to hear. "You've only been with two different women your entire life?"

He shifted uncomfortably. "What's wrong with that?"

"It's just...Well, hell, I don't want to have a bigger track record than the guy I'm sleeping with."

He arched his eyebrows. "What exactly is your track record?"

B.J. refused to answer. She glanced away. The answer was nothing to write home about, but it certainly doubled his measly two.

"B.J.?" he pressed quietly and set a hot palm on her thigh.

Feeling the need to distract him, she turned toward him and opened her legs in one smooth move, successfully gaining his attention where she wanted it. "If you want to taste me, you'd better get to work, Slim. I might not be so charitable and let you

166

proceed in another few seconds."

Not wanting to lose his opportunity, Grady immediately set his hands on her knees and bent down. He was very tentative at first; his tongue was soft and gentle. When B.J. arched and made a sound of pleasure, he paused and glanced up.

"Am I doing it right?"

"Don't stop," she yelled.

He sent her a slow, self-satisfied smile and lowered his head again.

****

"B.J.?" Grady whispered.

"Hmm?" she murmured drowsily, feeling as limp as a noodle.

Yep, Tornado Grady had struck again. In the last half hour he'd topped their first night together like it was nothing. Three times. Holy crap, she'd had three explosive orgasms right in a row. First from her own ministrations, then from his mouth, finishing with a round of good ol' fashioned sex...with her on top.

The guy was a Lothario, no question about it. Her time with him—as much time as she was going to get—would be one big roller coaster ride with loops and drops aplenty to keep her wanting more. She was going to love every second of it. She just hoped it didn't end nasty and—

"Will you marry me?" he asked, interrupting her wishful thoughts.

Her brows pulled together. "I thought I told you—"

She stopped dead when she rolled toward him and saw the ring in his hand. It had a huge white diamond on it and was the prettiest thing she'd ever seen. The thrill inside her about had her launching herself into his arms right then.

"I bought it this morning," he said. "I would've given it to you sooner, but I think you successfully

167

sidetracked me." The grin he sent her said he didn't mind the distraction in the least.

B.J. found it suddenly hard to breathe. Forcing herself to toughen up, she eyed the amazing ring with cool disdain and snorted. "I hope you don't actually think I'll ever wear any kind of jewelry."

He merely smiled, a lazy tilting of the lips. "But it's a wedding ring. Lots of men wear them too. So, I don't actually consider it jewelry." He shrugged. "Once you get used to it, you kind of feel naked without it on. Think of it as underwear. It's just another part of getting dressed in the morning."

B.J. sent him a dry look. "Ever heard of going commando?"

His eyes glittered with amusement. "Married people don't go commando."

She snorted. "Oh, really? And why's that?"

He shrugged. "There's always clean underwear around to wear when you're married."

B.J. threw back her head and laughed. As she was holding her stomach and chuckling, Grady took her hand and started to try the ring on. Immediately, she grew alarmed and curled her fingers into a fist, preventing him from finishing his unwavering task.

His probing gaze lifted to hers.

"You don't want to do this, Grady," she whispered. "I'm warning you. It'll just turn into a disaster if we get married."

Keeping his eyes on hers and not saying a word, he slowly pried opened her fingers. If his hand would've been warm and confident, she probably would've fought him harder. But as it was, his cold touch trembled with an uncertainty that tugged at her heartstrings.

They silently stared at each other as he slid the ring into place. It fit a little snug, making her panic and suck in a breath, thinking it would never come off again. Then she grew even more unnerved because she didn't really *want* it off.

The moment was too intense to suit her. Her pulse leapt uncontrollably, and she felt things for Grady she'd never felt for anyone. But with his chilly fingers still touching hers and the ring banded around her, she experienced a connection with him that was simply overwhelming. Only a person who had never possessed any compassion in their entire life would be able to turn him down at that moment.

B.J. thought she was doing well with the casual, uncaring shrug she managed. "Fine." Let the stubborn fool have his way for a little while before he realized how right she was. "But you asked for this. We'll try the whole marriage thing until it falls through. And when it does—which it will—I'm going to be right there in your face, saying I told you so."

Grady nodded. "All right then," he told her, blowing out a relieved—or was that a petrified—breath. "We'll get married next Friday."

"Next Friday?" she said dumbly. So soon?

Grady merely sent her a look that said, *Well, why wait?*

B.J. swallowed and immediately put on her cool face again, ignoring the leap of excitement in her belly. She gave another unconcerned shrug. "Whatever," she answered. "This is your thing, Slim. Doesn't make no never mind to me. We'll get hitched next weekend."

Chapter Fourteen

Grady woke at his usual time Friday morning. He rose and took a shower, just as he always did. Then he fixed breakfast and ate it alone. Nothing new there. An outside observer would assume it was a normal, average day for him. He didn't appear to be nervous or excited or even regretful about the fact he was getting married in mere hours.

What he honestly felt was reflective. He'd already visited Amy's grave the day before and informed her about his upcoming nuptials. He'd left the cemetery with a feeling of peace, confident she would approve of her successor.

He hadn't confessed how much he liked bedding B.J. though. Then again, there were a few things he'd never told Amy...or her gravestone...like the fact he'd blamed her death on her for an entire day.

Amy had wanted children right away. But typical, reserved Grady, he had to wait a few years. He wanted to build her a house first. Their dream home. And he wanted them to settle into their lives together before adding a new member. So Amy waited with him...impatiently.

The woman had loved children. She'd babysat for not only the Gilmores, but many other families in her younger years, and after high school, she'd gone to college for a teaching certificate. Her life revolved around tending to the young. But Grady had resisted the idea of starting a family so soon in their marriage, and he was able to hold her off for three years.

Then, one evening, he asked her at supper when

she was carrying a hot pie to the table for dessert. "Do you still want kids?"

Amy spilled her pumpkin special on the floor, she was so excited by his question. She jumped into his lap and started kissing him all over the face.

"Let's start now," she said, instantly ready to go forth and procreate.

But you know Grady. 'Right now' was not a phrase in his vocabulary. Amy was still on birth control. They had to wait until that cleared through her system and her body took over its natural cycle. Then Grady wanted to get them both tested for whatever was necessary, to make sure everything was okay.

Good wife that Amy was, she let him have his way. Grady's tests came back fine. He was fertile and full of healthy sperm. Dr. Carl said he was capable of producing fit, normal children. But the shock of all shocks came with his next words as he glanced at Amy and winced.

"Now, you, on the other hand..."

And thus started years of baby-making hell. Amy wasn't barren, but she had internal physical problems. Grady couldn't even remember all the technical terms the doctor used. It was inadvisable for her to attempt to bear children—that was all he understood.

So, Grady shrugged and suggested adoption. Amy looked at him like he might've just proposed they turn into swingers.

"I want *your* babies," she stated adamantly, letting him know good and well that no one else's would do.

"But Dr. Carl said you can't—"

"He didn't say can't," she interrupted quickly. "He said shouldn't."

"Then we *shouldn't*," Grady was quick to retort.

Amy merely held up a hand, refusing to listen to

his concerns. "I'm fine. We *will* have a baby."

Grady knew how desperately she wanted a whole gaggle of children—hell, *everyone* knew—so he gave in, and they began to try. For over a year, they tried with no success. And every month when her period started, Amy fell into a fit of depression. Sex became a duty, and he almost reached the point he regretted having to perform on certain days.

After four months of fertility implants, Amy called him at work and was so hysterical, he thought she'd been in an accident.

But when she calmed down enough for him to understand she'd only missed her period, he said, "Is that all?"

Upset by his lackluster answer, she hung up on him with a loud slam. He called her back and apologized profusely, saying he merely didn't want to get his hopes up until he saw a positive test. Amy, excited enough for the both of them, demanded he come home immediately, so they could take the test together. He did, and the test was indeed positive.

She remained pregnant for five months. Dr. Carl put her on bed rest ten weeks into term, and Grady feared he might strangle himself by the time month nine came along. He hated worrying about her. He hated how she could do nothing but lie in bed all day. But Amy positively glowed.

"It's only for a few weeks more," she assured him. "Then the baby will be born, and everything will be fine again."

Like a fool, he believed her.

During month five, Amy woke in the middle of the night with cramps and spotting, and Grady still believed her reassurances as he rushed her to the hospital. But she had a miscarriage as well as emergency surgery to remove one of her ovaries.

Amy was inconsolable afterward. When the doctor told her he recommended she never try to have children again, she turned her back to him and refused to speak to anyone—Grady included—for a week.

Things were never the same after that. He stuck by her side, and she eventually returned to the land of the living—or half-living, as he came to know it. But it was obvious the essence of the woman he'd married had vanished. A couple of years passed, and they fell into a new routine, not like how it was before, but Grady remained comfortable and content. He still had his wife; that was all that mattered to him.

Then his sister, Emma Leigh, turned up pregnant. He should've recognized that as a warning sign. But blindly, he assumed Amy was reconciled to the fact babies were not in their future unless they adopted.

She wasn't reconciled to any such notion.

He came home from work to find a glowing, happy Amy waiting at the door with a bright smile and positive pregnancy test in her hand. Gaping at the stick, he turned livid. She'd tricked him, gone against his wishes and stopped taking her birth control.

That night, the two of them had the biggest fight of their marriage. Grady couldn't believe she was so willing and even excited about risking her life for a baby they could just as easily adopt. And Amy didn't understand why he didn't want his own child, flesh of his flesh, blood of his blood.

"Of course, I'd prefer that," he argued. "But it's just not possible for us, Amy."

She laughed bitterly. "If it's not possible, then why am I pregnant?"

"You know you're just going to miscarry again," he countered. "And then what? It's going to crush you just as bad, if not more, than last time. I don't want to go through that again."

"So, what do you want me to do? Get an abortion?" She snorted. "That's not going to happen."

Grady gritted his teeth. "You shouldn't have gotten pregnant in the first place."

Glaring at him, she spit back, "Yeah, well, it takes two to make a baby, *darling*. You sure weren't arguing like this in the bedroom the night I conceived."

Unable to do anything but stand there and seethe, Grady stared at his soul mate, feeling so disconnected he thought he was looking at a stranger.

"If you don't want this baby," she hissed, "I'll go have it somewhere by myself." Then she turned and stomped away.

This time, they didn't speak for two weeks. Finally, Amy approached him one evening. With a bowed head, she quietly said, "Because you feel so strongly about this, I'll agree to look into adoption if we lose this child."

Grady pulled her into his arms and apologized for being a butt until he started to weep.

"I'm so scared," he admitted, burying his face in her hair. "The last miscarriage almost ruined us, Amy. I don't...I can't even breathe when I think about what would happen if we had to go through that again."

"Shh," she soothed and ran her fingers through his hair. "It won't be the same, Grady. I swear it. It won't be the same this time."

Once again, he believed her promise. And to an extent, she was right. It didn't end up like the time before. It was worse.

Their second child almost made it to full term. Six weeks before her due date, Amy went into labor. And Grady, like any excited, expectant father, rushed her to the hospital.

Since the baby was breech, they performed an

emergency cesarean. Grady was allowed into the delivery room where he watched the entire procedure. But problems developed, complications he didn't understand from the medical jargon the doctor and nurses used. More help rushed into the room to assist, and Grady was asked to leave. But he didn't budge. And everyone was too busy to scoot him along.

He watched Dr. Carl pull the limp, bloody form from his wife, and he continued to watch as they tried to revive the boy through chest compressions. When one nurse shook her head, Amy opened her eyes and asked to see her son. The doctor told her to relax.

"Just take it easy, Amy," he soothed.

Amy's weak voice repeated, "Baby."

Grady took her hand, but she didn't seem to feel the pressure of his fingers gripping hers because she was too occupied looking the other way and taking in the sight of their lifeless infant.

"No," she gasped in a hoarse voice and reached for Bennett. "No."

"Amy," Grady whispered, lifting her hand to his mouth and gently kissing her knuckles.

His only answer was the long steady beep of her heart monitor as she died. She didn't fight; she merely looked at her dead child and gave up. Not once did she look at him or ask for him. It was like she didn't consider him worthy enough to live for.

It took a while for him to forgive her for that.

Blowing out a shaky breath, he stared down at the picture book opened on his lap. He blinked when he saw a snapshot of Amy in her wedding dress, grinning up at him.

Frowning, he tried to recall when he'd left the kitchen and come into the living room to look through his wedding album. But here he was.

Without thinking, he turned the page. He looked

so damn young in those frozen images, and Amy was incredibly alive, glowing like a typical bride. Photo after photo, he flipped through the entire book. She'd wanted a big, all-out wedding. She'd planned every single detail down to those stupid sacks of birdseed to throw. She's decorated each bag with tiny flowers and colored ribbon.

Grady shook his head over the memory and winced, leaning forward to study the last picture of their hands, bearing their wedding rings. He'd spent so much time picking out her ring.

Lifting his face, he realized he hadn't undergone such consideration for B.J. He'd walked into the jewelry store and bought the first diamond he saw, thinking it'd do fine.

Experiencing a pang of doubt, Grady wondered what the hell he was doing. His courting mannerisms for B.J. were pathetic compared to the lavish ritual he'd expended on Amy.

It didn't seem fair for some reason.

But then he frowned and assured himself he had nothing to feel bad about. B.J. didn't deserve the same treatment he'd given Amy. He'd loved Amy with his whole heart. With B.J., it was just...what?

She was pregnant. They were getting married. End of story.

Okay, he couldn't honestly say there were *no* feelings for his soon-to-be second wife, because desire was a pretty strong emotion. And in truth, he liked being around B.J. It was actually refreshing to be in the company of someone who didn't pity him.

For a few minutes there, when he'd thought she'd only slept with him in Houston because she'd felt sorry for him, he'd been devastated. But she'd since assured him none of it had been sympathy sex. He believed her too, because she didn't act particularly sensitive toward him. Actually, she was the most unsympathetic-acting person he knew. Not that she was cruel and uncaring. But she stayed refreshingly normal, treating him like she treated everyone.

That was probably why she was the only person with whom he could talk about Amy. She'd didn't turn all soft, giving him a pitying look and making him want to snarl and snap at her. And though the effect she had on his libido was so intense it was frankly unsettling, he was still able to relax around her more than he had anyone else in the past two and a half years, since neither of them was worried about bringing up his dead wife. In fact, they talked about Amy openly as if she'd actually existed and not just as someone who'd died tragically.

Realizing how nice that fact was, Grady calmed. He blew out another breath and set the picture album aside.

"I can do this," he told himself.

He could marry B.J. He could start a new life with her. And he could survive past this era of constant grieving.

Chapter Fifteen

B.J. worried she was going to yak through the entire ceremony. Arriving at the courthouse half an hour early, she had to admit, she was a little unnerved when she discovered the ever-prompt Grady hadn't shown up yet. Not that she'd blame him if he cried off. But damn, even tomboys didn't want to get jilted at the altar.

Her stomach had already been weak up to that point. And she was cranky because she hadn't been able to have her morning coffee for going on three weeks now. But the absence of Grady's truck in the parking lot tipped the scales. She hurried into the building, found the nearest bathroom, and threw up until there was nothing left.

When she stumbled out five minutes later, weak and tired, she immediately started to unbutton her blouse. The white T-shirt she had on underneath seemed to be free of chunks, but she had to admit, a plain white T and blue jeans was not the best outfit for a bride.

She hadn't thought the new dark pants looked that bad with the blouse she'd originally put on. But with a plain white undershirt, the jeans suddenly looked less crisp and more...average. Glancing at her watch, she cursed when she saw how late it was. She probably didn't have time to go home and find a new top.

Suddenly, she laughed, realizing what she was doing. Waiting until she was twenty-seven was a little too late to finally start worrying about her appearance. But then she glanced up and saw Grady approaching. Her smile fell flat. He wore slacks, a starched shirt, and a tie.

Damn it.

She couldn't stand next to him and get married when she looked like this and he was decked out in that.

"I need to change," she said without preamble. Lifting the wadded blouse in her hand, she added, "I just got sick all over my shirt."

His blue eyes took in the shirt and then rose to her face. "Are you okay?"

"I'm fine," she nearly snapped, trying to hold back her impatience. She needed to get a move on it, though, or she'd be late for her own wedding. "I just need to go home real quick and—"

"You look fine," Grady interrupted.

She snorted. "Says the man whose damn-near wearing a tux. Just look at us, Slim. Talk about mismatched."

He merely quirked his lips at her distress. "I can't imagine you owning a dress."

"Because I don't," she said, appalled by the very idea. "But I do have some black slacks. I could—"

"B.J.," he said, grasping her elbow. "It doesn't matter what you wear. We're still going to be married either way."

B.J. blew out a breath. "Well, if you don't care, then I certainly don't give a rat's ass."

He grinned, and his smile immediately shot a spear of white-hot pleasure down her spine and through her arms and legs. God, she loved his full smile. It'd been in remission far too long. But what she liked even more was the fact she'd been the one to make his eyes crinkle and the corners of his lips tilt up.

"Amy always said you'd turn out beautiful," he murmured, skimming a purely male, appreciative gaze down her body.

B.J.'s heart stopped beating. For a full second, she could only gape. He'd just called her beautiful...or at least implied it. Be still her heart, the man had complimented her. What a day this was turning out to be. First a smile, then a comment on her looks. She was starting to feel like an honest-to-God bride.

Afraid tears would follow, she bit down hard on the inside of her lip.

She was beyond grateful when a voice called, "Grady!" from behind them, interrupting the moment.

Both B.J. and Grady turned to find his younger brother approaching. Caine Rawlings was one year younger than her, but they'd shared a few classes in high school. He was a famous photographer who lived in some big city, she couldn't remember which—maybe Dallas. But she hadn't known he was going to show today.

Obviously, neither had Grady. He stared at his brother in shock. "What're *you* doing here?"

Caine ignored the question until he'd folded Grady in a hard hug. Then he said, "I'm here to see you tie the knot. What do you think I'm doing here?"

Grady frowned in confusion. "I thought you couldn't make it."

Caine snorted. "Like I was going to miss my big brother's wedding." Then he turned and grinned at B.J. "Especially to this wild thing."

The two brothers were strikingly similar in looks, but Caine was shorter—probably the same height as B.J.'s five ten—and he was stouter than Grady. Plus his playful blue gaze had nothing on the intensely hot look Grady could give.

Grinning at her, he murmured, "Banner," and pulled her into a hug, much the way he had Grady. "Welcome to the family, kid."

She couldn't recall ever being hugged by Caine

Rawlings before. But it was strangely comforting, as if she really was welcomed into his circle of loved ones.

"Banner?" Grady repeated in confusion.

When B.J. glanced at him, she found him frowning thoughtfully. It took him a second to realize what his brother meant. Then his eyes popped open wide.

"Is *that* what the 'B' in your name stands for?" He swung toward his brother. "How in the world do *you* know her name?"

Caine merely grinned and gave a mischievous shrug. When Grady turned back, pinning her with an accusing gaze, B.J. sighed.

"I lost a bet with him in high school," she explained with a roll of her eyes. "And the wager was for me to tell him what B.J. stood for."

Grady looked back to Caine, apparently not liking the fact his own brother knew more about her than he did.

"Hey, she made me swear not to tell anyone," Caine defended, still grinning.

Grady swung back to B.J. "What does the 'J' stand for?"

She sighed again. "Didn't you pay attention to my name on the marriage license?"

He gave her a blank look. Then he scratched his head and murmured, "I didn't even think to look."

"Don't tell," Caine advised, sending her a devilish smile and a quick wink. "Not knowing will bug him to death."

Grady didn't get a chance to pry anymore, anyway. Everyone else showed up, seemingly all at once. Grady's parents, grandfather, and Jo Ellen appeared along with Cooper and baby Tanner. Her father strolled in next with her three brothers and sister-in-law, Phyllis. Thankfully, Buck and Phyllis had found a sitter for their little hellion.

Jeb and Rudy trooped directly toward her, while Leroy stopped a few yards away with Buck and his wife.

Rudy was the first to speak. Holding out two envelopes, he said, "Here. This one's from the Smardos. Junkyard would've liked to come, but he thought it best to stay away."

B.J. stared at the card in surprise. Well, hell, she hadn't expected to receive gifts for marrying Grady. Getting him felt like a special present all by itself. However long he could stand to be married to her, he was going to be hers.

"Uh...thanks," she said, feeling uncomfortable as she took the card her brother thrust into her unsuspecting hands.

"And this one's from me," Rudy said, pushing another card at her. "Actually, it's from all of us, but no one else had the balls to give it to you."

He sent a meaningful look toward Pop. But Jeb merely cleared his throat and scratched the back of his neck.

"So, uh, what do I got to do at this thing?" he asked.

For the first time, she noticed he was wearing a new pair of overalls and his thin, gray hair had been slicked back as if recently brushed with a wet comb. Feeling a sudden spark of adoration for him, she smiled.

"Don't worry, Pop. This isn't one of those conventional weddings. You don't have to walk me down the aisle or anything."

"Oh," he said, and for a second she could've sworn he looked disappointed. But then he blew out a breath and gruffly said, "Thank God."

B.J.'s grin spread. She was about to tease and put him on the spot by saying something like, 'unless you really want to,' but both men tensed, glancing over her shoulder at someone's approach. She turned and found Jo Ellen there, holding out two small wrapped presents.

As Jeb and Rudy subtly backed off, moving automatically toward the rest of their family, Jo Ellen grinned and handed the gifts over. "Emma Leigh says she's sorry she couldn't make it today. But this is from her and her husband, Bran."

She piled the package in B.J.'s quickly filling arms. "And this is from me, Cooper, and Tanner. Actually, it's really for the baby. It's a book. *What to Expect when You're Expecting.*"

B.J. blinked down at the second gift Jo Ellen had given her. "Really? Well, hot damn, I didn't know I could buy instructions for the little ankle bitter."

Jo Ellen laughed and then impulsively threw her arms around B.J. Since her hands were already full, B.J. couldn't hug back, so she stood there in stunned shock as Grady's sister kissed her cheek and said into her ear, "Welcome to the family. Oh, and thank you for not sleeping with Cooper."

B.J. pulled back in surprise. When Jo Ellen merely beamed, she blinked. Then she let out a chuckle.

"Did he tell you?" she had to know. "Or did you just listen in on our conversation?"

Jo Ellen snorted. "Like I could get him to confess something like that."

B.J. shook her head. "It wouldn't have happened between us, anyway," she said. "He was so hung up on you, it was pathetic."

Jo smiled, obviously pleased to hear such a report. "Then I'm glad you were there to cheer him up."

B.J. glanced around to make sure no one else was listening. But Grady stood gathered with his family, and her relatives were clustered in their own group.

"I really don't do sympathy sex," she muttered quietly so only Jo Ellen could hear. "I wasn't thinking one sorry thought when Grady and I—" Realizing she was about to discuss personal details with his sister, she snapped her mouth shut.

Jo Ellen smiled. "Well, that's good to know. Just as long as you did with Cooper."

"Okay, it was all about sympathy with Cooper," she relented. "That's true. And Ralphie Smardo too, but not—"

"I think it's time to get started," Granger Rawlings announced loudly from his wheelchair. "But before we all go into the judge's office, I demand a kiss from my soon-to-be granddaughter."

B.J. was quick to oblige the old man. She leaned over him and pressed her lips to his cheek, but he grabbed her hand and returned the sentiment, softly saying for her ears alone, "I'm glad it's you who'll be taking care of my grand-boy."

She blinked repeatedly as she straightened. She hadn't expected this kind of welcome at all from Grady's family. She'd just assumed they'd see her as some kind of opportunist leech, going after the sad widower and taking advantage of him. But with Jo Ellen's, Granger's, and Caine's approval, she felt pretty damn good.

Then she turned and caught Tucker Rawlings's eye. Grady's father gave her a quiet nod, his eyes full of all sorts of messages. She froze, suddenly remembering their "arrangement."

He'd already cornered her at her house earlier in the week with his lengthy prenuptial agreement. Having no problem letting Grady keep all his money and possessions in case of a divorce, she'd signed Tucker Rawlings paperwork. Thinking they'd get into specifics about child custody and her plane next, she'd been shocked when he'd merely nodded and left, leaving behind her own copy of the prenup.

She spent the rest of the evening reading what she'd just signed. And to her horror, the deed and child custody issues were all mentioned in the document. If she and Grady ever split, full custody of their baby would go to him, and in return her plane would be signed over in her name.

A cold chill washed over her. Swallowing, she set her hand protectively over her stomach. In the past few days, she'd come to realize she wanted her baby...she wanted it very much. And she wasn't about to give it up either. Not for anything.

Somehow, someway, she was going to have to make her husband keep her around for a good long while. Because she also wanted to be his wife just as much as she wanted to keep her baby.

It was the biggest gamble she'd ever taken.

Chapter Sixteen

The wedding was over five minutes after it started. It took longer to get everyone packed into the judge's chamber than it did to say all their vows and sign their names to the certificate. Rudy stepped forward and relieved her of her wedding presents and puked-on blouse. Then he backed her even more by being a second witness to sign the license.

"Does this make me your maid of honor?" he asked teasingly.

B.J. rolled her eyes. "Just sign."

Grady had his brother Caine stand in as his witness. And then it was all over and done. She was married. Feeling queasy, B.J. pressed a hand to her stomach and prayed she didn't have to race to a bathroom.

After all the legal paperwork was taken care of, Tara Rose declared they'd celebrate her son's wedding at the country club, all tabs paid by the Rawlings family. Her brothers eagerly stepped forward, salivating at the thought of a free meal. Rudy and Leroy headed straight for the bar as soon as they arrived. But B.J. pulled to a frozen stop in the doorway, feeling transported back in time.

The last time she'd stepped foot inside Tommy Creek's Country Club, the whole place had been rented out and decorated with blue and cream-colored balloons and crepe paper for a Rawlings wedding...for Grady's wedding. Realizing she was here again for the same exact reason, B.J. sent her groom a worried look.

But he'd obviously been here numerous times

since then. Because when he caught her gaze, he didn't looked sickened with nostalgia. He merely puckered his brow and took her elbow, looking concerned. "Are you still feeling queasy?"

B.J. stared at him a moment longer. He honestly didn't look overcome with misery, like this was the worst day of his life, so she shook her head. "No. I'm fine. Just hungry."

****

As marriages went, she couldn't say hers and Grady's was by any means normal. But she couldn't say she minded it either. It was nearly midnight when they broke away from both their families and finally arrived at his big house on the hill. Feeling self-conscious about going inside, B.J. lagged behind as Grady led the way to the entrance.

This was Amy's home. Grady had built it for her. Though dozens of people had been hired to construct it, no one had labored as hard as Grady had. B.J. still remembered driving by when it was being erected. Every time she'd looked out her window, there he was, shirtless and sweating, helping out and making sure every detail was just the way his wife wanted it.

Amy had been so excited to see it finished. B.J. remembered bumping into her at the grocery store one time. The woman gushed on for a good half hour about its progress, not even noticing how B.J. had nearly gone cross-eyed and started to drool from boredom.

Seven years later, the place was still in great condition. The brick siding had weathered well, and the trim looked as freshly painted as the first time B.J. had seen it finished. The dried wilting weeds in the flowerbed, however, about broke her heart. She stared at them as Grady unlocked the front door.

There was a swing at the far end of the porch, and she had a sudden vision of him, at sunset, sitting there, watching the sky turn all shades of the rainbow. He was the quiet type who would do a thing like that. He'd feel content, living out here by himself with nothing but a house full of ghosts and memories to keep him company.

Tension gnawing at her stomach, B.J. glanced once more at the decaying flowerbed. When she saw a green flowering plant in the depths of those brown weeds, despite the fact it was being choked out, she caught her breath, not sure whether it was a good omen or bad. She could either take it as a sign for new growth and hope, or as a haunting reminder that there would always be a part of Amy alive here, no matter how dead she was.

B.J. shivered. She was about to step over the threshold into Amy's life with Amy's husband. It felt almost wrong...forbidden.

She glanced toward Grady to see how all this affected him, but he'd already opened the door and disappeared inside. "Remind me to get you a key made," he called over his shoulder.

Wondering briefly if he'd carried Amy through the doorway of their first home after they married, she shook her head and forced the thought away. "Okay."

She didn't want Grady picking her up. She definitely didn't want him treating her the same way he'd treated Amy. She was nowhere near that important to him, so she'd better just forget any ideas otherwise.

****

After pointing out the kitchen and bathrooms, Grady showed B.J. the second floor.

"This is our room." He opened the first entrance on the right in a long hall full of closed doors.

He stood in the entrance, watching her stroll around the room and study the furniture. She peeked into the closet and was surprised to see all his clothes pushed to one side, leaving the other half completely bare. The skin on the back of her neck prickled as she wondered if this was where Amy had hung her dresses.

"I cleaned out a few drawers for you too," Grady said, bringing her attention back around in time to catch him opening a dresser drawer to show her it was empty.

She blinked in surprise. He'd cleaned the space out for *her*? That meant...leaving the closet half-bare hadn't been some tribute to his departed wife. It was done in order to welcome B.J. Feeling ashamed of her thoughts, she looked at the room in a new light and realized this probably wasn't even the master bedroom. There wasn't a bath connected, nor did it contain some of the amenities a homeowner would put in his private chambers.

He'd probably moved into this room after Amy died. That suspicion was confirmed when she moved back into the hall and motioned toward the half a dozen closed doors lining the walls.

"What're they?"

Grady shrugged, unable to meet her eyes. "Other rooms," he said on a mumble and started back down the stairs.

Though she was tempted to go peek, she decided not to mess with opening any closed doors just yet. She turned to follow him back down to the ground floor. But once she entered the living room, an open photo album caught her attention. Wandering closer, she jerked to a stop when she saw a picture of Grady feeding Amy a piece of wedding cake.

Unable to stop her curiosity, she stepped cautiously closer. Then she sank into the chair and pulled the album onto her lap. Grady turned, noticing her preoccupation, and immediately zipped his gaze guiltily to hers. He opened his mouth as if to apologize for its presence, but what came out was,

"I didn't mean to leave that out."

B.J. shook her head, letting him know it didn't matter. In a way, it really didn't matter. It'd been so long since she'd seen Amy.

Smiling at the picture, she said, "She sure was happy."

Grady closed his mouth and slowly eased down next to her. "Yes, she was."

B.J. turned the page and snorted when she caught sight of a huddle of women falling over themselves to catch Amy's bouquet.

"You know, you're the only person I can stand to hear talk about her," Grady said.

Jerking her head up, B.J. gaped as he gave her a half smile.

"Everyone else is always so sympathetic when they mention Amy. It...makes me sick. I mean, almost physically ill. I can't handle pity. It just...it makes me feel worse. But you...you actually talk about her like she existed. And you remember when she was happy and healthy and alive."

B.J. looked down at another photo but didn't see it this time. "I remember you used to be pretty happy yourself."

"Yeah," he said softly. Then he cleared his throat and pushed to his feet.

Quietly closing the album, she pushed to her feet as well. And they stood there in silence, both making sure they had their gaze set firmly on different parts of the room.

Unable to take it any longer, B.J. blurted out the first thing that came to her head. "You know, I heard only eighty percent of Americans actually have sex on their wedding night."

Grady lifted his face. She could see his mind spinning, and it suddenly dawned on her how suggestive her comment sounded.

"What are you trying to say?" he asked, his voice

cautious.

"I...I'm not trying to say anything," she answered, defensive. "I mean, I said what I wanted to say. I just thought it was weird so many people didn't..." Damn, she was only burying herself deeper.

"I think it's weird too," he returned quietly.

She nearly sighed in relief. Licking her lips, she darted a glance toward the doorway. "So...do you want to—"

"Hell, yes," he cut in, already reaching for her.

When his mouth slanted across hers and his arms crushed her to his chest, she finally did let her sigh loose. Thank God, thank God, she thought. Something finally felt right. She'd been tense and unsure of everything ever since saying I do. But every single insecurity inside her melted away in Grady's arms.

If only they could have sex all the time, then life would be perfect.

He had her tee and bra off by the time they made it to his—er, *their*—room. She'd stripped him of his tie and shirt, and they were each working on the other's pants. As he backed her toward his bed, he skimmed her jeans down over her hips and paused when he realized she hadn't been wearing underwear. He glanced up and treated her to a questioning look.

She smiled, hoping he'd appreciate his wedding gift. On a wink, she explained, "And you say only single people go commando."

He chuckled. Then he pressed his mouth to hers, and his kiss tasted like laughter, sunlight, and heaven. B.J. groaned and clutched his hair. After backing her onto the bed, he set a hand on her knee, moved her thighs apart, and knelt between her open legs. As he touched her with his tongue, she gasped and arched. For a novice at this particular art, the man was already a pro.

Wanting to reciprocate, she said, "Wait a second."

He stopped and looked up in concern, like he was worried she was going to stop him. But she merely wiggled her hips around until her feet were by the headboard and her face was in his crotch.

"I'll do you while you do me," she explained, spreading his fly apart and taking him into her hand.

At the first touch of her mouth on him, he went rigid and sucked in a breath. He whipped a hand out as if to pull her away from him by her hair. But instead, he tugged off her ponytail holder and buried his fingers in her thick locks.

"Oh, holy God," he groaned and tightened his grip as she stroked him with her tongue from base to tip. "Jesus."

B.J. glanced up at him then. He'd thrown his head back and the muscles in his neck worked as he sucked in a silent gasp of pleasure. "Let me guess," she said. "You've never had a blowjob before."

He let out a strangled laugh. "If Amy wouldn't let me go down on her, do you honestly think she'd go anywhere near my..." He groaned and closed his eyes when she reached out to stroke him with her index finger.

"Well, then maybe you should worry about me later," she suggested. "Lie back and fully enjoy your first BJ from B.J."

He shook his head. "No," he rasped. "I want your taste in my mouth."

Not one to argue about getting herself some pleasure, B.J. shrugged and watched him lean toward her. What followed was the best sixty-niner she'd ever experienced.

****

"B.J.?"

Grady's voice jerked her back from the brink of drifting off. She opened her eyes and drowsily mumbled, "Hmm?"

But, wow. She felt like a limp noodle. Lying there in his arms, she wanted to fall asleep so she could wake in that same position, rested and rejuvenated for another round.

"What's the 'J' stand for?"

She cracked open one eye. "J?"

"In B.J."

Unable to help herself, she chuckled. God, he never forgot anything, did he?

"Jewell," she relented, hoping that would be that.

It wasn't.

"Your name's Banner *Jewell*?"

"The Banner part was supposed to be Banana," she explained. "Actually, it was supposed to be bananer because that's what Pop calls bananas. But Jebediah Gilmore can't spell worth crap, so I ended up being Banner instead."

"Banner Jewell," he repeated to himself.

She sighed. "I'm going to have to tell you the whole freaking story, aren't I?"

He didn't answer, but his look said yes.

"Okay. All right. When my mother was pregnant with me, she was always hungry for bananas. She ate them like they were going out of style. Well, Pop would tease her and say I was going to come out one big bananer if she didn't stop. But my mom would rub her stomach and say, 'Don't talk about my little Jewell that way.' And Pop would counter, 'Don't you mean, your bananer?' I guess the joke was carried all the way through her pregnancy. So, when I was born, they named me Bananer Jewell. Except Pop spelled the name wrong on my birth certificate. And Bananer became Banner. And Banner Jewell quickly became B.J. Thank God."

"I like the name Banner," he said, sounding almost defensive about her bashing her own name. "If we have a girl, I think we should name her Banner."

"Hell no," B.J. said, jerking upright into a sitting position to glare down at him. "I'm not putting some poor child through that name."

He lifted his eyebrows in disagreement, but said, "Then what were you thinking for a girl's name?"

Totally clueless as how to answer, she muttered, "I don't know. I haven't even thought about it."

"Well..." He frowned, deep in his own thoughts for a moment. Then, "What was your mother's name?"

B.J.'s lips parted in shock. "Dellie," she said, surprised he'd want one of her family names for his child. Then she remembered they'd named his stillborn son Bennett, which had been Amy's maiden name.

Relaxing against him, she rested her head on his shoulder. "You really want to name her after my mother?" She closed her eyes as he began to sift his fingers through her hair.

"Sure," he said. "Why not?"

The gentle stroke of his thumb continued down the side of her throat, and she hummed her appreciation, adding a slurred, "Thank you."

"And what if it's a boy?" he asked next.

But B.J. didn't answer. She'd already fallen asleep.

Chapter Seventeen

Since she didn't have anyone or anything to fly anywhere, B.J. planned on going to her house the next day to pack up the rest of her things she hadn't already moved to Grady's place. But Jo Ellen called before she'd even left the house, asking if she wanted to go shopping for baby necessities.

Not particularly enthused about the idea of packing, B.J. agreed and drove to Grady's sister's house instead. From there, they trekked nearly an hour to the closest mall. By the time they stepped inside the baby outlet, she decided packing might not have been such a terrible idea after all.

"Holy hell," she breathed, stopping in the entrance to gawk at the rows and rows of infant paraphernalia. "Do I really need all this crap?"

Jo Ellen merely hooked their arms together and urged her into the store. "Let's start at this end."

To B.J.'s horror, they went through the entire place, stopping in every freaking aisle. Jo Ellen tried to teach her the art of comparative and bargain shopping, but it didn't take. She had to admit, though, the newborn bootie sneakers Jo Ellen discovered were adorable. Unlike Grady's sister, however, she was able to contain her oohing and awing, even if she did snag two pairs and shove them into her shopping cart. The only item to provoke an actual response from her was a bib exclaiming *I love my Daddy*. Jo Ellen merely sent her a knowing smile and tossed it into the cart as well.

By seven o'clock that evening, she was dead

tired. Her muscles ached in places she didn't know she had muscles, and her ankles were swollen as far as the skin would stretch. Feeling giddy, though, she realized the expectant Mommy bug had finally bitten. She started thinking about the baby to come.

Would it be a boy or a girl? Would it look more like her or Grady? Grady, she hoped.

Though Jo Ellen had successfully instilled her with excitement for a future of parenthood, she was still ready to drop into the nearest bed when she pulled into Grady's drive at a quarter to eight. She frowned when she realized damn near every light in the house was glowing.

Her new husband opened the front door before she had her truck parked."Where have you been?" he growled as soon as she jumped out of the driver's seat. "I came home early to help you move, but—"

"Just a sec," she said, shoving two shopping bags at him and bulldozing past. "I gotta pee like a racehorse."

He fumbled to catch everything and could only sputter as she sprinted inside.

When she exited, he was waiting by the door.

"You went *shopping*?"

"Yeah," she gave the breathless reply, still winded from her dash to the john. "Jo Ellen called this morning and talked me into going. I didn't want to be rude, so I said okay. Plus, she convinced me I needed to start getting ready for this kid now."

"Jo Ellen?" he nearly yelled the name.

B.J. frowned. "Yes, Jo Ellen," she repeated. "You know...your *sister*?"

His jaw dropped as he stared at her. Then he exploded. "Jesus Christ, B.J.! I've been going out of my mind with worry, and you were with my *sister*?"

She straightened. "You were worried? Why?"

He made a disbelieving sound. "Why do you think? I had no idea where you were. You weren't here. You weren't at your place. I called the hangar, and they hadn't seen you all day. For all I knew, you could've passed out again while you were driving and been lying dead in some ditch."

Taking a moment to swipe a harassed hand through his hair, he muttered, "Damn it, B.J." His voice broke in the middle of saying her name. "I even called the hospitals to make sure you weren't there."

She sucked in a breath. God, he was really upset. Feeling instantly horrible, she started to apologize.

"I...I'm sorry. I didn't realize you'd be so concerned. I didn't even think to tell you about my change in plans."

"Well, it's a common courtesy to let your husband know where you're going to be," he snapped.

Her back going rigid at his tone, she sniffed. "Well, excuse me, Mr. McPerfect. But I've never been married before. And it's been a long damn time since I've been accountable to anyone for anything."

Grady linked all ten fingers together and rested them on the back of his head as he stared up the ceiling and appeared to be silently counting to ten. When he was done, he blew out a breath and calmly said, "All right. But next time, could you please just...leave a note, call my cell phone, do *something* to tell me what your plans are so I won't worry?"

B.J. gave a jerky nod, lowering her face so he wouldn't see the red tinge of humiliation on her cheeks.

"Thank you," he gritted out.

She shifted uncomfortably, and Grady shoved his hands into his pockets. After sending her a brief nod, he pivoted on his heels and strode away.

She stayed there a moment and pulled herself back together. She should be delighted he cared enough to worry. But all she felt was a hollow loss.

He'd been married before. He was a pro at this husband-wife thing. It was natural for him to expect her to just slip into place as the patient, obedient wife...as another Amy. But she couldn't do that. It went against her chemical make-up to be anyone but herself.

She'd never wanted to take Amy's place. She felt like she was breaking some sacred rule, intruding somewhere she had no place being. He'd always be Amy's husband in her mind, and she didn't think anything could ever change that.

Feeling an unwanted emotion rise in her throat, B.J. hissed out a curse and curled her hands into fists until the pain of her nails digging into her palms wiped away the urge to cry. Once she had herself under control, she checked to make sure her ponytail was still on tight, and then she proceeded to carry the rest of her purchases inside.

Once done, she started to tote them up to the second floor. Frowning down the hall at all the closed doors, she opened the first she came across, merely looking for a place to store her purchases. She didn't realize she was looking for a place to start a nursery until she opened the door and found herself in an empty room with walls painted a pastel yellow and boarded with pink and pale blue letter blocks.

"Oh," she whispered in shock.

Stumbling in reverse to flee the room intended for Amy's baby, she turned and jerked to a stop when she found Grady poised at the top of the stairs, watching her.

"I..." she said. Feeling as if the wind had been knocked out of her, she lowered her head and tried to pull in a breath of air. "I was just looking for someplace to put this stuff."

****

It was on the tip of Grady's tongue to apologize.

B.J. looked like she'd just seen a ghost when she'd jerked herself out of Bennett's nursery. He should've showed her the entire house yesterday...should've opened all the doors, should've painted over the damn walls.

"You..." He paused and licked his suddenly dry lips. "You can put them in there if you want."

The violent way in which she shook her head made him feel even worse. He was such an idiot. Of course, she didn't want to put her baby's things in another's baby's room, a baby who hadn't even made it to a full day old. Bad karma.

Clearing his throat, he said, "The next door down is a guest room." Had always been a guest room.

Still not meeting his eyes, she nodded and started to turn away. But at the last second, she stopped and came back around, looking at him with an expression that nearly rent him in two. He'd never seen the tough tomboy B.J. Gilmore look so miserable before.

"Believe it or not, Slim"—her voice was shaky, a fact that bowled him over—"I still think this whole marriage thing was a stupid idea, but I don't want it to be a disaster. I don't want to fail as a wife. But you know what? I'm never going to be what your parents—what your dad—wants for you. I'm never going to wear a dress or paint my nails...or care what color the freaking curtains are. I'm never going to be Amy."

That last comment caught him by surprise. He stared at her in shock, and she stared back as if surprised those words had come out of her as well. She even opened her mouth like she was going to apologize.

Not wanting her to feel bad about saying what she'd needed to say, yet wondering where in the hell that little speech had come from, he said, "I never expected you to be."

B.J. stared back, and he thought she was going to cry for a moment. So he cleared his throat and added, "My father doesn't hate you either. He's just worried about me right now. And I don't...no one thinks you need to change just because you're married. I actually..."

He cleared his throat again and glanced away. He wanted to tell her more, like he appreciated who she was. He was glad he was with her and even excited about their baby. But it felt too soon to go that deep.

Before he could change his mind, he mumbled out a brief, "You're fine just the way you are," and turned away, jogging back down the stairs. When he reached the kitchen, he paced from the refrigerator to the stove to the sink and then back to all three in restless anxiety.

This was his fault. He shouldn't have made her feel like an outsider or left that stupid wedding album out. He'd messed up bad.

Of course this place was going to remind her of Amy every time she turned a corner. He should've gone to live with her at her house.

Running his hand through his already mussed hair, he wondered if he should go ahead and offer. He could live at her place if he had to. Or hell, maybe he should just build them a new house, free from any kind of past or troubling memory.

Growling out a sound of frustration, he turned again to march toward the refrigerator when he focused in on the telephone hanging on the wall. Falling to a stop, he realized he'd never erased the message with Amy's voice on it. Letting out a groan, he gritted back a shard of sharp pain in his gut.

Swallowing, he numbly moved to the phone, slowing with each step until he was there. His fingers came up, and they hovered over the delete button, debating. If he pushed it, he'd never hear Amy again.

Above him, he heard a muffled thump—B.J. flopping a bag of baby things on the guest room floor, no doubt. Grady stared up at the ceiling.

If he didn't push the button, what would she think? Realizing he wouldn't be able to move on and start his future until he let go of the past, he punched the button and gasped out a breath as he did so.

His heart pounded against his chest, and his finger stayed glued to the delete button for seconds after he knew the message was already gone. Letting out a shaky laugh, he pulled away and stared at the phone as if he expected it to exact some kind of revenge for his actions.

"I'll always love you," he whispered, hoping somewhere up there, Amy heard him. "No matter what."

Feeling a strange relief, like he'd just freed a caged dog and was watching it enjoy all the wide open space, he blew out a breath. Lifting his face toward the ceiling again, he smiled slightly and started for the stairs.

The door to the guest room was still open, and he could hear her moving around inside. Grady approached quietly. He stopped just before entering and peeked around the corner. She sat on the bed, holding up the tiniest pair of high top sneakers he'd ever seen. It was the awed smile on her face that caught him right in the chest though.

More than anything, he wanted to go inside, sit next to her and see all the things she and Jo Ellen had picked out. But she looked so happy, doused in her private thoughts, he felt himself stepping back instead. Since she was upset with him, he didn't want to ruin such a special moment for her.

He retreated to their bedroom, stripped to his

boxers, and crawled into bed. After shutting off the light, he lay there, wondering how the hell he was going to deal with this.

****

When B.J. went to bed, Grady was already lying under the covers on his side of the mattress with his eyes closed. She swore he was faking it. But she didn't want another confrontation just then, so she quietly slipped into an oversized T-shirt and eased onto the mattress beside him. He didn't stir.

It took her a long time to fall asleep. And when she did, she dreamed of him and Amy at a hospital, delivering a healthy baby. The smile on Grady's face was so radiant, she jerked awake with a gasp.

The first traces of light were starting to enter the room through the shades, so she crawled out of bed, feeling drained and sore. She took a shower, dressed and left the bedroom before Grady woke.

He joined her just as she poured milk over her cereal. Unable to look at him, she merely put the carton in the fridge and moved silently to the table. As she seated herself, she watched him out of the corner of her eye. He went to the back door, disappeared outside for a few seconds before returning with a newspaper.

She munched noisily, staring straight ahead as he fixed his own bowl of cereal and finally seated himself across from her.

Unable to take it anymore, she muttered, "I'm messing up, aren't I?"

In the middle of unrolling the paper, Grady snapped his head up. "What?"

"Are we fighting?"

He blinked. "Uh…" he stalled, looking confused. "What makes you think we're fighting?"

"Well, when you walked in here this morning, I noticed your hair was kind of messed up and I thought it looked really sexy. So, naturally, I thought about what it'd feel like to run my fingers through it and then, wham, this totally erotic fantasy popped into my head of me crawling into your lap, right there where you're sitting at the table and riding you like there was no tomorrow. But I held myself back because I thought...well, you're mad at me for not calling you yesterday. You probably don't want me anywhere near you."

He straightened. "I'm not mad at you."

"You're not?"

He shook his head.

She scowled. "So, why didn't you touch me last night?"

He laughed. "I don't know." He ran his hands through his hair, making it look even sexier. "I guess I thought you were mad at me."

"Why would I be mad at *you*?" she demanded to know. That kind of thinking was just...stupid.

He shrugged.

"I'm not mad," she said. "And I still want to ride you like there's no tomorrow."

He was already dropping his newspaper and scooting back his chair. "Then what're you still doing over there?"

B.J. laughed. Popping to her feet before he could change his mind and realize he really was mad at her, she rushed around the table and straddled his hips just as he unzipped his fly.

"Hurry," he growled, his eyes already unfocused and glassy.

B.J. kissed him hard and ground her middle against him, making him groan and sink his teeth into her bottom lip.

"I'm not kidding," he added. "Hurry. I need you. Now."

As he skimmed his hands up her torso and rid her of her shirt, she slipped off her panties. He reached for her hips and jerked her down. When she sheathed him with her heat, they both caught their breaths. To keep them from tipping over backward in the chair, he braced his legs wider, which spread her thighs in the process, leaving her open and vulnerable. The resulting effect caused her to clench around him.

His already glazed eyes dilated. Grabbing her hair with both hands, he yanked so hard tears of pain clogged her lashes.

"God. Oh, God," he rasped and jerked up into her, nearly bucking her off his lap. Squeezing her hips more securely around him, she stared into his eyes and came just when she felt him shudder.

He buried his face in her shoulder, and she wrapped her arms around him, kissing his temple.

"I think I like starting the day this way," he murmured.

B.J. threw back her head and laughed. But her chuckle died when he lifted his face and she caught his frown. He reached for her cheek and touched a tear at the corner of her eye with his index finger.

"I hurt you?"

Realizing he was worried, not angry, she let out a relieved breath and rolled her eyes. "God, Slim. Don't you remember trying to yank me bald? You damn near pulled my hair out by the roots."

"I did?" Eyes wide with concern and alarm, he reached for her scalp and eased his finger gently over her still aching noggin. "God, B.J., I'm sorry. I didn't realize—"

"Oh, can it, Rawlings. I loved every second. Sometimes, nothing hits the spot like a full dose of rowdy sex." To prove her point, she purred like a contented cat and stretched out her arms above her head. "Man, I feel great."

But when she glanced over her shoulder at the tabletop, she frowned. "Oh, damn. My breakfast went soggy."

Grady burst out laughing.

B.J. whirled around and gaped at him, a little shocked to hear him laugh so openly. She'd seen him smile and even chuckle in the past few weeks, but...she hadn't seen him really let go like this. Watching him laugh now caused something inside her to spark. And she fell in love...completely, hopelessly, irreversibly in love with her husband.

Chapter Eighteen

Tucker Rawlings couldn't stop pacing. But where the hell was his son? Grady never arrived late. He checked the clock on the wall, then the watch on his wrist, and cursed. If the kid didn't walk through that door within ten seconds—

The door opened and Grady entered. Tucker almost jumped out of his skin. Okay, that was Twilight Zone weird.

Whistling as he moseyed through the entrance like he hadn't a care in the world, Grady lifted his hand in greeting, and Tucker returned to his senses.

"Grady, where the hell have you been? The meeting was supposed to start fifteen minutes ago. Your mother's been trying to entertain a room full of investors with coffee and doughnuts, but they're getting restless."

"Oh, hell," Grady yelped and leapt into action, hurrying toward his office. "I completely forgot about the meeting."

"Do you have your presentation with you?" Tucker trailed his every step, unable to believe his ears. Grady never forgot meetings...and come to think of it, he never whistled either. Not since—

He slowed to a stop.

"It's in my office," Grady assured him, opening the door and flying into the room. He snagged the folder off his desktop.

Tucker shook his head, forcing his mind back to the task at hand. Meetings. Investors. Got it.

"Thank God," he said, but only paused again as he took in the features on his son's face. "Jesus,

Grady," he said, stepping forward and reaching for his son's crooked tie. "What've you been doing? You're a complete mess."

He straightened the knot and started to smooth out Grady's unruly hair before he realized his son was coughing into his hand and turning tomato red. Pausing, Tucker frowned in confusion until Grady lifted his head, letting his dad see the glow of contentment in his eyes.

Dropping his fingers, Tucker took a shocked step back. Then he shook his head and laughed. "I guess this means your marriage is going well."

Grady grinned as they shared a knowing look. With a nod, his son answered, "Can't complain."

Tucker chuckled again and grabbed Grady's shoulder, feeling a blast a relief. "Shit," he murmured and turned his son toward the meeting room. "Go give your presentation already."

As Grady tucked his file under his arm and hurried to comply, his father stood there a moment, staring after him. An emotion of immense pressure slipped off his chest and loosened the knot that had been there for two and a half long years.

Running his hand over his face, he made sure there weren't any tears in his eyes. But, God. He'd waited so long to see his boy happy again.

****

A Rawlings Oil company truck sat parked at the Gilmore hangar when B.J. landed her plane for lunch. She taxied to a stop near the entrance of the opened double doors and killed the engine. Rudy had agreed to go up with her today to take some aerial pictures but once again hadn't shown on time. So she'd gritted her teeth and dragged Leroy along. But her older brother had actually been halfway decent for once in his life. They'd gotten six farms photographed, and he hadn't made one rude comment about her marrying a Rawlings.

But all her morning's work was instantly forgotten as she stared at the parked truck.

Grady.

"Horny bastard," she muttered even as her heart sang at the thought of him coming to visit her at work. "Hey, Leroy," she called over her shoulder as she unstrapped her safety harness. "Can you get the equipment? I've got company."

"I guess," came the reluctant grumble. "But you owe me."

"Thanks."

Grinning, she popped from the plane and nearly sprinted down the tarmac. But as soon as she entered the hangar, she slowed to a stop. The smile dropped off her face as she stared at the man who was chatting with Pop. It wasn't Grady at all, but his father.

Tucker glanced over when he heard her enter. Instantly, he straightened from where he'd had his foot propped on a bench. Turning to face her fully, he gave a brief and solemn nod.

Not realizing she was holding her breath, B.J. returned the silent greeting. Her steps were much slower as she approached.

"B.J.," he said.

She didn't answer.

"Got a minute?" he asked.

She nodded, cleared her throat, and pointed to the closed door of the office. "We can talk in there," she said, irritated with herself for letting her voice go hoarse.

Tucker stepped back to let her lead the way. He was just like Grady, she realized, letting the lady go first. Her heart clenched in misery.

Grady.

She opened the door and started to enter, but immediately realized someone—probably Pop—had just brewed a fresh pot of coffee. Slamming a palm over her mouth, she backed out of the doorway and spun toward Grady's dad.

"We can talk out here," she amended.

He grinned at the humor in the situation, but politely asked, "Want to go outside to get some fresh air?"

She didn't answer immediately, still fighting back the nausea. Then she closed her eyes, blew out a breath and shook her head. "No. I'm good." Straightening, she faced him head-on. "Look, I don't know what you want now, but I'm not making any more deals. You can just keep the goddamn plane. Okay? I can't—"

"B.J.," he broke in. His smile faltered, and he shifted uncomfortably. "No. I, uh...to be honest, I'm here to apologize for all that."

B.J. nearly passed out at his feet. Striving to hold in her shock, she managed a casual shrug. "Well...don't worry about it. No harm done."

"No," he said. "There was harm done. I offended you and..." He paused and shook his head, looking ashamed. "I get a little overprotective and irrational when it comes to my children. I—"

"Mr. Rawlings, you have every right to worry about Grady. I don't blame you at all for anything. In fact, I probably would've thought less of you if you hadn't done anything. I—"

"B.J.," he said, stopping her again with his soft voice, shocking her into silence as he took both her hands into both of his. "I was wrong," he murmured, looking into her eyes with a penetrating blue stare so like his son's that she could only gape back, holding her breath.

"You're not some scheming gold-digger. You're not out to hurt or cheat anyone. You're just a woman who's in love with a man."

She sucked in a surprised breath. Wow, it felt extremely uncomfortable to hear anyone actually say that aloud. She sent Grady's dad a leery look. "You're not going to tell *him* that, are you?"

Tucker sputtered out a surprised laugh. After a moment, though, he squeezed her fingers reassuringly. "I'll leave that detail to you."

Her shoulders deflated, and she nearly fainted once again.

"Oh! Before I forget. Here. This is for you." Tucker yanked an all-too-familiar-looking document from his back pocket and tried to hand it to her.

B.J. backed away from the deed as if it had lice. Then she lifted her eyes. "I can't take anything for marrying Grady."

Lips parting in dawning realization, Tucker glanced down at his hand and then tried to shove it at her again. "Well, look at it as a wedding present then."

She shook her head. "I can't take it," she whispered.

Tucker looked distinctly uncomfortable as he continued to hold out his hand. "B.J., honestly. I don't want your plane."

He glanced in horror at her Cessna, and B.J. finally grinned. "I'll tell you what," she relented. "How about I make the same payments to you I was making to the bank and buy it back?"

"That would work," he said, his shoulders sagging as tension eased out of them. "That would work just fine."

"And about the prenuptial agreement," B.J. started. "I don't mind letting Grady have everything that's already his. But the baby—"

"I'll have a new agreement worked up by the end of the week," Tucker said.

This time it was B.J. who was relieved. "Thank you," she said.

He nodded. Thinking that was all the business they had to discuss, B.J. shifted when Grady's dad merely stared at her a moment longer.

"I, uh, came to give you something else too," he finally said. She frowned just as he added, "This," and enfolded her into a huge hug. Too bowled over to resist the fatherly embrace, she just stood there like an idiot with her arms hanging down limply at her sides.

"Thank you," he said into her hair, "thank you so much for bringing my boy back."

Confused, she pulled away and looked up at him.

He smiled, his eyes damp with emotion. "I never thought we'd see the old Grady again. He was so lost. But when he came into work this morning..."

For a second he looked too choked to speak. Then he broke into another brilliant grin. "He was smiling. You made him smile."

Emotions engulfing her, B.J. covered her mouth with her hands and burst into tears.

Chapter Nineteen

B.J. didn't want to blame it on Tucker's visit, but after he left, something inside her shifted. After locking herself in the bathroom until she'd stopped bawling and the red blotchiness left her face, she emerged a different woman entirely, humming as she returned to her plane.

Leroy paused to send her a strange look.

"What?" she asked as she moved by.

"You okay?" he asked, wrinkling his face and sending her the strangest expression.

She frowned. "Sure. Why?"

He shrugged. "Don't know. You're just acting awfully...girly all of the sudden."

B.J. rolled her eyes and turned away. "Well, thank God I'm a girl then."

She knew he continued to watch her, but she kept ignoring him. After a moment, he said, "Them pregnancy hormones are really messing with you, ain't they?"

When she glanced his way, he actually looked concerned, like there might really be something medically wrong with his sister.

"Shut up," she muttered and flipped him the bird.

His face cleared, and his shoulders slumped in relief, but he sent his own dirty hand-signal back in return. Then he turned and strode off. She could've sworn she heard him say, "Thank God," as he walked away.

B.J. stared after him for a moment, absolutely stunned. Her butt-headed brother had actually been worried about her. The sudden softness she felt for him shocked her even more.

Hell, maybe there *was* something wrong with her. If there was, she knew exactly what the source was. One Grady Jace Rawlings. If she'd acted a little too feminine today, it was purely his fault. The guy made her emotions go haywire.

She was in love with him, and that scared the piss out of her. Suddenly, she wanted to make this marriage thing work...not just work. She wanted to make it succeed. She wanted it to be permanent, and she wanted to be as important to him as...well, hell, as important as Amy had been.

Sobering, she straightened.

There was no way she'd find equal footing with Amy. No freaking way. But her heart still wished it...and B.J. couldn't ignore the yearning. Thinking up ways to get him to feel at least half as much for her as he'd felt for his first wife, B.J. put in a discreet call to her new girl buddy, Jo Ellen.

If anyone knew how to be feminine and win over a man's heart, it would be Grady's utterly feminine sister.

****

By five o'clock, B.J. had started taking steps to finding her inner female. She'd stopped by Jo Ellen's, and they'd talked for hours, discussing all the changes she could make to be less masculine.

Now, she knelt in the flower garden, muttering under her breath about all the freaking weeds. After visiting with Jo Ellen and then stopping by a boutique on the way home for a new nighty, she'd called Rudy for gardening advice.

Rudy gave her very strict instructions on weeding, what to pull and what not to pull. So there she kneeled, down on her hands and knees, sweating in the dirt. As she worked relentlessly, a very small, very green grass snake slithered across her hand.

B.J. screamed and jumped to her feet, immediately scrambling from the flowerbed. In her mind's eye, the reptile was ten feet long. She could almost hear the twitching rattle of its tail and feel the white-hot venom from its fangs as it bit her right under the arm.

Grady flew out the front door. "What's wrong?" he said, bounding off the porch, his eyes wide with concern.

B.J. didn't think. She just leapt, landing in his surprised arms and nearly crawling up his leg she clung to him so tight.

"B.J.?" Grady took her shoulders in his hands and pulled her back so he could look her up and down, probably for blood. "What's wrong?"

Reality finally returned, and she could only shake her head and move out of his concerned grasp. "Nothing. I'm fine." Yet she scanned the grass frantically as she spoke.

"You screamed," he insisted.

"I did not." But as soon as she spoke, she bit her lip, realizing screaming was a girly thing, and that was exactly what she'd been trying to accomplish.

Grady looked at her strangely. "I heard you scream."

"I do not...scream," she stated firmly. Okay, so, in some ways she'd always be a tomboy, because no way on God's green earth would she admit to screaming. "I might've let out a sound of surprise. But your goddamn wrong if you think I screamed."

Grady gaped a moment. Then he sputtered out a laugh and shook his head. "All right then," he revised. "I heard your *sound of surprise*. So, what surprised you?"

B.J. mumbled about the snake, and Grady moved closer.

"I'm sorry, what?"

"I said I saw a damn snake, okay?" she

practically shouted. It was humiliating. She, B.J. Gilmore—Rawlings—hated snakes.

Grady fell back a startled step. "You're afraid of snakes?"

"Hell, no," she growled and then snorted, appalled he would even suggest the idea, even though her hand had already raised to cover the spot under her arm where her snakebite scar remained. "I just don't like them."

He grinned, clearly amused, and she ground her molars. But damn it, she didn't want to be feminine weak; she wanted to be feminine strong.

"It's okay to be afraid of snakes, you know."

"I am *not* afraid." Her voice vibrated with irritation...and humiliation.

He lifted his hands in surrender. "Sorry. Honest mistake."

At her glare, he tried to stop smiling, but it didn't work, and his lips quirked up at the corner. She folded her arms over her chest and let her eyes narrow.

Shaking his head, he seemed to relent. "Okay, okay. I'm sorry. Really. Just tell me which way he went, and I'll see if I can get him out of here."

"I didn't see which way he went," she answered, looking at him as if he was insane. "The damn thing slithered right over my hand, and I was out of there."

Making a sudden gagging sound, she stared down at her fingers in horror. "Oh, God. I need to wash my hand."

As she raced inside, she heard Grady's laughter follow her.

"Bastard," she muttered, dashing to the sink.

Grabbing up the dish soap, she poured half the bottle over her fingers and commenced to scrubbing the skin raw.

****

Still chuckling, Grady shook his head again. For a full-blown tomboy, the woman had a healthy set of lungs on her. He hadn't heard such a high-pitched scream since Caine had put a spider in his sister Emma Leigh's hair when she was ten.

The prospect made him feel a little lighter. B.J. was such an independent, self-sufficient woman, he liked knowing she'd actually need him for something every once in a while. Hey, maybe if he was lucky, she'd "dislike" spiders too, and he'd get to play hero even more often.

Searching the ground for a long black slithering object, he thought back to B.J. at breakfast. She was definitely something else. One minute, she could be a seductive vixen, driving him out of his mind with what she could do with her mouth. Then she was shrieking her head off over snakes, only to switch back into the ultimate tomboy a second later, acting too tough to be scared of anything.

He enjoyed the mix. He enjoyed B.J. The woman was a breath of fresh air. He hadn't realized how much he'd missed companionship until she'd crowded her way into his life. But he liked having her around. And he liked catching her unaware when she paused in a room to look down at her still flat stomach in wonder, like she couldn't believe there was a little human in there.

Amy had talked constantly about her pregnancy, how her body was changing and what she was thinking. But B.J. remained quiet, hardly ever mentioning the fact she was carrying.

He found himself wanting to know what was going on her mind when she laid a protective hand on her stomach and stood there lost in thought. He wanted to know what her body was going through and what emotions she was experiencing, because he had a sneaking suspicion the baby secretly delighted her.

Still lost in thought, he almost missed movement out of the corner of his eye. Jerking around, he watched something slither across the lawn away from the flowers. Surprised such a small thing had made her let out such a big scream, he picked the snake up by the back of its head. It was hardly even a foot long.

He laughed. She was afraid of this little worm of a thing? It didn't seem possible. But as the front door opened and she appeared in the doorway, he lifted it to show her. She pulled to an immediate stop.

"Found it," he called.

"Good," she said. "So...go kill it."

He frowned. "I'm not going to kill it. Snakes are good to have around. They eat mice."

"I don't have a problem with mice. The mice can stay."

He was half-tempted to tease her about being so scared. He probably would've if he didn't fear getting a black eye for his trouble.

"I'll just carry it off then," he relented, grinning.

B.J. folded her arms across her chest. "Do whatever you want. I'm going to start supper."

"You don't want to finish weeding?" he couldn't help but ask.

After sending him a dirty look, she spun around and slammed her way back inside.

He took off across the yard, chuckling. After finding the snake a new home, he returned to the flower garden. It was only half weeded. Deciding to take up where she'd left off, he knelt in the dirt and pulled at a dead plant. It'd been nearly three years since he'd done this.

Amy had possessed a black thumb. She'd killed everything she'd ever tried to plant. After a while, Grady had banned her from gardening all together, claiming she was a hazard to the flowers. He'd been the one to keep the plants nice because his wife liked how they looked. But after she'd died, he'd forgotten about them for a good year, too distraught to bother with flowers. When he finally noticed all the weeds, he didn't see the point in repairing them because there was no one to grow them for.

But if B.J. wanted flowers, he'd grow her flowers.

****

"You know, if we were in Regency England and you were a woman, you'd be in half mourning right now?"

Grady paused as he entered the bedroom. "Excuse me?"

Lying with the covers tucked up to her armpits and a load of pillows propping up her back, B.J. lifted the paperback in her hand.

"It's right here." She pointed to the passage in front of her. "The first year is called deep mourning. You seclude yourself in your home, cover the windows with crepe and wear all black."

When he merely blinked as if she'd just read the words in a foreign language, she continued. "The second year is second mourning, and you can take the crepe off the windows. The third year is half mourning, and you can wear gray and lavender and mauve."

She glanced up and watched him unbutton the gray shirt he was wearing. As her eyebrows lifted with a see-what-I mean look, he shook his head with an amused lift of his lips. "What in the world are you reading?"

Holding her place with a finger, B.J. turned the spine and read aloud. "It's called *The Trouble With Bluestockings*. It's the first in a series. Jo Ellen lent it to me. And you know what, for a sappy romance, it's not half bad. There are some great sex scenes in here." She wiggled her eyebrows. "I'm learning lots of neat tricks."

After stripping off his button-up shirt, Grady tugged his undershirt from his jeans. "And why are you reading a romance novel?" he asked, sending her an odd look.

B.J. rolled her eyes and sighed. The man would never get it, would he?

"I'm trying to get in touch with my feminine side." Duh.

She nearly sighed aloud as he pulled his T-shirt off, leaving his chest bare. His defined pecs glistened in the dim light from her bedside reading lamp. God, he was so beautiful. He probably didn't even realize his striptease was turning her on like crazy.

"Your *feminine* side?" He snorted as he sat on the edge of the mattress to tug off his socks. "Why do you want one of those? I like you how you are."

Stunned, B.J. bolted upright, her finger unconsciously slipping from the page she'd marked. "No, you don't."

About to toss his socks toward the laundry hamper across the room, Grady turned to eye her with an incredulous lift of his eyebrows. "Excuse me?"

"You can't like me like this," she told him in no unnecessary terms. "Every man prefers *girly* women with their frou-frou hairdos and smelly perfumes. God, even Ralphie Smardo preferred Nan Lundy to me."

Grady froze. "What? Raphie Smardo? Why the hell is *his* name coming up in *our* bedroom? I thought he was only sympathy sex for you."

She cracked out a disgusted laugh, and to her mortification, her eyes watered. She blinked repeatedly "Yeah, but still...he didn't have to go and act so appalled afterward. You'd a thought I'd given him an STD or something. Let me tell you, it's a sobering realization when your own dorky best

friend thinks you're not woman enough for him. I
don't care how much I didn't want sex with him ever
again, he didn't want me either. He didn't want me."

Lips parting, Grady whispered, "Oh, B.J." He
reached out, but she only smacked his hand away
and scowled, suddenly wishing she'd kept her big
trap shut.

"Don't you dare feel sorry for me," she charged
and backed across the bed away from him as he
started crawling toward her. "Not you. Not the king
of Thou-shall-not-pity-me."

"Will you just...stay still!" he muttered, leaping
until he tackled her, trapping her under the sheets
so she couldn't even move.

B.J. growled and glared up at him.

He scowled back a moment before he buried his
face in her hair and laughed. "Jesus," he chuckled.
"You are something else, telling me what I do and
don't like."

"But—"

"Will you just shut up and listen to me a
second?"

Taken aback by his attitude, B.J. let her jaw
drop open.

His blue gaze sparkled as it met hers. "B.J.,
listen to me and listen good. You have the same
taste in movies I do. I get to see all the great action
flicks and haven't had to watch a single sappy
romantic drama yet since we've been married. You
prefer sports to the cooking and home decorating
channels. Plus you're fun to talk to because you're
into engines and racing, and you've never once tried
to stuff healthy junk like salads and vegetables
down me."

After pressing a light, quick kiss to her mouth,
he rested his forehead against hers. "You don't ask
me what I'm feeling every three minutes. If I'm not
talking, you don't think it's because I'm mad at you.

I like how you don't clutter the bathroom with a load of useless perfumes bottles because, to me, nothing smells as good as a plain, clean woman. It's like...you have all the perks and none of the downfalls. In fact, you just might be the perfect woman. So, don't go telling me what I don't prefer. I know what I like. And I like everything about you just as it is. If you even think about trying to change, we're going to have problems."

B.J. could only stare at him in awe as he leaned up to press another light, teasing kiss to her mouth.

"You really don't mind if I'm a tomboy?"

"No," he murmured against her mouth. "I really don't."

He kissed her for a few seconds longer, before B.J. pulled away. "Well, in that case," she muttered, wiggling out from under him to get free, "I'm going to change."

"Change?" Grady asked, frowning as he sat up to give her space.

When she ripped aside the covers to expose the silk and lace two-piece she was wearing, his mouth fell open.

"Holy God," he breathed, his eyes soaking in the skimpy bra and thong set.

"I'll be right back," B.J. said, popping off the bed to head toward the bathroom.

"Whoa!" he called, leaping after her and hooking an arm around her waist to drag her back. "Let's not be too hasty now."

He tugged until the smooth globes of her butt brushed his chest. Kissing the base of her back right above her panty line, he cupped her bare backside in his hands and started to lick his way up her spine.

B.J. gasped and sat down on the edge of the bed in order to let him continue. Bowing her head as he lifted her hair and ran his tongue along the back of her neck, she said, "But I thought you said you liked me being a tomboy."

"Mmm." He slipped his hands around to cup her breasts with both palms. "What does this have to do with being a tomboy?"

B.J.'s back arched when he slipped his fingers inside the bra to get to her nipples, causing her long, free-flowing hair to tumble over his shoulder like pure silk. "So, this isn't at all frou-frou or girly, huh?"

"Hell no," he growled, fumbling a little in his haste to shed the bra. "Amy, the ultimate supporter of all things frou-frou and girly, wouldn't have been caught dead in a thong. This is what I call drop-dead gorgeous."

B.J. purred when his caress found the center of her heat. Sliding her panties down her thighs, he nibbled his way up her throat.

"Do you want to know what I think of Ralphie Smardo?" he asked just before catching her earlobe with his teeth.

Sighing out her pleasure as she tilted her head to the side to give him better access, B.J. asked, "No, I'm not sure I do."

He chuckled and told her anyway. "I think he was scared because you're *too much* of a woman, and he knew he'd never be able to handle you."

B.J. lifted an eyebrow. "Oh, but you think you can *handle* me, huh?" Her voice held a certain challenge even though her eyes sparked with pleasure at his true meaning.

He grinned and tossed her underwear over his shoulder. "No, not really. But that's not going to stop me from trying."

Chapter Twenty

The next morning, Grady woke hard and hungry. And even though his stomach wouldn't stop rumbling, he decided to ignore his appetite in favor of the other pressing need. An hour later, showered and dressed, he whistled as he strode to his truck.

Before Houston, he'd always been eager to go to work, to escape his lonely, memory-filled house. But this morning, he felt reluctant to leave. B.J. was inside. It didn't matter if she'd be heading out soon herself to go to the hangar. She was in there now. And since she was, that was where he wanted to be.

He cringed, thinking he sounded pathetic for wanting to be with her nonstop. But then he realized, hey, he was a newlywed. Of course he wanted to spend every waking hour with his wife.

Realizing, yes, he was indeed a newlywed, it suddenly struck him they'd totally bypassed a honeymoon. He should ask her tonight if she wanted to go away for a few days...or weeks. He grinned. The woman would probably want to see a NASCAR race, which was perfectly fine by him. He liked her tastes and was happy about the fact he'd never have to attend another craft fair in his life.

Craving coffee, he decided to stop by the diner on his way to Rawlings Oil. Someone at the office usually made a pot, but whoever did couldn't brew to save their life...and since the smell made B.J. sick to her stomach, he couldn't make his own at home. As he stepped into the café, however, the smell of frying bacon, scrambled eggs and hot apple pie made his stomach growl.

He ordered a full meal with his coffee even though he'd already eaten once this morning. Grinning, he realized it was entirely B.J.'s fault. He wouldn't have worked up such an appetite if she'd kept her hands off him in the shower and hadn't demanded she wash his back because he'd missed a spot. After that, he'd felt obligated to offer the same courtesy. And pretty soon, they were cleaning each other against the shower wall. It didn't seem to matter that he'd been inside her only minutes earlier. He was always ready for more with B.J.

The extra-long shower and double breakfast made him late for work, but he wasn't too concerned. If he was needed so badly, he'd just stay later this evening. Being late was worth having such a wonderful morning.

He dropped by the office first thing. After checking his e-mails and answering machine to find no one had left him any pressing matters to attend to, he decided to head out and spend the day in the field. For some reason, he wanted to be active today. He felt energized enough he could probably go for hours without a break.

Whistling again, he stopped by his dad's office to let the old man know where he'd be.

"Hey, Dad." Knocking on Tucker Rawlings half-opened door, he poked his head inside to find the room empty, the screensaver on the computer flashing family photos across the monitor. Glancing out into the hallway, Grady didn't spot his dad nearby, so he stepped inside and snagged a Post-it note to leave a quick message. He'd just reached for a pen when he spotted B.J.'s name on an official-looking piece of paper sitting among his father's things.

Frowning, he changed direction and snagged the document. "What the hell?"

It didn't take him long to realize he was holding

a prenuptial agreement. Mouth falling open, he smoothed out the tri-fold, causing another set of papers to fall out the bottom, landing on the desk. He slowly picked up the deed to B.J.'s plane. A sickening feeling crept through his stomach.

Returning his attention to the prenup, he scanned every numbered line, feeling more nauseous with each addendum he read. "Oh, God."

"Grady?"

Grady lifted his head and found his father paused in the doorway. With a half-eaten doughnut in one hand and a steaming cup of coffee in the other, Tucker Rawlings had a guilty expression smeared across his features.

"What—"

"Dad, what is all this?"

Tucker set his snack on the corner of his desk and lifted both his hands. "Grady, I can explain."

"Oh, my God," Grady breathed. "You *paid* her to marry me?"

"No. I...I...I just wanted you to be happy. I didn't think—"

"And she just...she *agreed* to all this?"

Tucker stepped toward Grady, but Grady shifted backward. His father froze, his face an ashen gray. "I love you, son. I would've done anything to help you."

"How..." When his voice broke, Grady shook his head, still reeling in disbelief. "How does this help me?"

He couldn't believe it. He refused to believe it. B.J. wouldn't marry him just because—

His throat burning, he blinked rapidly as he looked down at the documents in his hands.

"Grady! Hey, there you are."

At the sound of her voice coming from the hall, he whirled and about passed out at the sight of his wife. She paused in the doorway, all five feet and ten lovely inches of her, grinning at him as she held up his briefcase. "I was walking out the door this morning when I caught sight of this sitting on the kitchen table. Thought you might need it for—" She broke off in mid-sentence, her smile slipping. After a quick look toward his dad, she turned back to Grady. "What's wrong?"

Grady held up the deed. "You made a deal with my dad?"

When her gaze latched onto the document, her face drained of color. She lurched a step in reverse.

"Grady," Tucker started, lifting both hands again like that pose could actually keep the peace.

"You stay out of this," Grady warned with a look that had his dad freezing. "I already know your side. I want to hear hers."

"But you really didn't hear my side. I haven't actually told you every—"

"Then B.J. can fill in the blanks," Grady growled as he stormed toward her and snagged her elbow, drawing her back into the hall and toward his own office. After ushering her inside, he let go his hold and shut the door behind him.

She stood in the center of the room, clutching his briefcase to her side, and silently watched him as he wiped a hand over his mouth and paced. Finally, he stopped short and seared her with a look. "So my father bought the deed to your airplane in order to coax you into marrying me?"

She gave a short nod, which made him clench his teeth. He wanted her to say something to defend herself. He wanted a reason to start yelling. But the damn woman refused to oblige.

Seething, he nodded in return. "Was this before or after I gave you the ring?"

"Before," she said in a low voice.

Pain shot straight up his windpipe. For a moment, he thought he was going to choke to death. When he realized he could still breathe, he huffed out a short breath. "So...that whole scene where you kept telling me no and I had to seduce you into saying yes, that was just, what...playing hard to get?"

Her jaw clenched. "No. That was me not wanting to give into your father's agreement."

"But you did anyway. You agreed to marry me. You signed your name right here next to this X, willing to give up the baby, *our* baby, for what? For a *plane*? My God, B.J. If you wanted the plane that much, I could've bought you the goddamn plane."

"It's not about the plane," she said, her voice breaking as she spoke.

"Then what is it about?" he growled. "The baby? Do you not want the baby? Is that what this is about?"

"No. I—" When she faltered, looking lost, his patience gave out.

"What is this about?" he yelled.

"Will you just shut up and let me talk?" B.J. hollered back as she wound her arm around and let his briefcase fly.

He tried to duck, but her aim was so deadly accurate, the tote hit him square in the shoulder. He grunted through the pain and caught it against him with both hands. Stunned mute, he could only stare as B.J.'s face flamed a hot, fuming red.

Hands clenching into fists at her sides, she said, "You...you stupid *idiot*. I'm getting sick of your asinine assumptions about me. You obviously don't know anything at all."

His mouth dropped open. She was mad at him? *Him*? "Just what do you think I'm supposed to know?" he asked incredulously.

She growled, looked around her and caught sight of a small pocket dictionary lying on his desk. Snagging it, she chucked that next. He ducked behind his briefcase, holding it up as a shield. The book bounced off the case and crashed against the wall behind him.

"What the hell?" he exploded.

"First, *first*," B.J. started through gritted teeth. "You accuse me of sleeping with you in Houston because you thought I felt sorry for you." Snorting out a disbelieving sound, she threw a stapler at him.

"Damn it, B.J.!" He dodged her aim again and yet again when she heaved a calculator. "Cut it out."

"No. I want you to tell me how it was sympathy sex when I wanted to be with you that night more than I'd ever wanted to be with anyone? When I've *always* wanted to be with you?"

Grady froze, having no answer. He stared mutely as she continued ranting.

"And now. *Now* you actually think I married you only because of some deal your dad wanted to make with me, as if I was some sissy-scared schoolgirl who could actually be intimidated by his bluffing threats. *God!*"

She glanced around her. When she caught sight of a container full of pens and snatched up the whole bundle, pulling them out of their holder, Grady braced himself.

"Don't even think about it," he warned.

Instead of throwing the pens, she squeezed them in her hand and quivered as she glared. "You're such a sanctimonious hypocrite," she charged. "How can you honestly be mad at me for thinking I married you for some other reason than love when you only married me because of this baby?"

The air rushed out of his lungs when he realized she was right. Dear Lord, she was so right. How could he expect her to have a pure purpose when he'd only been thinking about morality and obligations?

"I'll tell you right now," she said, breaking into his thoughts. "That deed to my plane, and everything else your father's said to me, had no part in my reasons for marrying you. And you're dead wrong if you think it did. The only thing I'm truly guilty of is falling in love with and marrying Amy Rawlings's idiot husband."

Grady dropped the briefcase. "What?"

"You heard me." With that, B.J. turned and stomped out of the office, slamming the door behind her.

Grady feared his heart might beat through his chest. But...damn. She loved him? B.J. loved him? Giving his head a shake as if to clear it, he blinked once and then hurried after her.

"Wait! B.J." He dashed from the office and soon realized that when his wife wanted to move, she moved fast.

Charging for the exit, he heard her diesel roar to life just as he pushed his way outside.

"B.J.," he yelled, sprinting toward her truck. But she put the motor into gear and peeled out. Changing directions, Grady ran for his own rig, muttering the entire time. "I swear to God, woman, if you get into a wreck and hurt yourself, I'm going to strangle you with my bare hands."

He followed her, grateful she took dirt roads so he could trail the plumes of smoke she left in her wake. He would've lost her otherwise. Still...his heart beat hard against his chest, hoping she remained safe and didn't hurt herself. He was sweating buckets and breathing hard by the time he spotted her truck parked and landed in one piece, sitting just outside the cemetery. If she'd gotten herself into a wreck before he'd caught her, he didn't think he could have handled it. He didn't think he could lose a second woman he loved in such an abrupt manner.

Parking behind her Dodge, Grady let the pent-up air out of his lungs as he killed the engine. Inside the limestone walls, B.J. sat on her knees in front of Amy's grave and bent over double, holding her stomach as she wept.

"Damn it, B.J.," he whispered and clenched his teeth. "You just have to make this as hard as you possibly can, don't you?"

Refusing to think about it further, he pushed open his truck door and slid out. She didn't even notice his approach as he entered the gate and started for her.

"I'm sorry," she sobbed, crying so intensely she squeezed her eyes closed. "I'm so sorry, Amy."

Though he'd been fearing what watching his second wife stand over his first wife's grave would do to his emotions, it strangely didn't affect him as he'd thought it would. Instead of feeling injustice and anger over Amy's absence, all he wanted was to go to B.J. and gather her into his arm, to take her away and dry her tears with his kisses.

"I never meant to sleep with your husband," she swore. "I never...I never meant for all this—"

"You know I'm not *her* husband anymore, don't you?" He stepped closer as she gasped and whirled to face him. "I'm yours."

Wiping furiously at her eyes as if she could hide the fact she was bawling, B.J. sounded defensive as she said, "What're you doing here?"

He didn't answer immediately. Taking a moment to rearrange his thoughts, he finally sighed and shoved his hands into his pockets, purposely keeping a few feet of distance between them because he knew he'd reach for her if he moved too close.

"A few months ago, I took a trip to Houston," he said. "And when I was there, I went to dinner with a woman who forced me to take a look at my life. She even followed me back to my hotel room, she was so determined to help me stop running from my feelings." With a small smile and self-conscious shrug, he finished, "I'm just here to repay the favor."

She snorted. "Well, you're dead wrong if you think I'm running away from my feelings, Slim. I said exactly what I wanted to say at the office."

Grady gave a nod of agreement but added, "Yet you were too scared to stick around and wait for my response."

Her eyebrows lifted. "Scared? Of *your* response? From what I saw, all you did was stand there and gape at me."

"You'd just finished throwing half the office at me," he defended. "It knocked me off track for a second. No one's thrown anything at me since Jo Ellen was fourteen and I told her I didn't like her haircut. She hurled a shoe at me and busted open my lip." He paused to touch his long-healed mouth. "Why do girls always throw stuff when they're mad?"

"I don't—" B.J. broke off abruptly and paused with a thoughtful frown. "Do we really?"

He grinned, charmed by her shock. She might be a tomboy through and through, but she was still one hundred percent female.

He loved watching her realize that fact.

When their gazes met, his smile dropped, and emotions swamped him. "I love you too, you know."

Her eyes went wide. Shaking her head, she took a step in reverse. "Don't," she begged, holding up a hand to block him. "Just stop."

He stepped forward and grasped her fingers, kissing them. "As I recall, that's exactly what I said to you in Houston. But you didn't stop. So, I can't either."

She shook her head, and more tears gushed down her cheeks. "But I can't...I don't...what do you want from me?"

He smiled softly. "Only everything."

She shook her head again. "No. I can't...I'll never be anything like Amy."

Not catching her meaning, Grady frowned. "What does she have to do with any of this?"

B.J. lifted one shoulder. "Nothing. Everything."

His shoulders slumped. "Listen to us," he said softly. "Talking in riddles and too afraid to just come right out and say what we really feel. Well, I don't want to hide anymore. You taught me that hiding my feelings doesn't do anyone any good."

Pulling her bodily against him, he ignored how she went stiff in his arms and held her close. "Yes, I pushed for this marriage because of the baby. But then...everything changed. I was so determined not to grow any feelings for you. I thought...I thought I could lose myself in your body and not lose myself in you. But you're so..."

He shook his head, unable to describe it. "When I saw that deed on my father's desk and thought you were only with me because of your airplane, it felt like someone had ripped my heart out of my chest. Here you'd just taught me it was okay to open myself up again, to risk love one more time, and you didn't even feel the same way about me as I felt for you. It hurt."

"I didn't marry you because of what your dad—"

"Yeah, I realize that." He grinned and kissed her temple. "If it wasn't the flying briefcase that convinced me, it was the stapler and the calculator and the dictionary."

Her muscles began to go lax against him. He let out a breath of relief. Smoothing her hair out of his way and kissing her cheek, he caught sight of the gravestone next to them. When he read the name Amy Rawlings and didn't feel like everything inside him was going to burst, he tightened his grip on B.J. gratefully. She'd somehow taken the pain away and filled him with life.

"Now, about this issue you're making with Amy," he said. "Just...don't. Okay? We both cared for her. Hell, I always will. She taught me *how* to love a woman. But she's my past, B.J. You're the rest of my life, and I love you with everything I have. Baby or no baby, deed to your plane or no deed, I love you. Now, I just want to be with you."

"But..." She pulled back just enough to see his face.

Placing both of his hands on either side of her head, he cupped her cheeks and gave her a long, closed-mouth kiss. When he finally pulled back, his blue eyes were rimmed with tears.

"I can't guarantee I'll never think of her again. Because I will, especially when I'm with you. It doesn't hurt so much to remember her when I'm with you. That's a gift you've given me, and I'm grateful for it. But I *can* guarantee you I won't automatically see her every time I look at you."

Grinning, he touched B.J.'s face, tracing her hairline with the very tips of his fingers. "God, I can't believe anyone would be able to see anyone else when you're around. You're so...alive. So wonderfully alive. Everything you do...it's all just...full of vitality. You're a survivor. You have a stronger spirit than Amy ever did. You fight! You're...you're B.J. And I adore everything about you."

He cleared his throat. "The day she died, in the hospital...she took one look at the dead baby and gave up. She didn't glance my way, didn't say anything to me. She just stopped living because she knew she'd never be a mother."

Closing his eyes, he nuzzled his face in B.J.'s hair, and she wrapped her arms around him, supporting him. "She could've fought to stay with me. I *know* she could've. She was alive and talking, right up until the moment she saw Bennett. But she didn't want to live. She didn't want to be childless. So, she chose death over me."

Blowing out a long, relieved breath as if

cleansed by the truth, he lifted his face and gave B.J. a trembling smile. "You wouldn't have done that to me," he said with dead certainty.

"No," she agreed. "You're right. I wouldn't have ever done that to you." As tears flooded her face, she grinned through the downpour. "Damn it, Grady," she said and then caught him off guard by launching herself tighter against him and hugging him hard. "I love you so much."

He pulled her close and kissed her hair. "Yeah," he murmured. "It's nice to finally be on the same page with you."

She snorted. "You're telling me. I thought I was going to blow a gasket with all this angst and frustration. I kept worrying it'd screw with the baby, and he'd come out with three toes hanging from his chin or something."

Grady laughed. Feeling free, as if he'd just been released from nearly three years of hell, he kissed her again. He knew the rest of his life would never be dull with B.J. at his side.

And he looked forward to it.

Epilogue

"I never want to go through that again," Grady said, mopping his damp brow with the back of his palm as he plopped into a chair next to the hospital bed. When he noticed his hand was shaking, he dropped his fingers, trying to forget how utterly petrified he'd been less than an hour ago.

A pale-faced B.J. paused from tucking a starched sheet around her and snorted as she looked up at him, her brown eyes underlined with deep purple grooves of exhaustion. "What did *you* go through? As I recall, I'm the one who did all the pushing."

"I had to watch," he argued.

Jesus, he'd had to watch her grit her teeth and cry out as the pain had split her apart. And, yes, his hands were at it again, shaking like they might rattle off his wrists. He glared down at them, wondering why they wouldn't settle down. The worry was over. Everything was going to be fine. B.J. had made it through.

"Okay then, Slim," she said on a yawn. "Next time I swear we can switch places. You give birth, I'll stand there and watch. How 'bout that?"

When he lifted his face to scowl at her, his expression froze at the sight of her tired eyes twinkling with love as she beamed at him. She reached out her hand, and he took her fingers immediately, though he had to grind his teeth when he saw the IV and hospital band.

Rubbing his thumb over her knuckles, he said, "No next time. This is it. I mean it, B.J."

Her grin turned ornery. "Yeah, yeah. You said that last time."

"Well, two's enough," he stated adamantly.

She rolled her eyes. "Having the second was your idea, if I remember correctly."

"Don't remind me," he muttered, paling to almost as white as she was. "If you'd had this hard a labor on the first, there's no way I would've suggested a second."

"Speaking of which," she said. "Where *is* Jace?"

"I think Jo Ellen still has him. Mom and Dad were going to pick him up this evening, and then I'll get him from them when I go home."

"I'm sure Tanner will appreciate that." B.J. chuckled. "It can't be cool for a four-year-old guy to have a twenty-two-month-old shadowing his every move."

"When I talked to Jo Ellen, she said they've both been having a blast," Grady answered, grinning. His son and nephew had been more than excited to stay the night together.

"And what about...about..." B.J. yawned again.

Grady couldn't blame her. She'd had a long, rough night, morning, and afternoon, delivering the most perfect baby girl he'd ever seen.

"She's being weighed and measured," he answered, reaching out to tuck a piece of hair behind her ear for her. "The nurse said she'd bring her back when she was done."

"Good," B.J. murmured even as her eyelids drooped. "I can't wait to hold her again."

Grady understood the sentiment. He'd been amazed when a red, squawking Jace had been thrust into his arms only seconds after breathing his first. But the boy had been his mirror image. His daughter, however, looked too much like B.J. for him not to feel a different kind of adoration.

As if sensing their restless anxiety, the door

opened and a grinning nurse pushed her way inside, toting a baby bassinet.

"Someone's getting hungry," she called.

As B.J. struggled to sit up, Grady popped to his feet. "I'll get her for you."

The nurse wheeled his child closer, and he reached for the swaddled form inside the cradle. But as he did so, his wife gasped.

"Grady!"

He straightened anxiously, his vision going spotty for a second because he swung toward her so fast. "What's wrong? Are you okay?" Oh, God. Was she hemorrhaging? Cramping?

She pointed at the baby's cart. "You misspelled her name."

He paused.

What?

Turning, he squinted at the nametag on the end of the baby tub. "I did?"

B.J. made a sound of impatience. "Yes, you did. It's Dell*ie*, not Dell*a*."

Grady turned back to blink at her. "Dellie?" he repeated slowly and sent her a strange look. "Your mother's name was Dellie...as in a meat deli?"

B.J.'s lips parted. "You're right," she finally murmured. "She'd kill us if we named her after a sandwich shop."

"We haven't filled out the records for the birth certificate yet," the nurse spoke up, "in case you need to change something."

But B.J. was already shaking her head and lifting her hand. "No. No, I like Della. Della Rose Rawlings. It gives her her own name." She grinned at Grady. "Besides, it's tradition in our family to misspell the girl's name."

"You sure?" he asked as he lifted the yet-to-be-named infant and then gently placed her in her mother's waiting arms. "I didn't mean to—"

"I'm positive," she answered as she looked down at her daughter's small, heart-shaped face. "I love it. I love the name Della."

As she opened her blouse and guided Della's mouth to her breast, the nurse faded out of the room, and Grady settled himself back into his chair to watch. Something inside him eased, and he realized his hands were calm and steady.

When B.J. noticed the direction of his attention, she snorted and rolled her eyes. But then she softened and lovingly murmured, "Pervert. I can't believe you get off so much on watching this."

"It's special," he said, and leaned in to kiss her softly. "Just like you. I love you, Banner Jewell. Thank you so much for our children."

She grinned against his mouth. "I love you too. But I gotta say, I didn't make 'em by myself. I did have a little help."

Grady winked. "As long as it wasn't Junkyard Smardo helping."

B.J. gasped and punched his arm. "Jerk."

He laughed and kissed her again, "Seriously, I thank you," he whispered. "Thank you for my life. I thank you for...everything. In the past three years, you've made me the happiest man, B.J. You've made me something better than I ever was."

She gave a rather feminine, rather dreamy sounding sigh and rested her head on his shoulder. "Well, a girl never gets tired of hearing that," she admitted. "Even a tomboy."

Dropping his eyes to Della Rose, Grady reached out and touched her thick head of super-fine baby hair. "I hope she turns out to be a tomboy too. Just like her mother."

B.J. pulled back to give him an are-you-insane look. "God, let's hope not."

"I'm serious. I hope she grows up tough and strong, and wraps some poor, hopeless guy around her little finger, so I can kick his butt for looking at her."

B.J. laughed. "You're so diabolical," she answered with a twinkle in her eyes. "Must be why I love you."

As they grinned at other and shared the next chuckle, Grady realized this was definitely the best moment of his life, though strangely enough, every new experience with B.J.—starting a family and building their life together—was fast proving to be the best he'd ever had.

A word about the author...

Linda is a contemporary romance writer from the Midwestern USA, where she lives with her wonderful husband and nine cuckoo clocks. The eighth and final child of dairy farmers, she was forced into having a vivid imagination if she ever wanted to do something one of her siblings hadn't already tried. She expects her first book and first baby both to be released to the world in 2010.